THE HERO
OF HEROES 2

JAMES PRINCE

Order this book online at www.trafford.com
or email orders@trafford.com

Most Trafford titles are also available at major online book retailers.

Scripture quotations marked NIV are taken from the Holy Bible, New
International Version®. NIV®. Copyright © 1973, 1978, 1984 by International
Bible Society. Used by permission of Zondervan. All rights reserved.

This is a work of fiction. All of the characters, names, incidents, organizations, and dialogue
in this novel are either the products of the author's imagination or are used fictitiously.

Print information available on the last page.

ISBN: 978-1-4907-6905-9 (sc)
ISBN: 978-1-4907-6904-2 (e)

Trafford rev. 02/17/2016

 www.trafford.com

North America & international
toll-free: 1 888 232 4444 (USA & Canada)
fax: 812 355 4082

CHAPTER 1

The love of the most has already cooled off since I last talked about it in my previous book. It cooled off to the point now the justice department has the will to imprison the greatest defender of justice since the Messiah was on this earth. Even doctors are taking more care of their money than what they do with their patients. Not only they want to imprison this hero, but they are planning also to kill him. Also, a good defence at the queen bench is not really accessible to the poor.

Accused of blasphemy and contempt of court for refusing to swear, he was condemned to spend some time in jail. But there is where fun started for him. Three law officers escorted him straight to his cell door of a maximal security jail, but as soon as he was looked in with double lock security system, Just asked them if this was secured enough to keep him in place. Only one thing though, Just was behind them outside the cell.

"You guys should seal this door a little more hermetically, just to see if it can really hold me in." "You think this is funny, but we are only doing our job and nothing more." "I know this, but part of your job is also making a report about how things went and there is where things began to be more interesting for me. All of them must know and understand that no one can simply lock up justice and suppress the truth indefinitely." "Do you mind going back in there, at least the time we complete this report?" "I don't mind going back in there, but I can assure you that this wouldn't stop me from doing my every day duties."

The three officers went to fill up this report and following up on this; the judge addressed himself directly to the Prime Minister, who ordered that an unbreakable sealed glass cell unit was immediately built with ventilation with the precise goal to contain this out of ordinary individual and to shoot on sight if he ever escaped again. Although, James, Just's father-in-law, who noticed his boss decision didn't like it one bit. He was still held back by the promise he made not to reveal the identity of the one who saved his government earlier, but this promise was a burden to him now, seeing what was going on. But Just came to appease him, saying he would himself settle the case of the Prime Minister.

The cameras were constantly pointed on this glass cell and the agents who were watching it steadily couldn't understand what was going on. They could see Just inside it and all of a sudden for some reasons they couldn't explain, they couldn't see him for four or five minutes at the time and then they could see him again.

They didn't know exactly if they were going crazy or if they were in a presence of an alien. When Just noticed their concerns, he decided to tell them next time he was going out again.

They asked Just who he was exactly and Just told them he was Just and that no one and nothing could hold him and that they were wasting their time and the country's money and this no matter what they do. Then he told them one last time that he was leaving this time for a longer period of time to go watch a hockey game and that he would be seated directly in front of the Prime Minister. He also told them he will stay there until the Prime Minister cancels the shooting on sight.

No point saying that this again created such a commotion during the hockey game, but of course, the PM couldn't do otherwise, seeing an army of policemen who were just waiting for the order, either to start shooting or to put their guns away. As soon as the order was given; Just returned to his cell waiting for the next call.

Superhuman who was told not to get involved unless things turned to be very ugly was doing nothing else than laughing his head off before the events. Then suddenly Just thought this game went on long enough and he asked Superhuman if he could just take this glass cell and put it in front of this penitentiary and smash it in a way everyone thinks this was done be an alien, so he can find peace again. This was quickly done.

James had a lot to say to his boss when he was back in office.

"How could you let such injustice happened in front of our own eyes? How could you let a judge from any court of justice condemn a man or an individual, because he has at heart the will of God and he wants to follow the Messiah and his teaching? This is simply an aberration." "You know as much as I do that I have been fighting for a long time now against the Superior court to no avail. The court always has the last word." "This is not a good enough reason to give up on justice and on just people." "You yourself should know that it is written: 'The rich, the poor, the strong and the weak, none will escape.'" "Is this mean that the court is more powerful than the government of a country?" "It seems to be the case, my friend James and you should be ready to forgive me if I can't do everything I would like to do, either this is fair or not." "But the order for shooting on sight this individual didn't come from the court, but from you." "Maybe so, but the pressure came from the court." "Is this meaning that you can't take the pressure?" "You just try to do differently when your life is at stake." "Then my advice to you is to ask this man for forgiveness and to offer him your personal excuses and then you'll see what he can do with all the threats that come your way. Maybe you don't know it, but he is as far as I know the greatest force of nature and don't you go believe what the most believes, that he is only an alien that we have to get rid of. I have seen what this man can accomplish and I also know his wisdom that measures up to the Messiah's one and this that you believe it or not." "Are you telling me that you know him personally?" "He saved me from a number of problems and he indirectly saved our government from a great number of problems also." "And in turn I condemned him to death, but I had no way to know all of this." "Now you do and you should act consequently." "Can you tell me in which circumstances you got to know him?" "I rather spare you from these details, but I can tell you that I would be lost, if it wasn't for him and your government too; so do what you can to repair what you've done." "Well, thank you James; you always have a good advice for me and I appreciate it, but I just don't know how to reach him." "I'll do my very best to put him in contact with you, but don't you ever betray him, because then; you'll make him the worse enemy you ever had and you'll be lost, that I am sure of." "I found him very arrogant though, to come to sit himself in front of me to avoid the shooting and to force me to cancel the shoot on sight." "Could you really blame him for using the best way and maybe the only way to succeed?" "Not really no, but nevertheless; this was very bold." "No one can argue this; he is for sure full of resources. I wouldn't have ever dared doing something like this, but I must admit it; this was the very best thing to do to get result, either you like it or not. Don't you ever forget too that he found you there where you were and if he could do this in front of twenty thousand people, more than two millions viewers and also facing the cameras; he can find you anywhere he wants to. Take my advice and don't make him your enemy, because then you'll be finished."

"Thanks James, we'll talk about this again later."

Of course this gave the Prime Minister a lot to think about, a lot to wonder about and to think about his next move, but he was not without thinking also that his opponents were very powerful too. He couldn't forget what his best minister, who is also a friend and his best adviser told him. But how could anyone stand up against such a powerful institution as the justice system? One thing is sure and this is that a government of a country is in place to make laws and laws he is able to make some even though the Superior Court is able to say that his laws are anticonstitutional. He knows too that when the Superior Court is busy debating about his laws, he can keep busy with more important matters.

I am pretty sure too that sometimes he would want to change this constitution that forbids him to act as he would like to; even if this was only to shut the mouths of those judges who seem to enjoy contradicting or to oppose him. If all of the judges know the constitution this well, how come most of the time there are four against five or five against four? Which ones of the four or of the five don't know the constitution this well? If it is one of the five, this means the decision could easily be overturned. The voice of a government should count in such a case.

It was James who made the first steps to discuss with Just about the whole situation. Just then realized that his father-in-law was squeezed between a rock and a hard place. Just knew though that James would never betray him, no matter what happens.

"Just, my friend, I had a long discussion with the Prime Minister about your case and he assured me that he couldn't act differently than the way he did." "Then he should understand that I too couldn't act differently than the way I did. I just wonder why the court decided to involve the Prime Minister in this whole thing. There must be a very Catholic reason behind this, which is unorthodox. I wouldn't be surprised to hear one day that this was done to embarrass him and they almost succeeded." "I wouldn't be surprised either, because this is what this court has done in many occasions lately. I'm glad you understand this, because I am sure that our Prime Minister didn't act to hurt you or to cause you any harm." "But if I wasn't who I am, I would most likely be shut to death by now." "Maybe not! Another one wouldn't have been able to get out of jail as easy as you did." "I hope they all understood by now that there is no point trying to lock me up." "I'll I can say now is that the Prime Minister is sorry and he would like to have a talk with you." "Are you absolutely sure that this is not a trap?" "If it is, you can always disappear, because you know that no one and nothing can hold you back without your will." "Maybe so, but I wouldn't want the Prime Minister to be embarrassed one more time because of me." "If he is embarrassed one more time, this wouldn't be because of you, but because of himself, so then he would get what he deserves. I wouldn't worry about this, if I were you.

Here is what I suggest you to do. I will let you know when he is alone for a certain time in his office and then, you can get a face-to-face talk with him. Even before you talk to him, make sure that all the cameras are shut down and there is no intercom that can catch what you're saying. If this doesn't work, ask your friend Superhuman to bring him to the fishing camp in Windigo; there you'll have total privacy." "This is a very good idea and maybe this is what we should do in the first place. I'm sure too that he can use a good day off. All you'll have to do is letting me know when he is the least busy and the camp is free." "I will inform you, I have the complete list of all the subscriptions in my office. I know for sure this camp is in great demands until the opening of the chamber again." "Aren't you afraid we could be accused of kidnapping?" "It takes what it takes, but don't you worry about this; he is the only one who can possibly make a complaint and because this is for his own good; there is no danger for this to happen. I will manage to spend the day with his wife along with Jeannette; this will lower her worries." "Do you at least know if he likes fishing or not?" "That doesn't matter if he likes it or not; it is about time that he experience a full day of peace." "You're not afraid that the whole country starts crying over him? They will most likely think he was taking away by the alien they think I am." "No matter what anyone thinks; the Prime Minister will reassure everyone as soon as he is back with a press release. I'm sure he will find a way to tell them how he wanted to go away from everything for one day." "Well then, I count on you to let me know when will be the proper time to proceed. I think I know how I will do it." "What's on your mind?" "I think the best time will be to intercept his limousine when his chauffeur is taking him home for lunch. Is there a whole suite who follows him then or only one car is taking him home?" "He is normally accompanied by two bodyguards who are well armed and of course the chauffeur who is also armed and they all stay near by permanently." "This means then that I will need the help of my friend the whole day if I want success as only a master can do it. I will discuss this with Superhuman and you in the mean time; you let me know when the fishing camp will be free for us." "I will."

"Superhuman, my friend, I have a delicate task for you and this is not with a nobody." "Well, tell me what this is all about and I'll see what I can do." "I need to have a private discussion with our Prime Minister. I talked about it with his closest Minister, who is also his main adviser and we came to the conclusion that the only way to do this would be to kidnap him and to be able to do it I need your help." "Well, this is true; it is a very delicate situation. How do you plan to do this?" "The plan is to intercept his limousine, take it to the fishing camp that you already know, leave there our man and to bring back this car to the governmental garage with his chauffeur and his two bodyguards and hold them there for something like eight hours. Then you could bring it back to the camp, pick up the man and put them all on the road to continue their route. You'll also have to take away from them all ways of communication, so no one can be alerted. I'm hoping that during this time I'll be able to convince our Prime Minister that all I'm doing is for his own good and for the good of his government." "Then let me know when and where and I'll be there, but I'm telling you, this is not my favourite mission." "Maybe so, but I am telling you that this is very necessary, because I kind of understand that the Superior Court is demolishing our government and all of our efforts to keep it in place and our man seems to be completely defenceless before it. This is not fair and I just don't like it." "Good then, have a good fishing day!"

"Alright Just, this will have to be on Thursday at noon hour, when he is going home for lunch. This will be the perfect time. Jeannette and I will already be with his wife to keep her company and to support her and also to keep her back from alerting the authorities." "Alright then, I'll tell my friend and you guys pray that his bodyguards are not too zealous with their weapons."

As previously figured out, Superhuman without any apparent effort took this limousine with all of its occupants to the fishing camp of Windigo and put down this huge car on the ground near the lake and he went to hide himself behind the building to give them time to recapture themselves. The two bodyguards then gave the order to their boss and to the chauffeur to stay inside the vehicle to give them time to look around and see if the surrounding is safe. In a wink of an eye Superhuman was on them to disarm them and to take away their communication units and at the same time he ordered the big boss to come down of the car and to go inside the building where Just was waiting for him.

Superhuman also gave an order to the chauffeur to get down of the car and to put his hands behind his head and to walk away from the car. He gave the same order to the two bodyguards, because he wanted to have the time to search that car and make sure there was no weapon or communicating system in there. As soon as he was done, one of the bodyguards had left, but he quickly got him back and brought him back with the other two.

Then as a gentleman that he is, he started to reassure them and to explain to them that this was just a routine exercise of confidence and trust to make sure they were doing their job well. He asked them then to take their respective place in the car and he brought them all back to the governmental garage in Ottawa where he had to keep them all for the next eight hours.

Then Superhuman went to Wendy's and he ordered eight double cheese hamburgers with four fries and four drinks, but when he was back a few minutes later, there was no one left in the garage. The three had managed to start the car, ran it through the garage door and flew the place. Superhuman found them a mile away, picked them all up again and he brought them back where they should have stayed in the first place.

"I treated you with good manners, but don't you force me to act differently, because you won't like it one bit. I assure you that your boss is treated well and he is in security and it is for a national security that he is taking this one day off. You will get him back in about eight hours in good shape and rested." "You don't think that we should tell his wife?" "So she can alert the whole country and create a panic through all of it. I don't think so and besides, there is already somebody with her, some friends to keep her company. So don't worry about this one."

At the camp sight, this was a total different story.

"Do you have in mind to kill me after all of this?" "Well, not at all Prime Minister, on the contrary, I'm offering you a wonderful day of fresh air and fishing on one of the best fishing lake in this country. I hope you like fishing though." "I especially like it when I am with good company." "Then you'll like this one more than anyone you have been with, but don't try to play games with me, because you wouldn't win anyway and I can find you anywhere I want, if I want to." "What do you want anyway?" "I just want you to understand that I am on your side, that I have always been and if I had to act the way I did at the Bell Center, it is because you didn't give me any other choice. You should think twice in the future before ordering a shoot on sight." "I quickly understood that if they would have shot, they would have hit me and I didn't really like the sensation to be the target of all these firearms." "This is exactly what I wanted you to feel, so you can cancel this order. Do you know that before God, this would have made you a murderer, if they would have shot me under your order? You would then to his sight be worth no less than Hitler or Saddam Hussein who are responsible for thousands of murders." "I didn't see things from this point of view." "It is not because we are Prime Minister of a country that we have the right to kill people. But it is beautiful out there and we should get the equipment out and go fishing, the fish is only waiting for us."

The two men got everything they needed out and they took place in the fishing boat. Just knew already where to go for good catches as he knew this lake for many years. In less than ten minutes Just had already three nice twenty inches pickerel, leaving the Prime Minister perplexed about what he was seeing. I have to say too that each man had chosen the lure of his choice.

"What's happening Minister, the fish doesn't like your lure?" "I don't seem to have a magic touch like you do."

13

"Let me set yours, just to give you a bit of magic, even though magic has nothing to do with it, if you allow me." "I have nothing else to lose; do as you please." "Fish has very good eyes and it can also smell the difference between a real and an artificial worm."

Just installed him a red and white number five Meps and he added a small piece of worm to the hook. He asked his fishing companion to throw his line fifty to sixty feet behind the boat and in less than ten seconds, a very nice twenty-two inches pickerel hooked itself to it, leaving this man overexcited to the point of falling backward.

"Be careful Minister, you have to show it who is the master, not the other way around." "I never had such luck fishing. This must be the best catch I ever had and I am overwhelmed." "Give it the time to get a bit more tired and it will be easier to pull in. Bring it closer to the boat now and I will net it for you. This is a very nice catch, let me measure it up. 22 and a quarter inches, this is the biggest so far. Good then, I will return over there; the pickerel is there and it seems to want to bite." "I've got another one." "Hold it steady, I have one too. I will let the anchor down here; it is a very good spot. Let me get mine in and then I'll help you with yours."

The two men continued until they reach their limits and then Just said:

"We are not allowed to take anymore Minister, we have our limits." "Call me Steph if you don't mind." "I don't mind, but then you too call me Just, this is my name."

"This is quite a bit different, nevertheless, if you want me to call you this way, I will. You don't think we could continue a bit longer?" "We could catch and release, but then we should use barb-less hooks; this way the risk of hurting deadly the fish will be a lot less. We could lose a few, but it doesn't really matter, does it?" "Just for another hour, if it's alright with you?" "But after this I want to cook you a few before we leave." "Alright then, let's see how many we can catch in one hour."

The two men fished joyfully during the next hour. Just got another twelve and Steph got fourteen more.

"I never thought I could learn to fish at my age. I will come back here at least twice a year from now on." "Don't go brag too much about this lake and these catches, because this place will be invaded in a very short time and the fish will disappear just as fast and your colleagues will not be happy about it." "You're right, but what a fishing day! I can't believe this." "Let's go cook a few before the others get here. They might just get to be hungry too." "It is already six thirty. I can't believe how fast time goes by when we are happy on a lake. We could wish to stay on much longer." "I can imagine it feels good to be away from every day problems for one day." "I didn't think about them since we got on this lake." "This is the magic of fishing, but now I have to bring you back to reality, back to our problems a little bit. I believe that your personal enemy, which is also the main enemy of your government right now is the

Superior Court that condemned me wrongly and keep trying to humiliate you." "I don't think though that we can do anything against it." "Maybe you can't, but I do." "How can this be possible? And even if this was possible, you cannot involve me in this." "I don't need your involvement at all. All I'll need is to know when will be the time for them to make a decision concerning your government. If the cause seems to be fair to me, I can make the decision fall on your side and this no matter what they are thinking." "I don't know how you can do this, but this is interesting." "I better not say anymore; just to avoid your involvement. Let's go cook this fish."

The two men put all the equipment away in respect for whoever comes next and Just showed Steph how he was making his filets and then they went in to cook the fish just in time for the return of the other four.

The chauffeur and the two bodyguards were stunned to see the harmony that exists between the two men. When the Prime Minister asked his three employees to swear secrecy about the events of the day, Just violently opposed him and he apologized at the same time for his intervention.

"It is not right to swear and it is not right to make people swear either. The Messiah said not to do it and whoever does it is antichrist. Now, if these three men are trustworthy and they are men of their word; I don't see why a solemn promise from them wouldn't be enough."

"What are you guys saying about this?" "We can promise, if this is alright with our Prime Minister." "Then do it."

"I promise you, Prime Minister not to reveal to anyone ever any of the events we saw and heard today, my word of honour."

The other two men repeated the same words and the Prime Minister said grace for the meal and for the most wonderful day he spent on the lake with Just. They all had the best fish meal of their life.

The other three though admitted going through the worse nightmare that day. Just asked them to forgive him, but he had no other possible choice, because their boss and his surrounding are under permanent surveillance, even at his home.

They all took a good meal and Superhuman brought them all down where they had left.

Just went to join his father-in-law and his wife in the home of the Prime Minister, but mainly to tell them the man was sound and safe and on his way home.

During this time there was a little discussion in the limousine.

"They must have a very powerful flying saucer to be able to carry us this way, so far and at this high speed." "I never heard of such a bizarre thing in my whole life and I never lived through something like this either."

"What about you boss, did you hear of something like this?" "As far as I know and from hearing from certain witnesses, the flying saucers exist and many are swearing haven seen them." "But if swearing is antichrist, should we believe them?" "We can surely think and say that what we lived through today is very strange." "But why can't we say anything about it?" "We don't want to have the journalists and the scientists in our way for years to come. They could be on our case day in and day out. As you already know, I don't like them this much. They are stickier than the bats." "That's a good one and I never heard it either."

"Here we are, Prime Minister." "Take us home Charley, my wife must be worried to death and I hope she didn't alert anyone. Now that I know how, I'll cook her some pickerel tomorrow. I know she will like this. Don't forget it in the car; it tastes a lot better when it's fresh."

In his house, his darling was all excited to finally see him come in and she threw herself in the arms of Jeannette in tears, but these were tears of joy. Everyone could tell though that the pressure was very high in the last few hours.

After going through the heavy metal gate, the driver took the car in the ministerial underground garage of the property and for three particular people; this was the end of a very disturbing day.

The hardest to come for these three will be to keep secret what happened that day. It is not easy for anyone to keep a secret, but these three are professionals and they have seen a lot before.

It was with tears in her eyes that the Premier's wife threw herself in the arms of her husband and the other three thought it was time for them to go home too. And like many other stories; 'All is well that ends well.' We can sleep well after spending a day on the lake and it is almost like after making love. Fresh air, pure air, this is what we find on a lake in the North on top of fresh fish.

CHAPTER 2

But the Judges of the Superior Court weren't happy at all about the decision of the Prime Minister to cancel the shoot on sight. So they decided to order it themselves and they also increased the sentence by two more years, because the prisoner was then an escapee.

Just then got very mad, something that rarely happens to him. He then went on the spot to the closest police station to tell them he was on his way to the Superior Court before the nine judges to find out who voted for his condemnation.

"What is your name?" "When I'm here, no one calls me, I'm here." "We need to get your name before we can proceed." "I am Just contrary to many of you. These should read Solomon's story. Now it is my turn to ask questions. Which ones among you voted for my condemnation?" "We don't have to answer to such insubordination." "I think on the contrary it would be good for all of you and for me to know who is unfair among you, because very soon a squad team of policemen will be here and they will shoot. It would be then a good thing they could shoot on sight as you wish and preferably shooting on the guilty instead of shooting on innocent people." "I don't want to hear anymore from this crazy nonsense man." "You better sit down before I sit you down myself." "I would just like to see this."

In just a wink of an eye, Just was with him, grabbed him by his clothes with one arm, lifted him up four to five feet in the air and drove him down on his chair that couldn't resist even though it was very solid. This man was close to passing out, but he managed to recover all of his senses.

"You wanted to see this; you saw it."

I want to know who voted for my condemnation and this will happen now. Lift up your hand; who ever is for it. Four of you! Now lift up your hand, who ever is against it. Four of you! And you, why didn't you want to vote?" "I didn't want to vote in a case as stupid as this one." "Then you are absolutely useless. If you were against this case, you should have voted against it. Cowardice is just as bad as hypocrisy and you shouldn't occupy the seat you are sitting on." "I am welling to go away, if you allow me to." "One thing at the time, if you had voted against, we wouldn't be discussing this right now."

Then the squad of policemen came in and they all had their gun in hand. The head officer asked for an explanation. But at the same time one of the judges who voted for his execution stood up and yelled they all have to obey the court order and shoot on sight, but at the same time, Just went to stand in front of this judge. After the shooting, this judge looked like a strainer and Just went to stand behind the squad. He then started to applause the action of the squad.

"I suggest now that we go through another vote. Who wants to vote for the cancellation of my condemnation?"

All the hands were up.

"Who wants to vote against the shoot on sight?"

And again, all the hands were up.

"So, this means I am a free to go man?" "You are free to go and this will make us happy if you do." "Thanks a lot gentlemen and I hope to never see you again."

The whole story was on the front page of all the newspapers the next day and on every media there is. All the policemen involved in this shooting were treated for nervous shock. All the judges who survived were saying being lucky to be alive and one of them resigned immediately, saying this job wasn't made for him anymore. I was wondering who would name the next two missing judges. Will they have a better sense of justice in the future? Well, only the future will tell.

It is not given to everyone to be fair, but anyone who can't be shouldn't be detaining such a position, no matter which cause is to be judged. I heard a lot of judgements given unfairly and more than once I wished I could have acted like Just has done it, just to be able to give justice to the one who deserved it and this either it concerned me or not.

Some people would say that we have to submit to the authorities. No one has to submit to the injustice; either it is enforced by a student in a school yard, by a teacher, by a parent, by a boss, by a judge or even by a government.

Hurrah for the Zorros, the Robin Hoods and the musketeers of this world; who gave their life for justice. See what the Messiah said about Justice in Matthew 5, 6. 'Blessed are those who hunger and thirst for righteousness, for they will be filled.'

Thanks to my two heroes, I am filled. If there is not too much justice in this world; there is plenty in my books.

Paul said that we have to submit to the authorities, but Peter and the John of Jesus said exactly the contrary. See Paul in Romans 13, 1. 'Everyone must submit himself to the governing authorities, for there is no authority except that which God has established. The authorities that exist have been established by God.'

BS. This would mean that Hitler was put in place by God to kill more than fifty millions people.

See now what Peter and John said about authorities in Acts 4, 19. 'But Peter and John replied, "Judge for yourselves whether it is right in God's sight to obey you rather than God."'

Jesus and all of his disciples were basically fleeing the authorities constantly that wanted to kill them.

I must admit though that very often we are crushed by the authorities, but we don't have to submit to them. Submission is for wrestling and martial art tricks.

A few people blamed me, saying that the Jesus in the story of the young boy possessed by a demon that I talked about in my previous book didn't have to pray, because Jesus is God and God doesn't pray and He is capable to order demons to move out of a person. This is a real example of a blind who doesn't want to see.

First thing, if you read carefully the story of Jesus, you'll see that Jesus was praying the Father in heaven.

Besides, know that the God who put his words in the mouth of a prophet couldn't have said one thing and have done the exact opposite. This prophet who is the Messiah, the Jesus of Nazareth, who gave these words to us and among these words there are those ones here in Matthew 6, 1. 'Be careful not to do your 'acts of righteousness' before men, to be seen by them. If you do, you will have no reward from your Father in heaven.'

This Jesus in this story of demon possessed boy clearly did his act to be seen by men. See again the story in Mark 9, 25. 'When this Jesus saw that a crowd was coming to the scene, he rebuked the evil spirit.'

Neither God nor Jesus did his actions to be seen by men. In fact, God created everything before he created the man and we can read it at the beginning of the Bible.

The devil would have done the exact opposite. He would have created the man first and he would have told him: 'See how powerful and strong and good I am; you are seeing from your own eyes that I have created all those things for you, now adore me.'

This is what the devil did when he met Jesus in the desert, bragging about owning all of the kingdoms of the world. You'll find other proofs of what I am saying in 2 Corinthians 11, 16-31.

Neither God nor Jesus did things to be seen or admired by men. Neither one preached one thing and did the opposite like Paul did it and of course, you want some proofs of this.

Here is one. See and read carefully Galatians 5, 2-4. 'Mark my words! I, Paul, tell you that if you let yourselves be circumcised, Christ will be of no value to you at all. Again I declare to every man who let himself be circumcised that he is obligated to obey the whole law. You who are trying to be justified by law have been alienated from Christ; you have fallen away from grace.'

What an abomination to say such a thing. The fact is that you are alienated from the devil, if you let yourselves be circumcised and become a child of God like Abraham and his descendants did it.

Well, Paul's grace he can put it where I think, there where is his fat part, because you will be alienated from the false christ, if you let yourselves be circumcised.

See now what Paul did to Timothy in Acts 16, 3. 'Paul wanted to take Timothy along on a journey, so he circumcised him because of the Jews who lived in that area, for they all knew that his father was a Greek.'

One has to be a hypocrite like Paul to call Peter a hypocrite. One man was arguing with me lately, saying that Paul has a good teaching. For sure, when a person is blind, it cannot see and even less if that person doesn't want to see. Do you want to see more of these? There are a lot of them.

Here is one more in 1 Corinthians 7, 39. 'A woman is bound to her husband as long as he lives. But if her husband dies, she is free to marry anyone she wishes, but he must belong to the Lord.'

See now how free she his according to Paul again in 1 Timothy 5, 11-12. 'As for younger widows, do not put them on such list. For when their sensual desires overcome their dedication to Christ, they want to marry. Thus they bring judgement on themselves, because they have broken their first pledge.'

Women are guilty one way or the other, according to Paul anyway, poor them. They would do well to get out of this beast's claws anyway. It is a lot easier, a lot less complicated and a much lighter burden just to stick with the Messiah's messages. See again Jesus in Matthew 11, 28-30. 'Come to me, all of you who are weary and burdened, and I will give you rest. Take my yoke upon you and learn from me, for I am gentle and humble in heart, and you will find rest for your souls. For my yoke is easy and my burden is light.'

Nevermind all the rest, just that message from the word of God should be enough to go towards Him.

Jesus frees you; Paul condemns.

Jesus saves the lost sheep; Paul, a worthless shepherd.

Jesus leads to God; Paul hand people to Satan.

Jesus preaches the Law; Paul preaches against it.

Jesus preaches God; Paul preaches Paul.

So it is yours to choose, but we cannot choose two masters, because we can only serve one of them at the time. See Jesus in Matthew 6, 24. 'No one can serve two masters. Either he will hate the one and love the other, or he will be devoted to the one and despise the other. You cannot serve both God and the devil.'

No, you cannot serve God and serve the devil, so you have to make a choice and this choice will follow you through eternity and the consequences too.

There is a very important message coming from Jesus that seems to me is ignored by way too many people and you can read it in Matthew 7, 15-20. 'Watch out for false prophets. They come to you in sheep's clotting, but inside they are ferocious wolves. By their fruits you will recognize them. Do people pick grapes from thornbushes, or figs from thistles? Likewise every good tree bears good fruits, but a bad tree bears bad fruits. A good tree cannot bear bad fruits and a bad tree cannot bear good fruits. Every tree that does not bear good fruits is cut down and thrown into fire. Thus by their fruits you will recognize them.'

And this is how I discovered a lot of bad fruits, a lot of lies and contradictions in Paul's writing. A good man doesn't hand men over to Satan and even less condemning an angel of heaven to hell, because he teaches a different gospel than his. See 1 Corinthians 5, 5. 'Hand this man over to Satan.'

See also 1 Corinthians 16, 21-22. 'I, Paul, write this greeting in my own hand. If anyone does not love the Lord, a curse be on him. Come, O Lord!'

We can read the same thing in Psalm 104, 35.

Someone lately and before me called this a good teaching.

Can someone seriously say that this is the way to call sinners like Jesus did?

See also Galatians 1, 8-9. 'But even if we (Paul and company) or an angel from heaven should preach a gospel other than the one we preached to you, (full of lies and contradictions) let him be eternally condemned! As we have already said, so now I (Paul) say it again: If anybody is preaching to you a gospel other than what you accepted, let him be eternally condemned!'

In another word, Paul is inviting him to his home, which is hell.

One such message in itself from Paul should have been enough to alert all human beings that such message was from the devil. As far as I am concerned Paul's gospel and company is nothing else than lies and contradictions, misleading, just like Jesus said it in Matthew 7, 15; 'They are ferocious wolves.'

I strongly believe the reason why all of the Christians churches and others kept the teaching of Paul was because it allowed them to get richer and it allowed them also to become paedophiles. Jesus' teaching is the total opposite.

They seduce you with their bad fruits, their lies that resemble the truth, weeds that look like wheat in your garden.

Just like this one for example. See Paul in Romans 10, 13. 'For, "Everyone who calls the name of the Lord will be saved."'

It looks true, but look now at what the Messiah said about this in Matthew 7, 21. 'Not everyone who says to me, 'Lord, Lord,' will enter the kingdom of heaven, but only he who does the will of my Father who is in heaven.'

Now, is this contradicting enough for you? Is this clear enough? 'Seek and you will find.' The Messiah said.

I did and I found a lot.

Jesus told us to seek the truth and if he said so, it is because the truth is hidden and if you look for it, you too will find a lot of these abominations from the devil. It is also very normal that you have been taken by the seducer. What is not normal is for you to put your head deep in the sand like an ostrich and to ignore the truth once you've seen it.

Always remember what the Messiah said, that no good tree can produce bad fruits and no bad tree can produce good fruits. The truth doesn't come out of the mouth of a liar. So if you see something good that seems to come from Paul; it means it is not from him, but from one of Jesus' disciples.

It was very easy for Paul or for any Roman in a position of command in those days to intercept and to steal some messages; some writing and letters from the Messiah's disciples and to use them the way they liked as certain religions and like Paul did it.

I wrote a bit earlier; 'Paul, a worthless pastor.' This brings me back to Zachariah 11, 17. 'Woe to the worthless shepherd who deserts the flock! May the sword strike his right arm and his right eye! May his arm be completely withered, his right eye totally blinded!'

See now what a certain pastor did to his sheep in 2 Corinthians 2, 12-13. 'Now when I (Paul) went to Troas to preach the gospel of Christ and found that the Lord had opened a door for me, I still had no peace of mind, because I did not find my brother Titus there. So I said good-by to them and I went to Macedonia.'

One could wonder if Paul was there to preach or to see Titus or yet to pick up the money. Titus might have been gone with it. We know that Paul was troubled by it and this enough to abandon them all, even though the

Lord has opened a door for him. Someone might say it is just a presumption from my part, but the story in the Holy Book doesn't give any other reason for Paul to abandon them all. Now I know it is because God loved and speared them.

But the fact remains that Paul is a pastor who abandoned his sheep, leaving them without a pastor, no matter what the reason was. We can also recognize Paul's writings by the way he spoke about the Messiah and this in a way that no other of Jesus' disciples have done. Instead of saying; 'Our Lord Jesus Christ.' like the other apostles, Paul was saying; 'In Christ, for Christ, by Christ, from Christ and even the Messiah's name backward, Christ Jesus.

Now, getting back to the worthless pastor as it is written in Zachariah 11, 17 and the right eye that he lost; I would like to bring you to a little story that is written in Galatians 4, 14-15 that might just be connected to it. Paul is saying to the Galatians: 'Even though my illness was a trial to you, you did not treat me with contempt or scorn. Instead, you welcomed me as if I were an <u>angel of God</u>, as if I were <u>Christ Jesus</u> himself. What has happened to all your joy? I can testify that, if you could have done so, you would <u>have torn out your eyes</u> and given them to me.'

Paul knew very well what happened to them, but he wouldn't tell us in his lying gospel. This is the way the Galatians felt before they found out that Paul was a devil disguised as an angel of heaven. It was most likely because Paul was missing an eye, a right eye that was completely blinded. A Jesus' disciple who knew about Paul must have told the Galatians about him and there is when the change of heart came about. This disciple opened their eyes and this is what a Jesus' disciple has to do, because this kind of disciple is the light in the darkness, the light of the world. See Matthew 5, 14. 'You are the light of the world; a city on a hill cannot be hidden.' But many devilish people want to turn it off.

Let's go see now about the one who has a withered right arm also mentioned in Zachariah 11, 17. We can find it in Acts 28, 3-5. 'Paul gathered a pile of brushwood and, as he put it on the fire, a viper, driven out by the heat, fastened itself on his hand. When the islanders saw the snake hanging from his hand, they said to each other, "This man must be a murderer, for though he escaped from the sea; Justice has not allowed him to live. But Paul shook the snake off into the fire and suffered no ill effect."

The islanders figured Paul out right when they said he was a murderer and I did too. And of course the devil is not honest enough to tell the truth that a viper can do no harm to a dry, to a completely dead arm.

No, I didn't find all of these things on my own. The Lord guided me to the things I must see and this has the purpose to help you open your eyes and I hope with my whole heart that it is working for you.

But I found more yet. I found the place where Paul himself admitted that he is lost. This is something I was not expecting at all. It was when I was looking in the New Testament where the writer was talking about Jesus in terms of; 'For Christ, by Christ,' etc. This I know that none of Jesus' disciple has done.

One has to go look first in the so called rapture of Paul in 1 Thessalonians 4, 16-17. 'For the Lord himself will come down from heaven, with a loud command, with the voice of the archangel and with the trumpet call of God and <u>the dead in Christ</u> will rise first. After that, we (Paul and company) who are still alive and are left will be caught up together with them (the dead in Christ) in the clouds to meet the Lord in the air. And so we will be with the Lord forever.'

First of all, I say that we are not dead in Jesus, but we are alive. Second, if we rely on what Jesus said in the parable of the weeds, it is the lost souls that will be taken away and thrown into the fire, then the dead in Christ with whom Paul is in the air and on the clouds. See Matthew 13, 41-42. And third, see what this demon said, this Paul said about the ones who are dead in Christ in 1 Corinthians 15, 18. 'Then those also who have fallen asleep in Christ are lost.'

There is a French Canadian expression that says having your head in the clouds means being somehow kind of lost.

And Paul really said he will be with the dead in Christ, with his lord in the clouds, then he will be lost. I knew it, but to tell the truth as usual, I never expected to find such an obvious proof as this one.

I could tell you a lot more about Paul, his lies and his contradictions, but I don't want to neglect talking about my heroes, which is a lot more fun anyway.

CHAPTER 3

Jeannine, Just's cherished wife was about to give birth to her first child, but her delivery became one of the worse nightmares to her gynaecologist. The little girl came out normally from her mom's belly, but her doctor overexcited about it became suddenly worried to death. The little girl was in his arms and one second later she was gone. All stunned about it, he turned to Just trying to understand what was happening and even to tell him he had nothing to do with it. Although, Just quickly understood that his little girl who was just born has the same power he has. At the same time the new mom was screaming with pain and her gynaecologist bended down on her to examine what was the problem. Then he yelled; "There is another one, she has an identical twin. I don't understand this; the scan was showing only one foetus."

So the doctor preceded to delivery another baby and when he took her in his arms he said; "She is exactly like the first one." And while he was saying this, the little baby disappeared from his arms one more time.

Just then asked the doctor to let him alone with the mother for a few minutes. The doctor thinking he was going crazy himself didn't insist any longer and he went out to breath a bit of fresh air, because the incomprehension was making him sick. Just asked him not to go too far and he will come to talk to him in a few minutes.

"Little girl, your little game lasted long enough and if you keep it up; you're going to kill your mother and this is something I wouldn't allow. So come in my arms and we'll make a little trip to the future, so you can see that after all, life is not this bad outside your mom's belly."

So this little baby, this little girl came out of her mom's belly on her own this time and she came to snuggle up herself in her father's arms who quickly rapped her up with a cozy and warm little blanket.

"Call the nurse Jeannine; I must make a little trip with this little girl, but we'll be back within a minute, a minute and a half. Don't you worry my love, I'll bring her back soon, but it is very necessary that she understands what's happening to her; otherwise she wouldn't pull out of it and neither would we."

So Just brought her five years farther in the future, so she can see how much fun she gets appearing and disappearing and playing this game with the other kids her age. But at the same time, he could see how the depression was getting to his wife because of his long absences. He could see also at the same time his little boy of four who has the same power and then he brought back his little girl who needed badly her mother's breast.

"Here's your little girl darling. She understands now the importance to make her first steps in this world that could seem terrible for a baby in her condition. I am persuaded too that if all the babies of this world had the power to do it; they would all return where they came from, there where it is nice and warm and fed freely and without any effort. There is a good reason why their first move is crying."

Then Just left his baby in her mother's arms and he went to meet with the gynaecologist who proceeded to the delivery of his baby; knowing very well that he needed an explanation.

"I am willing to explain to you my baby's condition, but first, I need the certainty from you that this whole story will stay between us." "What I have seen from my own eyes is either a miracle or witchcraft. But I know very well that it is impossible for a new born baby to return in her mom's belly, unless there is a way that is totally unknown to me and this is beyond me, I must admit." "Before I tell you what this is all about, I need the assurance of confidentiality from you." "This might be a hard thing for me to do, but I can assure you that I won't tell anyone of all I witnessed here or what you are going to tell me about it. I don't want to be locked up for mental illness." "I have the power to move myself as I want to and where I want to." "Doesn't everybody have this power, except maybe for the paraplegics?" "You don't understand. Wait for me for five seconds and I'll be back….Here is a business card from one of your colleagues in Paris; I just came back from there." "Are you trying to drive me crazy?" "On the contrary, you're not an idiot and I wouldn't have put the health of my wife and baby in the hands of a dumb doctor. Far from me is that idea, but I'm trying to make you understand the situation. I understand that this is not an easy thing to understand, because there is only one case in this world and this is me and also my daughter now. This is why she could get out of your arms when she wanted to. She can and this is possible for her through her thoughts. Let me show you something in a different way and in a bit simpler. Just stay put on your chair and I will move myself around this room and this without walking any step what so ever and where I want to. I'm here, I'm here now, I am behind you. It doesn't matter where, either it is Paris, London, China, Japan or Norway or anywhere. In fact, Just before I came to see you a few minutes ago; I took my baby five years in the future, so she can settle down, just to give her confidence in life. Otherwise she would have continued to go back in her mom's belly and she would have ended up killing her mom and this is why I intervened. I also saw that you didn't understand what was going on." "To tell you the truth; it is not understandable either." "I agree with you and this is why I am here. You must understand too that it is very important to keep a lid on this story; otherwise we'll never come out of it." "I agree there too." "Now I hope you'll still be here next year, because there will be another similar case, but it will be a boy this time. At least now; you are worn ahead of time." Laughs......

Just returned near his wife and his new born baby, who was sleeping peacefully, having her head leaning against her mom's breast. What a picture this is, he thought!

"Don't you move darling; I'll be back in three seconds."

And three seconds later, just was taking pictures of his daughter and her mother, because he wanted that his wife Jeannine could see too what he was looking at, which means a picture of reproduction, the main will of God for his creation. It is the picture of life and love, the picture of a man and a woman who became one flesh, a child, a new human being who is for the time being a child of God. May she can stay this way forever! This is something I wish from the bottom of my heart.

But Just didn't have peace of mind, remembering what he saw five years in the future just after the birth of his daughter whom he named Justine. Seeing his wife depressed because of him being too busy with the problems of this world was a burden to him and he thought it was time again to have a good conversation with God about it.

"My Lord God, your Messiah, the Jesus of Nazareth said one day that I will find rest for my soul if I join him and if I receive his instructions, but today I am troubled, because I saw my loving wife depressed because of my absences answering your calls. And as You perfectly know it Yourself, if I leave her alone so many times, it is because the love of the most has cooled off again. What I mainly saw is that it is cooled off to the point of keeping me so busy that I have to neglect my family." "How is your soul?" "My soul is at peace at the present time, but my spirit is troubled presently and I am worried for my own family and I don't want to give a reason for Paul to be right when he said; 'It is good for a man not to marry.'"

"Don't you worry about those small details, because I'm not about to abandon you. Remember one more thing this Messiah said and it is written in Matthew 6 from verse 25-34. 'Therefore I tell you, do not worry about your life.'

Don't worry about these things either; because I know your needs better than you do yourself and I never forsake my faithful children." "How can You explain what I saw about my wife five years ahead then?" "I showed you what I wanted you to see, because I wanted to have this conversation with you. As far as your obligations concerning your duties; don't worry about them either, because both of your children will help you with that and this from their young age and you'll be able to rest on them. This will be for them only a fun game, but this will allow you to spend good times with their mom. You'll see then all the importance and the good reasons for having touched a woman, just like all of the patriarchs touched their wives. See what Solomon accomplished by touching all of his princesses, his wives and his concubines. He actually acquired more territory for his country by touching his wives, touching his princesses than all of the other kings of Israel reunited did with their armies and their wars and he is known as the wisest of all. So go peacefully and always remember that my main wish is for men to be <u>fruitful</u>, to <u>multiply</u> and to <u>fill up the earth</u>. This is the main goal of my creation, so say it for everyone to know. And you are right to mention Jesus of Nazareth, the Messiah and his messages, because what he said is coming from my own mouth; it is the truth. Talk to you soon Just and never forget that I am always there for you and for all of my children."

The main reason for the devil to have men to commit so many murders and to declare so many wars, like Hitler did it, is to avoid the earth to be filled, because so is the will of God. It is for the same reason that Paul said it was best for a man not to touch a woman. The devil knows that when the earth will be filled; this will be his end.

I asked a pastor from a Baptist Evangelist Church once what he was thinking of Solomon and he answered; 'Not much.'

He might go to heaven, because as far as I think; he is poor in spirit. See Matthew 5, 3. 'Blessed are the poor in spirit, for theirs is the kingdom of heaven.'

Then Just returned to his wife and to his baby happier than ever. Not only he was very happy with his conversation with God, but he was also at peace in his soul and mind and it was true that his burden was much lighter.

"How are you doing darling?" "I am marvellously well sweetheart. Since you brought back this little girl, she seems to accept life near me now, but I admit that she scared me a lot earlier." "This is luck from heaven that I was there, because she would have killed you and the doctor couldn't do anything about it." "Lucky for us too that you understood quickly what was going on. We have to understand the poor little girl; it is not easy to get out of a nice warm nest on a cold morning and this is surely what she felt." "I can't tell; I don't remember my first day in this world." "I'm sure that you were a lot stronger than her. So, what I understand, according to what happened is that she has the same power than you have?" "This is it darling; you will be able to control this one only if she is docile and obedient. So, it will be my duty to keep a close eye on her and to direct her in the right direction, but I'm not worried, because the Lord reassured me about her.

Our next child will be very similar." "This is a good thing to hear and I thank you my love."

Then Superhuman and his wife Johanne entered Jeannine's hospital room to congratulate the new mom.

"Ho, how gorgeous this little baby is!"

At the same time the little Justine disappeared and her father picked her up under the bed and he told her that these people were his best friends and she was to never be afraid of them, especially when her father is around. Then Just put her back in her mother's arms.

"You'll have to excuse her, because she is a little shy of everything and everybody that she doesn't know. And because she is like her father; she just moves away every time she is not sure of her surrounding. She did the same thing to my doctor earlier today, who was totally stunned about it. Luckily, she seems to recognize her father's voice. He must have been talking to her every day for the last seven months." "This means then she inherited her father's power and she is as pretty as her mom. This is excellent news."

"Come Superhuman; let's leave the two women talk about their own adventures; we can go out and talk about ours, if you don't mind."

"See you in a bit sweetheart; I won't be long and I won't be far." "Good, because we never know what is going to happen with her."

"How did the delivery turn out?" "The first one turned out very well, but I thought the second one would kill me." "No, you had two?" "No, I had one twice." "But this is impossible." "Ho yes it is, with a baby like this one. She didn't like the temperature, so she returned where she came from."

When hearing these words, Justine went to snuggle in her father's arms. She didn't seem to like the way the conversation between her mom and her friend was heading too much.

"What are you doing here you? You need much more your mother than your father at the present time and I bring you back immediately. You must stay in your mom's arms for the time being."

"Excuse me for a sec., my friend; I'll be right back."

"What happened for her to leave you this time?" "She doesn't seem to like our conversation." "Try not to talk too much about her; she seems to have a sensitive heart this little one, but I'll have another mouth to mouth conversation with her very soon."

"Excuse me young lady; I didn't mean to offend you and I'll be more careful in the future."

"My son could squeeze so hard that he was hurting me. And ho my God, did my breast suffered, especially when I was two minutes late. He sure could keep me on time this one even better than his dad. On the other hand, he helped me so many times with the things I could hardly lift. You should have seen him when I needed to move the piano to clean behind it. Today he can lift the front of a car with no problem at all, but he must put some gloves on, not to tear his hands apart." "I only hope that our children will be as good friends as we are." "I don't worry about this one, because I think they will be united at least in the justice." "In fact, her name is Justine and if she carries her name as well as her father does; I won't have to worry about her either."

"Excuse the disturbance Superhuman." "Ho, this didn't bother me one bit. I just came back from a beach of Miami where I made flying for about ten miles a shark that was getting ready to eat a child. One of these days, when I have a bit more time ahead of me; I will try to give them a good lesson. They seem to think that human flesh is good food for them." "You only have to get them out of the sea for ten minutes or so and let them dry a little on the sand under the sunshine; so when you'll put them back in the water, they'll be happy to get the deepness of the sea again. And because they all have a very good memory; they might remember maybe that it is better for them to stay away from shore, no matter how high is the temptation." "This is fine, but they are millions." "How many can you throw in one hour?" "I don't really know, a thousand maybe." "This will be a thousand less threatening and there are no millions of them that come to eat on the beach." "You always have a good advice for me and I am so happy that you are my friend and congratulation for becoming a dad today." "I am very happy too that you are my friend, but I was wondering when these congratulations will finally come." Laughs.....

A good handshake followed and at that moment Superhuman wondered how strong Just might be. He already knew that Just could stop him one day, but he didn't think that he used physical strength to do it. They both compared their speed, but they never thought of comparing their strength. Of course, this was only a man's thought. Superhuman always thought that there was no one wiser than Just, but after this handshake; he realized that Just too had a very strong hand grip. Superhuman thought that this might be a subject he will talk about one day, but that day wasn't the time. The time was to joyfulness and not about comparisons. Then the two men returned to their wife.

"How are these two charming ladies doing, especially the new mother?" "Can't be any better; the little girl is sleeping peacefully now." "I wished I could have had a little girl too, but our boy made so much damage when he came to this world that the doctor told us to put an end to pregnancies immediately, if we want the mother to stay alive. I know Johanne doesn't like me to talk about this, but friends are made for confidences too. And we don't have better friends than the two of you." "I am sorry for the two of you that your family is ended, but if Just agrees with me, I would like you to be legal guardians of our child. She will be your child in one sense this way, but she's ours first." "This is the greatest joy someone gives me since Just offered me to be part of his clan. We are happy to accept and be sure that I will watch over her like I do for the apple of my eyes." "Don't you ever forget that she has a very special power." "This will be more of a problem when she enters her teenage years."

"I must take her for another little trip in the future, so she can understand that she doesn't have to be afraid and disappear every time that something new comes up. She must understand that unless there is an imminent danger, she doesn't have to be scared if her father is around and that she can rely on him." "Are you only sure that this couldn't affect her to go like this in the future and come back to normal afterwards." "Don't you worry guardian and don't take your new role so seriously; just remember that she still has her mother and father. I brought her already to the age of five and as you can see for yourself, she's doing fine and she can sleep peacefully. No, I only want her to get through her mind that she doesn't have to worry when she is with her parents, that's all." "This is what Batman thought too when he was a child, but this didn't stop his parents to be killed." "Batman's parents weren't Justine's parents." "This is true too, I agree. He didn't have Superhuman as a guardian either." "This is an extra reason to stop worrying for her." "You're right and she couldn't have a wiser father than you either. But you must understand that I already love her as she was my own daughter." "I'm happy about that, but I am the father."

Then Jeannine's parents entered the room too and the head nurse came in to tell them that a maximum of only three visitors at the time was allow in the room of a new mother.

Then Johanne and Superhuman said good-bye, promising to visit again soon.

"Hi sweetheart, how things with you?" "For me things are fine and for the baby too, but my gynaecologist is a bit troubled." "How can he be troubled; he is not the father?" "No, but he saw something he shouldn't have seen." "If he is a gynaecologist; he must have seen a baby coming to this world before today." "He has never seen a double delivery like mine." "What is so strange in welcoming a baby nowadays?" "Welcoming a baby once is fine, but doing it twice is rather strange and rare and troubling even for a gynaecologist, don't you think?" "No, don't tell me that she is like her father?" "Yes mom and she's not easy to keep in place, just like her father."

"Well, this is good news. Having a superhero in the family is great, but having two is twice greater." "This is what you think dad? I rather think she will have difficulty to play like any other kids her age."

"Don't you worry about that sweetheart; I already saw how much fun she has playing with the other kids her age and believe me; it is better than I have ever done myself. I already know too that for her to help me with my mission will be only a fun game. She will actually have a happy life."

"Well, all of these are wonderful news and I am very happy to be the grand-father of such a special child. Grand-ma might have a hard time to play hide and seek with her, but she can always teach her how to play the piano."

"Well, I don't want to sound too insolent, but I sincerely think that the new mom needs some rest now. Having two different deliveries in the same day are rather exhausting." "You must be right about that Just and I thank you for taking such a good care of our daughter. She deserves it and she deserves you too."

"Make sure you rest enough my girl and you call me if you need what so ever." "Count on me mom, but don't you worry, because even if I only need a smile; Just brings it to me in one instant and he can spend the night in my room without anyone noticing it. And besides, he respects my need to sleep and to rest. He is a wonderful man and thanks to him, I had my life spared today, but I will explain all of this to you later on mom, Bye."

The couple of grand-parents would have liked to spend more time with their daughter, but they also understood the goodwill of their son-in-law who has at heart the health of his wife and this is a very good thing.

Just was wondering how many times he could bring his new born baby in the future without causing any mental damage to her. This didn't seem to have any side effect the first time, but we never know, because there is no antecedent to the matter. This didn't seem to bother her at all the first time. On the other hand, if he could this way give her confidence in life and trust in her parents and friends, then she couldn't be anything but better. When he saw her at the age of five; she rather looked physically and mentally healthy. Although, just like any other parents in this world; Just must learn to have trust in his children too and he must know that being over protective with them can lead to bad behaviours.

I personally left home very young with only a quarter in my pocket. This hasn't been easy and neither always funny, but I have learned to help myself more than once. I quickly learned that work, no matter what it is, allows us to pay our way and since I was introduced to work very young, work has never scared me.

But I wanted to be on my own and this is what I did. I mainly wanted to get off my father's grip, because he didn't really have the most sense of justice, at least as far as I was concerned or with my mom. I just know today that if I didn't get out when I did, things would have turned out very bad for both of us. We have to honour our parents, but some how, they have to be honourable too, at least a little.

Although, as far as I can remember, I know now that God has always guided me; I mean lead me to get in when it was time and lead me to get out also when it was time. And all of this, I am sure is done through the thoughts. God is a fair Father and He is also my Father and Him I love with all of my heart. So I say to all of the children of the world that no matter how is your earthly father; there is a Father who is in heaven and who loves you more than anyone and he is infinitely good, infinitely just, infinitely perfect and He will never let you down. It is not very important either if you see Him or not, because he sees you and He hears you. What is the most important is that you listen to his voice, because his voice will lead you to his marvellous kingdom.

"Tell me James, why are you so happy to have a grand-daughter with such a power?" "Well, think about it for a minute Jeannette; we will never have to worry about her and for any reason, except if she gets sick maybe. She will always be able to get out of any awkward situation without the help of anyone; contrary to all of us who sometimes need people like Just and this in more than one occasion as you witnessed it yourself. Can you imagine how we would have turned out without him?" "I don't even want to imagine it; the ruin is not funny for anyone." "It is though what could have happened and very often depression is next, but we were very lucky. I only wish that this little Justine becomes as valiant and as generous as her father." "I am not worry about this one at all; with parents like she has, she can do nothing else than to turn out alright." "May you be one hundred per cent right." "Her father who can travel in time might just be able to reassure us about that." "The fact remains that he might not want to." "We'll see. Good night!" "Good night to you too!"

Children, no matter who they are don't ever know to what extend their parents and their grand-parents worry about them and about their wellbeing. Many even seem to be ungrateful, but we don't really know the bottom of their heart, because most of them learn to express their feelings much later in their life. Some of them remain discreet all their life; I mean the ones that we have to squeeze the facts out of them. They are so closed within themselves that they are dangerous for themselves and for others.

I am not the one who would blame Just to know more about the future of his daughter. One thing is sure and this is, if I had the same power, I might have had the chance to change a few things in the life of my son and also a little bit of my attitude towards him. Although, for many years I seemed to be for him the nicest and the strongest dad.

I even composed a song that concerned him and his feelings towards me. It is written in French though, but I will translate it for you.

When a Dream is over

When a dream is over, what is left?
The sad reality that poisons
The existence of the ones who can't dream
A childhood of fun games that went out too quickly.

1
I have a fifteen years old son who is not like before
When he was only three and jumping in my arms
To him I was then the strongest of all dads
The one who knew everything, the one he mainly loved

2
Now he's grown up and he is facing life
Don't understand all the time what my love is about
When he'll understand, he too will see
That to become a man, it is only his turn.

Chorus
When a dream is over, what is left?
The sad reality that poisons
The existence of the ones who can't dream
A childhood of fun games that went out too quickly
A childhood of fun games that went out too quickly.

I made one about my dad also and it's called;
My Father in The Gathering Evenings

Ho how I loved to hear my father
Singing in the gathering evenings
He was not the most educated
But there was none like him to talk about things
How he knew to talk about roses.

Songs about our first parents
This was what he sang back then
Talking about their sins
And what happened to them
And to talk about women
How he knew what they claim.

Then I was sitting in the stairs
Trying hard to stay awake
To listen to his fiddle
This was giving me shivers
There was nothing as tender
How much I loved to listen.

I could listen for hours
Without seeing the time going by
He was taking me into my bed
When I fell asleep
And then I was dreaming
How short were the nights.

I learned since to sing too
Like him in the parties
And I learned to make songs
I sing when I have the occasion
Just like in my childhood
I was so lucky to have the chance
To have my father in all the gatherings.

CHAPTER 4

The first time the Lord asked me to write for Him; I told Him that all I could write are some songs and that they were full of grammatical errors, but He reassured me by saying there were lots of people who could correct them. Today I know that there are a lot of people who like to point them out to me, I mean my errors. Most of them mention more my grammatical errors instead of talking about what is the most important, the content, the very important Jesus' messages and the lies and the contradictions they have never seen from a so called apostle. They act like little demons, who are trying to discourage me, but for me, it is way more important listening to the voice of the Lord and I am not at all the one who gets discouraged easily. Like one could say, I have seen worse.

I write mainly about the word of God and because it is endless; I will most likely write to the end of my life, at least, I hope so. To write, this is of my capability, but when comes to the distribution of my work in all of the nations of the world, this is way beyond me, for now anyway. Then I leave this to my God and I am not worried about it, because He has a way to cross borders a lot easier than me. I know too that what I'm doing is according to His will, so why should I fear?

When the Messiah asked us to make disciples for him in all the nations; he didn't tell us how to proceed, but he told us <u>he will be with us to the end</u>. This is enough for me, because he (the word of God) is with me every day. I learned too, a very longtime ago that when one door is closing, another one gets opened almost instantly.

"How are you doing today sweetheart?" "Can't be any better, my love. This little darling is just like an angel of heaven and she slept just like an angel too. She woke me up only once in the whole night. Can you believe this?" "Of course I can, if you say so. There is hardly anyone as frank as you are. I went out a couple of times, but I kept an eye on both of you almost all night. She woke up a few times, but I picked her up and I coddled her and when she was wriggling a bit too much, I just put her back near your breast and she seemed to be satisfied with it. To tell you the truth; I understand her very well." "The two of you make a nice pair. I will need a boy next time to balance things up in the family." "Let's just hope he will be on your side." "If things are the way I want to; there will be no one against the other in my family." "I hope so too sweetheart, but I cannot forget the

Messiah's message that we can read in Matthew 10, 34-38. 'Do not suppose that I have come to bring peace on earth. I did not come to bring peace, but a sword. For I have come to turn a man against his father, a daughter against her mother, a daughter-in-law against her mother-in-law—a man's enemies will be the members of his own household. Anyone who loves his father or mother more than me (the word of God) is not worthy of me; (the word of God) anyone who loves his son or daughter more than me (the word of God) is not worthy of me (the word of God) and anyone who does not take his cross and follow me (the word of God) is not worthy of me. (The word of God)'"

And according to my own experiences, this is exactly what the word of God did, because many members of my family don't speak to me anymore and this is because I preach the truth and they have received the lies with wide opened minds.

"These words from the Messiah are very hard and I hope my family will be spared from this scourge from God." "The Messiah knew already that one person out of two will accept the word of God and because that more often than otherwise, when a person doesn't agree with the other's belief, it becomes the enemy. If there is a prayer to our God that I would like to suggest you; this would be to pray that all of our children accept the word of God, the truth, then they will agree with us and this is the only way to avoid this scourge." "But we won't be able to force anyone to believe or not in what so ever." "My plan of course will be to prove to them that God is the Creator of all things and if this is up to me; God will talk to them as He talks with me; then they will understand. But I must tell you that God already told me they will help me with my mission; then I am reassured about them and you should be too." "I haven't realized to what extent I am lucky to have you as a husband until now. I am sure blessed among all women in the world and if God didn't hear me; tell Him yourself." "Come on darling; God is listening to all who speaks to Him with sincerity. You shouldn't doubt this, not even for a second. Don't you ever think that I am a person like the Virgin Mary or any other idol, who would be a mediator between God and people, because the Messiah said: 'No one comes to the Father except through me.'

Can you see darling that no one goes to the Father in heaven except through the word of God. This is why it is so important to spread it, to propagate it as much as possible and not to suppress the truth. The Father receives you just as well as He receives me; don't doubt it. And besides, you and I are only one." "You are a wonderful husband and mainly my favourite hero." "Well, I hope so. I have to leave, but I'll be back soon."

Then Just got a very urgent call and he himself called Superhuman right away. A passenger train operator in a moment of furious madness, instead of stopping his engine as he was ordered to, got on the restricted rails for the time being and this at a very high speed with the purpose of causing a frontal deadly accident with a commercial train loaded with many waggons full of fuel.

While Just was busy reasoning this operator; Superhuman with an extreme effort kept busy trying to stop the commercial train. He who mentioned once not knowing his limits came very close to find out that day. But one could tell that the operator of this train didn't want to collaborate, because even if his train wasn't going forward anymore; the drive wheels were still turning full blast and this to the point that the flames were raising high on both sides of the locomotive and the heat became almost unbearable. This hero was wondering if he could hold it yet for some time and in a moment of anger; he simply lifted the first locomotive and he let it down beside the rails. The train was still pushing forward, but at least this way it was easier to hold it.

During that time the other train was speeding at one hundred and sixty kilometres an hour and the operator didn't want to hear anything, but Just seeing this train wasn't very far from the other train anymore just pulled this operator off the controls and he knocked him off with a punch in the forehead. Then Just asked the assistant operator to take over the controls and to stop this train immediately, but this assistant in a moment of panic said that he didn't know enough to get involve and this was his first day on the job.

Then Just had to think and to think fast, because there were more than six hundred people on board. So Just went in a passenger convoy and he asked them to activate the manual emergency brakes right away.

Then he went in the commercial locomotive to neutralize the other operator who was dying out of fear.

"Cut the gas immediately or I'll throw you straight through this window." "I can't do that; we are invaded by aliens." "Cut the gas idiot; he is not an alien, he is a superhero who just saved your life. He is my best friend and you do what I said, now."

This operator obeyed well despite his willingness and Superhuman went to stop the other train right away that was still coming pretty fast.

"Get me the communication with the controller and do it quick."

"Alert, we are invaded by some aliens and they took over my engine."

"Shut up you stupid man and let me have this unit. Go sit down before I smash you; you're a shame to the masculine gender acting like a young girl who just pissed her panties."

"Hey controller, I don't know your name, but let me explain the situation to you here. An operator at a passenger train tried to create a frontal accident between his train and yours and believe it or not, if we didn't intervene, there would have been most likely the biggest train accident in history." "But who are you exactly?" "Me and my friend are only superheroes and your operator here thinks we are aliens. I think he's got his head in the clouds somewhere, but on the other hand; I have to admit that he saw some very unusual things for a simple human. I don't tell you my name simply because we prefer and by far anonymity by necessity, just to be able to continue our duties peacefully." "I saw on our radar there was a train out of control, but no one was answering my calls." "It was in fact an operator out of his mind who was controlling the other train and it is up to you now to either send him to a mental test or to get him locked up. I had to knock him down to make him leave the controls and my friend just stopped his train. You must send two other operators on this sight now, because this one here is too troubled to continue; he is totally hysterical. He too needs some psychiatric care." "I don't know who you are exactly, but I thank you in the name of all the ones you saved the life and also for sparing us from a lot of damages." "Ho, this is nothing, but you are welcome. It is mainly to save souls that we came to their rescue."

Then Just bound up this operator on his seat to make sure he doesn't do anymore harm by getting back to the controls of this train again. He went out afterwards and he put this locomotive back on its rails and this to the stupefaction of Superhuman.

"Well, the least I can say is that you have some mussels too." "This happens sometimes, but contrary to you; I must have both of my feed solid on the ground and I can't propel myself up in the air like you do to thousands of kilometres away. I can hardly jump twenty feet high." "This is quite impressive anyway." "Don't even mention it; because this is something I try to hide most of the time. I rather use my mental capacities than my physical ones. God supplies me with strength as I need it and I don't really know to which extent He would go, but this is convenient in times like these. It is very rare that I can't control an individual with my thoughts, but with these two idiots today; I must admit that I failed and I don't understand why." "Maybe it is just because they are not up to par up there." "That is a good point and you might just be right. I should go confront him to see how he is recovering. Do you mind staying here until the two new operators get here? I will go talk to him and then I'll have to go see my young family right after." "Say hi to both of them for me, will you?" "I sure will. See you soon my friend and make sure you're going to rest after this."

"What happened to me?" "You were knocked down with a punch in the forehead, don't you remember?" "I do have a headache, but I don't remember being hit. Why is my train stopped over here?" "You do remember that this is your train, but do you remember what you were doing with it?" "I was operating it just like I always did." "I rather say that you were taking it directly to a sure catastrophe, towards a head on accident with the other commercial train that is there ahead of us." "What is this train doing there?" "It is waiting for you to clear the way, so it can make it to its destination, but some of your manoeuvres have forbidden it to do so." "I don't believe any of this. Who are you to accuse me this way?" "I am the one who stopped you and if I didn't do it; there would be six hundred and more people dead right here right now. You'll have to be examined to find out what happened in your head, but as far as I know; you'll never control another real train again." "I wouldn't let some aliens like you ruin my career this easy, because I am highly qualified to do my job." "Maybe you were before this incident, but it is no longer the case and I'll see to it." "Get out of my way and I'll show you what I'm capable of."

"Would you come here for a minute, Superhuman? I have a little problem to settle before I go." "What is the matter over here?" "This individual who caused all of our problems here today wants to take over the controls of this train again and we have to stop him and release him to the authorities. But myself, I have to go to more important things right now." "This is no problem; I'm taking care of him and I'll see you later." "Thanks my friend and see you soon." "You are welcome, but this is nothing."

"Come here man; we have to go out for a little tour." "Leave me alone you bastard." "The more you're going to wriggle the more I'm going to squeeze you, but it is yours to choose and believe it or not, I can squeeze." "Ouch, ouch; you're hurting me." "You just have to follow and it won't hurt so bad."

A squad of police officers and two other train operators arrived by helicopter and after hearing Superhuman's declaration of the facts; when he was asked who he is; he jumped on the top of the locomotive and started to run towards the back of it. But the authorities wanted to know more about him and when Superhuman saw the helicopter coming after him; he simply flew away and he disappeared from their sight."

'Just be happy to put everybody back on tracks.' Was he saying to himself and life goes on.

"This must have been pretty bad for you to be held back this long?" "This was just lives of more than six hundred people. A mad man who was mad at everybody and I don't exactly know why just yet. He doesn't seem to remember it himself. I might have hit him a little too hard. How is our little sweetheart?" "I had to lecture her, because she was playing her disappearing little game again and I didn't like this at all." "Did she stop since then?" "She didn't do it anymore, but I think she was just looking for you. She might have felt what I did; find your absence a bit long. She's only two day old and she's already spoiled." "She will settle down in time; we only have to give her a bit of time. I'll have to talk with my mom about it to see if I was acting the same way.

If you don't mind, I would like to turn the TV on to see if they talk about that incident on five o'clock news. Here they are."

'Good evening ladies and gentlemen. I'm Jacques Mars for your five o'clock news. There are people who believe in UFOs and in aliens and many others who don't believe in them, but a very strange thing certainly happened this afternoon on a rail track that the authorities can't explain yet. This incident happened between Quebec City and the City of Trois-Rivières at about ten miles west of the old Capital. A passenger train that according to many people who were on board declared that this train was travelling at a vertiginous speed and they admit having the fright of their life. The operator keeps repeating that he doesn't remember any of this and he was put under arrest until the preliminary inquiry. Although, according to a mysterious witness, the two operators should be under psychiatric care. The operator of the passenger train for leading his train at highly dangerous speed towards destruction and risking this way the life of many people and the other one for being excessively scared, thinking he was attacked by some aliens. This he said was the reason why he didn't want to stop his engine even though his locomotive was off the rails.

This operator of the commercial train said haven seen a man stopped his train; since he was refusing to do it and also he said haven seen the same man lifted up his locomotive and let it down beside the tracks. Of course everybody who was near by just burst out laughing, but wait a minute; there were deep prints on the ground that demonstrate he is telling the truth and we actually have numbers of pictures that prove it. The prints on the ground leave us with no doubt; his locomotive has been off the tracks. But by which miracle this locomotive returned on its tracks? According to this operator, another alien came inside his locomotive without opening any door and forced him under threats to turn his engine off. And as he said; this last one is the one who bound him up on his seat.

The authorities are admitting also that another eyewitness ran away and disappeared just after given his version of the facts of the events. They also say that it is absolutely impossible for one man to lift such weight.

But all I can say about this story is that it is to say the least very mysterious, because for sure; this locomotive was at one time off the tracks and it was on its tracks when the authorities arrived on this sight. I don't know if this is a bubble gum mystery or the mystery of caramel into a chocolate bar or others, but it is definitely a mystery.

The police authorities and the Railway regulation and Safety–department of Transport are promising to inform us as soon as they have something new about the events and they are asking for the help of the public to bring light over this.

Then we are reporting another murder in the town of........'

"It would be so nice if we had good news from time to time." "More than six hundred people who have their life saved by my favourite hero; I think I can call this very, very good news, don't you?" "If you want to, but to know that such crazy people could be at the controls of a passenger train; this is rather scary, don't you think? There was another crazy man who was at the controls of an airplane not this long ago and this with many people on board. He flew it straight to a mountain purposely, killing everybody. If only one of them could have reached me in time; I could have saved them all." "Do you have any ideas about what is going through their mind to act like this?" "I am not a psychiatrist, but I have a good idea of what a devilish religion can do to people who are poor in spirit. It is written that a day will come where people like these will kill others thinking they are doing a service to God. See John 16, 2. 'In fact, a time is coming when anyone who kills you will think he is offering a service to God.'"

I received an Email longtime ago and the message in it was saying that the only way for a person to be welcomed in heaven was to bring as many people along with us as possible. Let me tell you that there were many murders-suicides since in the world. I erased it from my computer immediately, thinking this was the best thing to do, but I should have told the police about it. The police might have been able to find this crazy one who I think is working to promote this new suicidal religion.

It is just the same thing with those crazy people who tell others that being a martyr by killing oneself in blowing up a lot of people at the same time assure them paradise and they are poor in spirit enough to believe it. All of this is the work of the devil who is a murderer from the beginning. How can someone sound in mind believe that killing someone or committing suicide could bring him eternal life? Only a satanic religion can preach such wickedness and unfortunately they exist.

I think it is more than due time for all the muslems, especially their leaders to tell those satanic killers that being a muderer, killing innocent people or commiting suicide doesn't make theme martyrs worthy of heaven, but useless martyrs worthy of hell. All religious leaders who refuse to do this should be considered terrorists too.

"There is a lot of madness in this world and even if I am very fast; madness is growing faster than I can fight it. Not only the knowledge is increased, but madness has increased too." "Forget about all of this for a minute my love and come to kiss me, would you? This is not bad."

"It's rather nice, if you want my opinion. Tell me, did you have visitors today?" "A few of my friends came to see me, but one of them has the bad habit of talking a little too loud and she was scaring Justine, so I had to tell her a couple of times to quiet down and she didn't like that, so they didn't stay very long." "You were right and they must know and understand that our daughter is our priority and this is it.

I can't wait to see her fill up some missions like I do and with me." "Give her some time; she just started to live this little one. Hey, I think this disturbs her to hear us talking about her. Did you see the way she turned around so abruptly?" "I think you are exaggerating a little; she is way too young to feel these things." "I could have the tendency to think the same thing, but this is not the first time she's doing it to me. She hears perfectly what we are saying; I can assure you this. She reacted very quickly to my little fit and to my impatience earlier today too." "If this is the case, she has more power than I had at her age. I remember getting mad at my dad when I was two, because my parents were arguing over me." "And what did you do?" "I slowly claimed up to his face and I told him to shut up." "You must have made him furious, what did he do?" "He slowly put me back down on the floor and he went out the door without saying another word. Then he came back home four days later to wipe tears off my mother's eyes and life continued nicer than ever. I learned that day that it is best to go away when we are too mad to talk things over and to get back together when the storm is passed. When nature gets into a rage; it is best to be out of it, because there is usually damages done to whom ever is stuck in it." "I personally have never seen my parents fighting about anything and if they did it; this was certainly not done in my presence. But they must have had some fights too, because it is hard to believe they could spend twenty-five years together without any hitch." "For this to happen, the two partners have to be perfect and perfectly made for each others, which is basically impossible. Something I wouldn't be able to accept is a spouse that doesn't support me. Even if two horses are very strong, if they don't pull in the same direction, they can't pull much and they won't get anywhere. They will have to be separated, because otherwise, things will get ugly for them. If people could understand this before things turn ugly; there would be a lot less marital disasters in this world. It is much better to separate than to kill each other. There are times when it is best to speak up and other times when it is best to keep quiet.

Coming back to the little Justine, don't neglect to tell me if she causes you anymore trouble, because I would have a hard time forgiving you if you don't. We made her together and we have to raise her together." "I agree with you at one hundred per cent and if you could feed her; I would gladly let you have her for that too." "I'll do it in about seven months." "Did you see her? She pinched my breast again." "This means it is time for her and you to go to sleep. I'll come back to see you later."

And Just kissed them both before going to meet with his mother about his childhood.

"How are you today, my favourite mother?" "Now that I see you; it is much better. You know that a mother is always a mother, no matter how strong her son is, don't you?" "Since then, you should have learned not to worry about me, don't you think? You already know that I can get out of any situation, at least you should." "Well, according to the pictures I have seen on television today; I understood that your life was at risk." "My life is practically at risk every day mom, but the One who gave me this power shows me also how to get out of danger. But I would rather like to know how I was as a baby and this from when I was born. You have a grand-daughter who is rather agitated and I was wondering if I was too." "I can tell you that you weren't normal at all; that's for sure, but when you were disappearing from my sight, I was going out of my mind with fear. I sometimes wondered if I wasn't crazy for sure. This was making your father very mad each time." "I am kind of remembering this and I remember too telling him to calm down." "He was so upset that he thought of giving you for adoption. I violently opposed him about that, but he calmed down after a while and he accepted your condition. When you started helping him with all kind of chores; he could have given the world for you. He loved you with all of his heart; this you can be sure of." "But how was I in the very first days?" "You were mainly very agitated. Your father was saying that you were nothing but a ball of nerves. I couldn't contradict him, but when I heard him saying this; I saw you clenching your hands into fists and they became so white that it scared me. I understood then that you could hear what we were saying and react to it each time. I asked him that day to be careful when he was speaking about you, but he didn't want to believe me. We have to admit that this wasn't too easy to believe either. He too then started to think that I was kind of crazy. I can tell you one thing; we had a lot of arguments about you. They say that mothers are too protective and I was one of them. I would have never accepted that another woman raises you instead of me." "I know that I owe you a lot mom and don't you ever hesitate if you need me or anything and you know how to reach me at anytime." "I only need to see you and to talk to you a little more often. I am very lonely and this is not funny every day." "You should join my mother-in-law's foundation; there is one lady missing since Jeannine gave birth to Justine." "I'm not really sure to be accepted by the other ladies." "They have nothing against you and I am sure that you too can bring something good to them. Just be careful about what you are telling them when you talk about me. When we are saying things that are hard to believe; very often people don't believe it and they think we are lying and liars. They would like us to swear on our mother's head. This is very frustrating and I know it, because this happened to me more than once. Don't forget it. I'll see you soon. Bye!"

"Mother-in-law Jeannette, I have a favour to ask you. Since Jeannine is absent from the foundation for the time being and this for many months to come, what would you say to replace her with my mother who is lonely and alone at home?" "I'm not too sure this is a good idea and that she would be accepted by the others." "You don't have anything against my mom, do you?" "No, not at all, but many people found her very strange at your wedding." "Maybe you could just explain to them what happened to her. Imagine what they could say and think about James, if he would tell people everything that happened to him since he knows me. Then think of what my mother went through since I was born. Thousands and thousands of times she was laughed at when she was talking about my achievements. Then she just gave up and she withdrawn into herself. None of this is her own fault and no one can certainly blame her for this." "Don't worry Just; I'm going to take her under my wings and I will introduce her to all the others and woe to anyone who will mock her." "I knew I could count on you, pretty mother-in-law." Laughs………

Then Just returned to his little family. In reality, he is never very long without being near it anymore. When he got there this time, at his wife hospital room; both Jeannine and Justine were sleeping peacefully and Just sat down to contemplate the two of them. It was at that moment only he realized Justine was as pretty as her mother, but that she has strong personality traits of her father.

Is there any point saying that some were saying that she looks just like her mother and others were saying that on the contrary she looks like her father? To me, I think it is just normal and natural that she has a part from both of her parents. When a child retains the best part of its mother and the best part of its father; chances are very good that it becomes a very good person. But, if on the contrary, it retains the worse of both, then this is very scary, because two demons are worse than one. Every human being has a best and a worse side. The better of one side and the worse of the other give normally an average acceptable in our society. Apparently too, two negatives give one positive; so a child born from two of the worse parents could become a very good person into this world, who doesn't want to be like the parents at all. I have seen some of them as well. I think too that a person becomes what it wants to become.

What I mean by this is that my parents raised me to the best of their knowledge, but they have nothing to do with what I became. My mother will be ninety-four in a few days, but she never ever thought I would become a writer, and neither did I, especially not one that would write about the word of God. She even wishes that I quit doing it; seeing the disturbances this causes in the family. But just like the Messiah said it in Matthew 5, 13-16. 'You are the salt of the earth. But if the salt loses its saltiness, how can it be made salty again? It is no longer good for anything, except to be thrown out and trampled by men. You are the light of the world. A city on the hill cannot be hidden. (I won't hide either) Neither do people light a lamp and put it under a bowl. Instead they put it on its stand, and it gives light to everyone in the house. In the same way, let your light shine before men, that they may see your good deeds and praise your Father in heaven.'

I sure hope that by my deeds, meaning my books and my messages in them, my hymns to the Lord, that many people will praise Him and that the flavour of this salt, the word of God will be agreeable to them. I want my light to be seen in the whole world, in all the nations and this despite the disagreement of the members of my family. I also want my light to shine until my last day and if this is possible until the end of this world. Then after this, the glory of God will shine everywhere and from everywhere for all the ones who turned to Him.

"Have you been here for long?" "About an hour I think." "Why didn't you wake me up?" "If you were sleeping; it is most likely because you needed to and it is not me who is going to deprive you of it." "It is a fact that she keeps me awake more than I used to, but I like to spend time with her."

At the same time, Justine was kind of caressing her mom's breast, as if she was telling her mom that she appreciates this ball of milk.

"Did you see what she did?" "What's that?" "She caressed my breast like she wants to tell me she likes it." "Let me remind you that I often did this too." "Maybe so, but this was not for the same reason." "I agree with you there, but I understand her very well." "All I wanted you to understand is that she hears us and she understands what we are saying; which is I think amazing coming from a few days old baby." "She sure is a special baby; she's my daughter and you are very special too; you are my wife." "Yes, and you are the most amazing husband in this world. What have you done out of the ordinary today?" "I met my mom and yours." "And what was this for?" "My mom because I wanted to understand Justine's strange behaviour, according to what she lived through herself with me and your mother because I want her to replace you at the foundation with my mom." "Are you sure she will be accepted over there? There are quite a few gossipers among these women." "I obtained your mom's word that she will be treated decently." "It is maybe time that a clean up is done inside this foundation anyway." "This is what I kind of understood. Miguel de Cervantès declared; 'When the gossipers are fighting among themselves; the truth is coming out.'

I once said something very similar when I said; if you want the truth from someone; make him either mad or drunk.

I sure hope they will be fighting about the word of God, if this can make the truth to come out for a few of them. This wouldn't be such a bad thing after all." "I don't like fighting period, no matter what the cause is." "Maybe so, but you told me not this long ago that you will defend the truth till the end." "This yes, this is true, but it is also written, which is coming from the mouth of the Messiah, which is from the mouth of God and you can read it in Matthew 5, 9. 'Blessed are the peacemakers, for they will be called sons of God.'"

"You are absolutely right, but don't you forget that very often a good fight, a good discussion or a good war is necessary to obtain peace and that God is the Almighty. But if the Almighty is fighting the wickedness in this world; this is mainly to make justice prevail and it is fortunate for us too. If wickedness would always win; this would be the complete downfall of all justice and human rights and only the wicked would be happy." "There is a good reason why you are called Just and I can't wait to reach my bed at home with you." "This is just a question of a few days now. You know as well as I do that they don't keep people in hospital longer than necessary anymore and if it wasn't for your double delivery; you'd be home by now."

At the same time Justine was making fists so hard that they became all white and Jeannine worrying asked Just to look.

"Don't worry too much about this; I did the same thing. She just didn't like what I just said, but I'll have a very serious discussion with her soon. There is nothing like a good discussion between two reasonable people to understand each other well and she will understand; I can assure you this. I have to leave now, but I'll be back soon. Bye darling and you too little Justine. Take good care of your mother or you will have to deal with me."

CHAPTER 5

Superhuman, how are things with you?" "So, so, my wife is blaming me for reproving and punishing my son too harshly." "What has he done that is so reprehensible?" "He has threatened to hit his mother and this is something I would never accept; not the threat or the action." "I don't pretend to be an expert, but would you allow me an advice to you?" "From a friend like you; I will always and at any time." "Then bring him to a place where he can measure up his strength and at the same time a place where he can let off steam, maybe on a punching-bag. He could be more conscious this way of his strength and the danger of killing someone if he hits. I am sure too that he doesn't want to hurt his mother and even less killing her." "This, my friend Just is a very judicious advice and I thank you from the bottom of my heart, but do you know a place where I could bring him? He is only eight years old." "Why don't you bring him to our friend Jonathan's dojo?" "What an idea, but how come I didn't think of it myself?" "Some times when we are too caught in our own problems; we don't see how to get out of them. It is then that we need a good friend and this is what friends are made for. But don't you wait till it is too late; do it even today if you can. If he ever passes his frustration on his mother or on another student at school; this would be disastrous for everybody. Do you know what made him mad at his mother? This would help us see clearer into the situation." "Just wait three seconds and I'll come back with an answer to your question……"

"Tell me Johanne, what made Hercules so mad at you?" "I didn't want him to stay out later than nine o'clock at night and he didn't appreciate this." "Is that all? Then he has a problem that we have to solve immediately. See you in a bit."

"His mother doesn't want him to stay out pass nine o'clock at night." "We all went through this, but far away from me the idea to beat my mom for that. It is then urgent that you act quickly about this." "You are perfectly right and besides; if he ever hits his mother; it's me that would become furious against him and this is one thing it is best to avoid. I hope Jonathan will have time for him." "Jonathan is a friend who always has some time for a friend. He knows the rules." "I will start by talking to him. Thanks for everything." "You are welcome my friend and at all time."

"Jonathan, I have a new mission for you." "Ho yeah, how many are they?" "Only one, but he is almost as strong as you are and maybe stronger." "This is rather scary, who is he?" "This is about my son who has some attitude and frustration problems as well and we have to correct these problems as soon as possible." "You already know that I don't train anyone who doesn't believe in God and this is essential to me." "Ho, I think he loves God too alright, but he has a hard time controlling his emotions and this is why Just and I are thinking that maybe a rigorous training will be beneficial for him. He needs something that will keep his mind busy and at the same time will make him spend some energy that he is overloaded with." "Good then, tell him to come to see me and I will see afterwards what I think of it." "I will have to bring him up myself; he is only eight." "He's only eight and you think he is as strong as me and even maybe stronger? If I didn't know you as much as I do; I think I would just be laughing in your face." "We still have to measure this up; I mean your strength against his, but one thing remains sure; he is very strong and I am afraid he hurts his mother some time and this is the very reason I want you to take care of him." "He would have to be obedient in everything and I hope he can understand this." "Discipline can only be good for him and I count on you to fill his life with it." "I have a young brother who is very strong too, but he is so slow that it is not even funny. He can make a good living though, because he can make the work of three ordinary men as a lumberjack in the bush up north. He amazed everybody one day when he took the horse off the load and he hauled it himself. Alright then; bring him to me and I'll see what and if I can do something with him and I'll keep you informed." "This will have to be in the evenings or else on the weekends, because he's going to school every week day." "I never work on the Sabbath day, unless I have to save someone; you know this already, don't you?" "Yes I do and it's the same thing with me, but will you have a few evenings for him? He comes out of school at four o'clock and he can be done with supper at five. So he can be with you from five till eight fifty-five. His mother wants him to be in the house by nine every night and I agree with her." "You are right about this one; the children who stay out after that time end up for most of them in jail. This is not very funny for the parents either." "But why exactly are you instructing only the ones who believe in God?" "I want people to use this art of mine for what is good and for the justice. I learned from my father at a very young age, when I was only four that we don't teach someone how he could beat us, because if that person is mean it will do it or at least, it will try." "So your father was a very wise man." "There is none like him and if there are; there are not too many." "Alright then, tell me when to bring him over." "I will be available for him every Tuesday and Thursday night of every week and this from six fifty-five to eight fifty-five; unless of course I receive an urgent call." "If you allow me; I will take your calls in those evenings." "Of course I will and I hope your son will like this art. What's his name?" "He's called Hercules." "Just like the legendary Hercules?" "We named him this way because he stood up on both of his legs the day he was born. We knew back then that he will be very strong and there was no mistake there. We still have to see to what extent he is." "I will put him to test right at the beginning; we'll see."

The next Tuesday evening, Superhuman was there at Jonathan dojo with Hercules for the beginning of his training. The young boy didn't really know what to expect. One thing he knew though is that he likes all the strength and the nimble exercises. So, as he thought; 'I will be happy here.'

"It would be best Superhuman that you leave me alone with him, so he is not intimidated and I will tell you my impression as soon as he is done with the first session; unless of course that he prefers you to stay. What do you think of this?" "Well, ask him what he thinks of it."

"What do you say Hercules? Do you prefer your dad to stay here with you or not?" "I would like him to stay here for the first five minutes and then he could go. I just want him to see what I can do."

"Alright then Superhuman, you can stay for the first five minutes to see what he can do and then you'll be able to leave as he wishes. Do you agree?" "Of course I do and if you have any problem at all; you just give me a shout and I'll be back." "Alright then; we all are in agreement." "This seems to be the case."

"Did you ever punch on a punching-bag Hercules?" "No, but I can break some wood 2×6 with my fists. This I often did." "Do you mind hitting this one here?" "Not at all; this is why I'm here, am I not? I am here to exercise, am I not?"

Hercules hit this punching-bag that went way up to the ceiling; something Jonathan has never seen any man accomplish. His father said that a hit half as hard as this punch could kill his mother or anyone by the way.

"But I will never hit my mother and now that I know what I know; I will never hit anyone either. This could bring me a lifetime jail term, according to my teacher anyway." "So you already know what your strength could do to you?" "Of course I know and this is what pisses me off the most. The other students are disgusting me and there is nothing I can do to shut them up without a huge risk. I have to count on a friend to defend me and the others are calling me a coward. There are times when I get so mad with rage that if I didn't love God; I would shut them up once and for all." "But why didn't you talk to me about this son?" "When do I have a chance to talk to you one on one dad?" "This is the way it is when we are taking care of the rest of the world; we are lacking time for our own family, but I thank you my son; there is going to be a change in our lives from now on. I cannot promise you that we are going to spend full days together, but we will spend a lot more time than before. Keep on training for now and tomorrow we will be talking about this, if it's alright with you." "This is more than perfect dad, but don't forget to come to get me before nine, so mom doesn't make me mad again." "I'll be here at eight fifty-five to pick you up my son, but please, don't break anything; I cannot afford to replace the equipment."

Superhuman went home to discuss with his wife Johanne the possibility to send their son to a private school.

"You don't think this will be too expensive for our income?" "I'll see if I can find a job that I might be able to work on between my missions. It is a question here of the security and the future of our son." "So you think that Hercules is in danger?" "Yes, he is in danger to hurt and even to kill someone with his herculean strength. We cannot afford such a thing and it is up to us to see that he can control himself." "Alright then, look for work and I will look for a private school for him, but I think we should ask what he thinks of it first." "You don't think it is up to us, his parents to decide what is good for him?" "How would you react if anyone imposes something on you?" "Not very well; you're right." "For once!" "Do you feel like your rights are violated too?" "I can tell this happens some times, but I am not a complainer; you know this." "Maybe so, but I would like for you to tell me when something is not going your way." "I will try, but this is not always easy." "What stops you from expressing yourself?" "Most of the time when you are back at home, most of the crisis is behind me and I don't talk about it. But go, go find some work and we'll talk about this later."

Then Superhuman went to pick up a newspaper and he looked in the employment section. There were a lot of demands for people to wash dishes in restaurants, but this was not his cup of tea at all. Then he remembered Jonathan who talked about his strong brother who works as a lumberjack.

'This would be my kind of work.' Was he telling himself. 'I will talk to him later on tonight.'

Johanne came back home very disappointed about her search. Not only the private school is very expensive; I would even say that it is only for the rich, but on top of all; there is no room available and the waiting list is very long.

'There is only one solution left.' She was telling herself. 'I will teach him until he is ready for high school. Everyone can learn from the Internet; I'm sure I can learn to teach too.'

And this is the way the problem was settled, for as long as the boy accepts this solution.

At exactly eight fifty-five, Superhuman was at the Jonathan's dojo to pick Hercules up and to get some information about his brother's job.

"Dad, you gave me the nicest gift you could in my entire life. I never thought I could ever be this happy." "There are a lot of little things that can make a person happy my boy and you will discover a lot more yet. I have to speak to Jonathan in private. Do you mind to go wait for me in the car for a few minutes?" "You're not going to pull me away from this training, are you?" "I will tell you more in a few minutes my son, but I can assure you that this is not my intention at all. Go boy, go, I will join you in two minutes."

"How is he progressing?" "He is very talented, there is no doubt there. I sure can make a very good Masked Defender out of him. His problems can very easily be solved too with this training. This will allow him to control his emotions his strength and his moves." "I have a very important question though, how much this will cost me?" "For you my friend, it will be a friendly price and this means nothing at all. This will be my pleasure to give him this art freely. Nothing pleases me more than to see a young fellow this talented being interested in it." "Then I owe you one." "No my friend, a friendly price means nothing at all to me and it is completely free. I think so and I say so." "I need to find a job and if it's possible paid by the piece. So I thought about your brother who works in the bush. Do you think he could recommend me to his boss?" "I wouldn't like him to lose his job in your favour." "I would make sure that this doesn't happen." "In this case, I don't see why you shouldn't meet him. He's got a house up North in La Tuque and he comes down from the bush every Friday night and he returns every Sunday morning. I'll call him and I will let him know that you are coming, because it is best I talk to him first. He is not very social and this is because he is very timid, he is hung about his look, but he is a good guy." "Alright then, just let me know when I can meet with him." "I should go now; my son is waiting for me out there and thank you for everything." "That's nothing at all, my friend."

When Superhuman arrived at his car, he found Hercules who was holding a man by the hand and was begging the boy to let him go.

"What is the matter her Hercules?" "This man wanted me to follow him to his car and I think he wanted to abuse me. I didn't like this at all. He was doing some strange things with his hand in his pants too and this was disgusting. So I gave him my hand and you can see what's happening." "Hold him back for another few seconds; I'll get a piece of cardboard and something to write on. I'll make an effigy for him and I'll take him to the police station. What do you say?" "This will be the cherry on the cake for the end of this day dad." "My boy, I think you heard this phrase once or twice before today. Do you at least know what it means?" "Of course I do. It is something like: 'All is well that ends well.'

It doesn't always look like it, but I often listen to you dad." "This is fine; can you hold him a bit longer?" "I'm just having a lot of fun dad. When he stands up to hit me; I squeeze him a little more. Don't worry; go and do what you have to do."

So, Superhuman went to get what he needed to make this effigy, a marker, a roll of duck tape and a piece of cardboard on which he wrote: 'I am a paedophile and a few minutes ago I tried to abuse a young eight years old boy. His father delivered me to you.'

Superhuman placed one of those cardboards on his chest and another one on his back; then he taped everything very well, including his arms altogether before taking this pile of shit to the police station. He sat him down at the door step and he rang the bell. He then retrieved himself a little to watch from a distance what will happen. As soon as the door was opened and the package was picked up, Superhuman knew this guy was done and his job too.

Then Superhuman returned to his son very proud of him for haven caught his first prize. From this moment on Superhuman knew his son was on the just side. For Superhuman too, this was the cherry on top of the cake.

"I think your mom and I will have another cherry for you tomorrow my son." "And what is that?" "We will talk to you about it tomorrow. According to your commentary, you appreciated your training tonight?" "This man is very special dad. He showed me a little of what he can do and

I think this is extraordinary. He told me his father started to teach him when he was only two years old. He also said that with my talent I can reach him before long. Can you believe this? This must be the nicest compliment I have ever received up till now." "I hope this won't be the last one my son, but I am telling you that I am sincerely proud of you today." "Truly dad, this is another cherry on top of my cake." "Your cake will end up covered with cherries; I hope you like them." "This kind, I am crazy about them." Laughs…….

"Excuse us for being late Johanne, but we had a little problem to solve and I assure you that this was worth it." "Well tell me, what happened again?" "Nothing, I can see that you are tired out and we'll talk about it tomorrow."

"Go to bed son; it is very possible that I have another discussion with your mother tonight." "But dad!" "Go son; this is best for all of us and don't you worry; I assure you that everything will be settled by tomorrow."

"I wanted him to be in by nine o'clock at the latest." "He is only late by ten minutes and he was with his father; so why are you so excited about this?" "The rules are the rules; this is what you keep saying yourself." "To every rule there is an exception; so come down a little from your high-horse and calm down, so we can talk politely. Come listen to the news with me instead before going to bed." "I am very tired; I rather go to sleep." "Make an extra effort and come to sit with me, would you?" "Alright then, but don't blame me if I fall asleep on you." "Have I ever done this?"

"We received tonight a statement from the local police station saying that they received the most interesting package all rapped up and delivered to their doorstep. Let me read it to you; 'A paedophile wanted by the local police for more than ten years was delivered tonight on our doorstep. We would like to thank the people responsible for this achievement. The fingerprints from this individual are confirming that he is the author of a dozen of these horrible crimes of sexual abuses on children of both sex committed in and around our community. A blood test will no doubt confirm all of this tomorrow. We sincerely believe that your children will be more in security from now on. Good night and sleep well.'

This is it ladies and gentlemen. We will keep you informed as soon as we have more on this subject and I can assure you that we would like to know who accomplished this exceptional achievement.

A not identified but reliable source is telling us that this man was caught around nine o'clock tonight trying to lure a young child of eight years old into his car. He had to be brought to the hospital to repair three broken fingers of his right hand. A unanimous employee from the hospital confirmed this fact afterwards.

Many of us here are wondering if it is the father of this child who caught this monster in action, but why would he hide himself? Such heroic achievement has to be rewarded and we think he deserves a medal for his action. He might want the identification of his child to be kept secret and in this case, no one can blame him. But who ever you are; I'm sure the population say thanks to you."

"Are you telling me this is Hercules who broke the fingers of this s.o.a.b?" "Yes my dear and I delivered him to the police station." "But how could he get this close to Hercules and this easy, if he was in the dojo with you?" "After his training I asked him to wait for me in the car for two minutes, because I needed to talk to his instructor one on one and it was then this guy approached him." "You left our son alone at night in the car?" "Yes my dear and if I didn't do it; this monster would be abusing another child as we speak, because this was his cruising night. But why are you looking only at the dark side of everything? Your son is a hero with an extraordinary strength and you don't have to worry about him like this all the time, because he can protect you way more than you can protect him." "But he is only eight years old." "Yes, he is only eight, but he can put to pieces any grown man. You'll have to get this into your head one way or the other and soon or later and it is better soon than later. Your son, as you say was super happy tonight before he entered this house and if I let you go as usual; you will destroy his confidence completely. He had two or three cherries on his cake, but I think you made them all fall to the ground." "What are you mumbling there?" "I'm not mumbling at all and I know exactly what I'm talking about. A cherry on his cake for him was the overjoy he experienced maybe for the first time, but with your woman attitude of the desperate mother; you ran him down and not just a little. Don't lead him to be an effeminate; he deserves better than this. He was told tonight that he is full of talents, but this was not done by you." "But he is only an eight years old child." "It is when he is a child that a boy learns to become a man, so don't prevent him of this.

To change the subject, what did you find on your side?" "Nothing at all! All the private schools are full for years to come and the list is endless. I thought I will have to teach him myself until he is ready for high-school." "I don't like this idea at all." "Can you tell me why?" "Yes, for all the reasons we had this discussion tonight. If ever Hercules gets mad at you; this could turn to be very ugly. I think you could with your attitude towards him, exasperate him and make him furious. So, this is out of the question for the same reasons. I will find another way." "This means that you don't trust me?" "No my dear; this means that I make sure you are safe. I saw tonight with which power Hercules could hit and I'm telling you that with a hit only one tenth of his strength could be fatal to you. I'll have to talk to him about this as soon as tomorrow morning, so he can understand well the extent of the seriousness of what a hit from him could cause to someone and the consequences." "So, what you are telling me now is that you do all of this for my protection? And here I thought this was done out of pettiness, meanness." "I have always loved you and this hurts me to see that you doubted it, but I love our son too. I have hundreds of tempting invitations every year, but I am still here with you.

The reason why I had to talk with Hercules' instructor alone was about a possible job in the bush with his brother and I didn't want that Hercules thinks he is responsible for our problems of shortage of money. He has enough problems on his own, especially with the other students in the schoolyard who piss him off without being able to defend himself, because he is conscious of all the harm he could cause to these little shitheads. For this reason, when he comes home from school, what he needs the most is not authority but comprehension. I will watch over him a lot more from now on and don't think this is blaming you, because it is not, but he is at an age when he highly needs his father and I realize it for the first time tonight. They say: 'Better late than never.' And I am glad it's not too late for him and I. Now you can sleep; I am done lecturing." "Now I am not sleepy anymore. What would you say if....?" "If what?" "You know what." "Do you really think so?"

The next day at the afternoon news, the police was saying it could attribute the sexual abuses on children to a dozen cases from the man arrested the previous night, but they couldn't hold him responsible for all the other cases. This means that surely the man arrested last night is not the only abuser to commit those despicable crimes. The police officer is saying that scourge is definitely diminished, but unfortunately not irradiated completely. This also means the general alert is still on for the time being. The police is sorry for telling the population in its excitement that most of the danger was over last night and it's telling the population to remain vigilant with our children, because those sick people are very dangerous."

Next to this last report, Superhuman decided it was time to put an end once and for all to this infection for the parents and the children in this town.

After meeting with Ben, the timid but very gentle brother of Jonathan; where he learned that instead of hiring, the company was laying off many of its employees.

Superhuman knew very well that he could cut by himself up to fifteen cords of wood in a single day; which could have brought him a very good salary and he wouldn't have had to work every day to support his family. So he had to find something else, but first, he wanted to settle the paedophilia problem in his town before anything else.

Then he put altogether a plan, but he needed the help of Just for more security and listen to this; the help of a child as well.

Knowing now what his son is capable of, he was not the least worried to involve him in his plan. The only thing was that he couldn't talk to his wife about it, at least not before the whole business was settled. Besides, his son was so proud the night before for catching one of them; one of the most wanted by the police that it would have been cruel for him to leave his son out of his plan.

Then Superhuman wondered where and when such a sick person would likely be in operation to trap one of his victims. The arcades are suitable between six and nine o'clock in the evenings and also in and around the schoolyard between three and five in the afternoon. Parks and swimming pools are also suitable in the hot days of the summer.

Superhuman has no problem at all lifting a car and smash it to the ground, but this is a much different story if his son is inside this car. On the other hand, Just could go inside the car without being noticed at all; something that is a lot more reassuring for the father.

The first attempt to catch one of those bastards was done near a very busy arcade. As expected, Hercules received an invitation to go out for a ride in a car. Pretending to be very innocent, Hercules followed a middle age man up to his car and he took place on the front seat of the passenger side. Just took place unnoticed on the back seat and he was listening to the conversation between the two.

"Do you see this? Do you know what this is?" "I think this a police badge." "You are right and you must know too that you can tell me anything, because I am here to protect you. Tell me, who do you like the most, the girls or the boys?" "It depends, I like boys better to play balls with them and I like girls better to play seek and hide."

Just didn't like at all the way this conversation was turning and he went out for two seconds to tell Superhuman that he thought this individual was just pretending to be a cop and he went quickly back to the back seat of this car in a position to learn a bit more.

Superhuman went to the police station to find out if one of their police officers was working near an arcade.

"Yes, there is one on the south side of the town and another one on the east side as well. We are taking seriously care of the peadophilia problems of our town." "Do they have the authorization to take a child in their car for questioning?" "No, not at all and it is even illegal to do this." "That's all! Thank you very much." "But who are you?"

Even before this officer had finished his question, Superhuman was already far from him.

At the same time this man was putting his hand on the boy's thigh; he started to scream out of pain, but because he is left-handed; he succeeded to draw his gun and there is when Just intervened.

"I'm going to take this one if you don't mind too much sir." "But who are you, goodness?" "Tonight we are paedophiles hunters and it appears that we just caught one of them. I think you'll have to trade your badge for a very small and cool room. Are you married?" "I do have a wife and three kids." "Well, you just threw the shame on them and if your wife divorces you; I won't be the one to blame her. Now you are going to go through what the other one went through last night." "No please, not this; I'm the one who picked him up and put him behind bars." "I'll bet that if you didn't let him go it is because you don't like the competition, otherwise you would have let him free."

It was shortly after this that Superhuman was there with two other pieces of cardboard and duck tape to repeat the last night experience. He was not too sure though, if the police force would protect one of their co-workers instead of protecting the children of the community.

But to his surprise, another statement came announcing the arrest of another paedophile that was bound and delivered at the door of the police station the same way the other one did last night. They held back though the information that this is one of their officers. I think that was done by precaution, because it is better to have solid proofs before accusing someone.

But the next day, a blood test was confirming that we were facing another case of paedophilia. The DNA test was the formal proof that this officer was responsible for eight other victims of sexual abuses on children of both sexes. The officer has been suspended from his job without pay; he was stripped of his police badge and he is kept behind bars.

But the best one came up the next day, when another individual pretending to be a lawyer came to the jail and insisted to meet with this fallen cop. He mainly wanted to know how someone, who ever it is managed to catch him in the act. He told him that his arrest was most likely illegal and he had a good case for his defence. The stripped officer started to tell him, but he suddenly stopped and he guessed that the man in front of him was also a paedophile.

Then he called a guard and he asked for this so called lawyer to be going through a DNA test too. This led to another arrest. Three in three days; this must be a record, but I don't know. It is nevertheless exceptional, no? This fake lawyer didn't find out how the cop got caught, but at least he found out how he was.

These three paedophiles who are now arrested are responsible for all the sexual abused cases of this town but one and this according to all the DNA tests ran on them so far. One unsolved case remains; one abused six years old child that has nothing to do with these three paedophiles already arrested.

Unfortunately though, this young person, this young victim was infected with aids and this gives us an extra reason to stop the one who has infected this child as soon as possible and this before he infects someone else. This also means that Superhuman cannot take anymore risk to involve Hercules, because the risk is just too high from now on. When a simple scratch can cause the infection; this is not a fun game anymore, because most of the infected ones are infected for the rest of their life.

If it wasn't for the confidentiality of the blood tests executed on patients in the medical clinics; there would be a much better chance to find out this mental case, because to commit such a dirty crime knowing he is infected; one has to be real mentally sick or really vicious. But that we want to admit it or not; there are a lot of vicious people in this world.

What is incomprehensible thought is why the confidentiality of an infected with aids patient is more important than the health of a young child.

Just who sees justice differently than the governmental and medical authorities decided to take things over for this last case. He first went to see the parents of the sick child, because he needed to know by what blood group the kid was infected. Then he went in a specialized medical blood clinic pretending that he might be infected himself. This was mainly to see how and where the files were classified. He knew very well that once he knew who committed this sordid act; the rest will only be a formality. He knew too that he had no choice but to act anonymously, because this way no one could be blamed for leaking information.

Just knew very well too that all the doctors are held to the professional secrecy by law and their whole future depends on it. It is just as bad for a priest who hears the confession of a murderer; he is not allowed to say anything. It seems to me though that such a case should be reported to the authorities without any prejudice and this the sooner the better.

But Just knew now what he needed to know to confront the one responsible for the sickness of the young six years old boy.

"What kind of man are you to give such a disease to a young child?" "I don't know what you're talking about." "Ho, so, you are a hypocrite on top of all." "I still don't know what you are talking to me about." "You're not remembering haven abused a young boy named Mario? What did you offered him to attract him to you, a quarter?" "I don't know any young Mario; this is the truth." "Do you have aids or not?" "I have aids alright and I am dying from it, but I have never abused any children; I can assure you this." "Are you gay or not?" "That yes, but I am not a paedophile. I even stopped all of my sexual activities as soon as I found out I was infected. This makes more than four years now. My lover almost died from grief and he had a huge depression about it. He wanted to continue a platonic love relationship, but I just knew the temptation would be too high and I left him to give him a chance to start a new life for himself." "It is best for him to enjoy this life, because when it comes for the next one; he won't have a chance to be happy, I mean to be gay. This I can assure you it." "How can you be so sure of such a thing?" "This is because I know the truth, I know the word of God and his word never lies. But coming back to our business here; how do you explain that your blood test led me up to you, if you have nothing to do with this nonsense child sexual abuse?" "How come you are in possession of my blood test? It has to be completely confidential." "The ways of the Lord are impenetrable, but they can penetrate anywhere the Lord Almighty wants too." "Then they should be able to tell you that I am not the one you are looking for." "I will end up finding who he is and if this is you; I will come back to make you pay for this crime." "I told you and I assure you that I am not the one you are looking for." "Can you help me find the guilty one?" "This no, I cannot betray one of my close ones even if I wanted it with my whole heart." "Well then, if you are not responsible for this crime; I'm asking you to forgive me for accusing you wrongly, but I think you've said enough for me to know where to look now. Good luck!"

Just didn't have to think very long to realize that if the one he just finished questioning is not the guilty one;

it has to be one of his close ones with the same blood group. This could be his father maybe or a brother or even a close cousin.

No other with the same family name appeared in the phone book of that town. This could be one of his close ones, a paedophile coming from outside of town that came to visit him, but how to find him? This was the whole question.

Then Just returned to see his first suspect to ask him one last question.

"I want the exact name and the exact address of your last lover." "I am not obligated to give you this information." "Maybe so, but you already know that the ways of the Lord can penetrate anywhere; so I'll find this information one way or the other; might as well give it to me and save me a bit of time. All the good actions can reduce suffering in hell." "I already live through the sufferings of hell; one more, one less, it doesn't make much difference." "This is what you believe, but I know better than this. It is written that whoever gives only a glass of cold water to the one who needs it won't lose his reward and these are words you can believe in, because it is the truth." "His name is Joël Dugenre and he lives at 666 of the Devil Street, but you didn't get this information from me." "I can be discreet when I want to, thank you."

Just knew already what he wanted to know by visiting this man ex-lover.

"Hi Joël!" "Hellooooo, what a nice looking man! Are you looking for a partner by any chance?" "I don't look for a partner by chance or by any other way. I am looking for information that I'm sure I can get from you." "Well then, if you are not gentle with me, why would I help you with anything?" "It is up to you, but if you do not want me to twist your neck; you better tell me what I want to know." "You are just a mean man, go away from me." "Then I am going to twist your neck; I have no other choice." "What do you want to know?" "Do you know your ex-lover's brother?" "My ex-lover, you're going to make me cry. You are just a big mean man." "Yeah, yeah, I'm a mean man, but tell me quickly what I want to know and I'll be soon out of your way, alrighttttt?" "What do you want to know about him? He doesn't like me; he likes only the little ones." "Do you know where he lives?" "Well yeah, he lives near the Sacré-Cœur school. He loves children so much; this drives him crazy. He talks about them all the time." "Do you know his address by any chance?" "I sure do; he lives at 667 of De La Cour Street. This is very near to the schoolyard." "Ho my God; protect them please." "What?" "Excuse me; I was just thinking out loud." "I remember his address because it is very similar to mine. I visited him a couple of times with my ex-lover." Tears.....

"You can rejoice now and be gay again; this is all I needed to know from you and I thank you. You were helpful to me."

From then on, Just was certain that this time he knew where to find the person responsible for the misfortune of the last victim of this aggressor who was not yet identified or arrested. A mad sick man who most likely was going to make many guys happy behind bars, for a time I mean and spread this disease even more. Some people would say they deserve this. I would say so too, except maybe for the innocent young victims like this young boy. He is caught with this disease that he never looked for and that he couldn't avoid. But Just who knows the director of that jail will inform him about this special customer who is certainly not the most desirable.

Then Just called Superhuman who kind of became an expert in delivering unhealthy packages.

"Superhuman, my friend, I know where to find the missing man; I mean the last paedophile to be delivered to the police authorities. Since no one knows better than you the way the deliver such merchandise safely and discreetly; I'm leaving you the pleasure to do it as soon as you feel for it. We don't need any other proof, because the DNA in itself will be sufficient to get him convicted." "Are you sure to have the right candidate?" "I am absolutely sure this time. I made a mistake at first by accusing his brother who has the same disease, but from a word to another, I was led to the guilty party." "This one is infected; I will have to change his effigy a little." "I leave all this into your hands; you know better than I do how to proceed, but be careful anyway, because you sure don't want this disease."

The new cardboards had this new effigy: 'I am the paedophile who has infected the little boy named Mario; the one you have been looking for now for some time. I am delivered to you by a hero unknown to me. PS. Lock me up and isolate me because I am very dangerous.'

It was without any problem that Superhuman proceeded to the arrest of this sick man and made him go through the same process than the other two earlier. But this time the local police head cop could finally tell the people of the population with certainty they could sleep well, because all of the children sexual abused cases by paedophiles were solved. He told all the parents of the population too that with the reputation his city just acquired concerning these twenty-four cases of sexual abused; there was no chance or no risk, I should say, for another paedophile to come to live in our community.

'Thanks to one or more unknown heroes, this plague is now something of the pass and I would like to thank them personally; who ever they are for their success in a field where us, the members of the police force have miserably failed. It is with great humility that I'm asking the people of this community to beg these heroes to remain among us, if this is possible to them. Good night ladies and gentlemen and may God blesses those who are allowing us to sleep well tonight.'

Superhuman made sure to register correctly on video tape the whole show that he would like to show it to his son along the years, so he knows there is happiness in doing what is right.

CHAPTER 6

There is a sexual abused case and a murder case of a young eight years old girl that happened in the town of Kelowna in British-Columbia that I remember. I just discovered an article on the Internet saying this happened in August of 1994. A man by the name of Murrin was accused of the crime, judged and acquitted after a long trial and also after a very long five years investigation. But a very stubborn cop continued to say after all this that Murrin was the one who committed this sordid crime. As far as what I think, it is his own blindness about his own wrong conviction that forbidden him to look somewhere else. The police of this community is so convinced that Murrin is guilty of this crime that the investigation is still on going, but at a dead end. I also thing that if the case is still open; it is because they didn't really find and punish the true abuser and murderer.

A woman who was one of the juries fell in love with Murrin during this trial and I think that a guy who can find a woman to be his life companion this easy and in such situation like the one he was in; doesn't need a young girl to satisfy his sexual needs.

On the other hand, a man who is disturbed to the point of wanting to go through the wall to make sure no one can see his little member; this one has an extra reason to attract a young girl who doesn't know the difference between the normal and a smaller size.

I have seen from my own eyes this man. Not that I was interested or anything like that, but this was the very first time in my entire life that I was seeing a man acting like this. We were in the basement of his house and there were a few other men around. I told myself at the time; 'This man is really disturbed.'

I was there in that house with my life lady friend and this was at her friends' house. We were all there to play music and sing.

This disturbed man is one of those the lead investigator asked to get a confession out of Murrin, the one who was accused of the crime. Three guys didn't go to easy on him, because Murrin spent eleven days at the hospital. Anyone could have said anything at all under such punishment. This was no less than torture. In comparison to Murrin's body injuries; I spent one day in the same hospital after a hernia surgery. So Murrin's injuries were like being hit by a truck.

The stepfather of my lady friend of the time, who was also a homosexual and a paedophile; one thing that was known by the whole family and who is dead for quite some time now also said that he too was thinking it was this disturbed man who has committed this crime. Homosexuals and paedophiles can recognize each other and they know their habits and their own signs among themselves. He too was a very good guitar player and he too knew the disturbed man very well. He too has abused all of his children, three girls and one boy and their mother was in total denial and she backed up her husband rather than protecting her children. As far as I am concerned; the two of them deserved jail time, but when the children became adults; they didn't want their parents to be charged. The four of them have a certain degree of mental illness, but only the last one is his real daughter.

Some people will say; 'Why didn't you report this earlier?' Well, I have done it, this was anonymously, but I did it and this didn't do any good. Like I said earlier; the lead investigator in this case was just too stubborn and he was convinced the guilty one was Murrin, so he didn't look any farther. I think he has miserably failed and the murderer-paedophile in this case is still on the run. If only this cop would have forced the one I mentioned to pass a lie detector; maybe they could have found the real murderer and abuser of this young little girl and by the same token, saved other young children's lives.

But the truth might come out some day; since the case is still opened. All I have are some clues, which led me to my own conclusion, because I saw and I heard some things others might not have seen or heard, but I don't have any proof and I cannot do anymore about it. I wouldn't want that an innocent man pays for a crime he didn't commit anymore than a guilty man runs away from a crime he has committed. Just like Just, I like justice and I hate injustice.

When came the next Thursday night; Hercules was taken to the dojo by his father for his second training session. No point saying that he was over excited to be there. Jonathan had a few recommendations for him though and one of them was to learn to control his strength, that this training was mainly meant for ability and flexibility and to keep his strength for strength competitions. He made him understand too that Masked in Masked Defender means anonymous. This means that he cannot scream over the roofs who he is and what he does.

"So, if you have understood all of this, then we can continue, if not; you can always come back when you got it." "Ho, I understood all of this alright sir and let me tell you that I only live for this anymore and I wouldn't want to miss any session." "You understand too that if I'm not here for you one night because I am held up somewhere else; you would have to take it like a man; otherwise you are wasting my time." "I understood that too sir and don't you worry; I will do everything you tell me to do, like you tell me." "Then you will be a model student and who knows; you might just be able to replace me one day as an instructor.

I must tell you that because of your great physical strength; you must never, never be implicated in a fight unless this is for your self-defence or to protect someone who is mistreated. I must advise you too to never hit anyone, because with only one hit you could easily kill someone and end up in jail for manslaughter; which would tarnish our reputation enormously. Use your grip instead or a push and your speed to avoid the hits. You cannot do boxing or karate either, because of what I saw the last time you were here; you would kill your opponents. Can you manage all of this?" "I told you sir; I will do everything you say the way you say it." "Then let's continue. Show me how high you can jump."

There are rings suspended at the ceiling of the dojo at sixteen feet from the floor and Hercules went to grab one of them in only one jump.

"Wow, but how are you going to come down from there now?" "You only have to put a few mats on top of the others under me and I will let myself down on them." "And you are not scared of hurting yourself?" "I did the same thing hundreds of times in my friend's dad's barn. Over there I let myself down on two to three feet thick of hay, but this in one of my favourite games." "Did you friend saw you doing this?" "Of course he did, but don't worry about that; he promised me to never tell anyone, not even his parents." "This is nevertheless something to worry about." "I trust him as much as I trust you sir." "And how much is that?" "This is one hundred per cent sir." "Would this bother you if I put him to test by trying to make him talk about you and your strength?" "He is my best friend and I know I can trust him completely sir." "Do you think he would like to take this training with you?" "We have been doing everything together already for the last three years sir. He cannot jump like I do, but I throw him up in the air where he can grab the beam too and like me he let himself down in the hay and he likes that a lot. He bursts out laughing every time. I can talk to him about it tomorrow, if you want me to. He was the only one who came to my defence when the other students were pissing me off at school and I was raging with madness. He knows part of my strength and he knows I could cause a lot of damages, if I would react to them. He is very wise for his age." "I think I would like him to take this training with you. I also think you would make a very good team. Alright then, talk to him about it and ask him to obtain his parents' permission and if he passes the reliability test; then I will train you both together. What do you say?" "I say this is wonderful sir and I assure you that you won't regret it."

Charley, Hercules best friend passed the reliability test with a high score and the two of them are very happy to live this experience together. They are learning tonight a way to defend themselves against all kind of attacks without hitting or hurting anyone, but in a very efficient way to make them understand that if they want to; they could very easily hurt them badly. This is a lot easier for Hercules who only has to hold one's hand to make himself understood. But this became easy for Charley too, because with his wisdom; he only asks his opponent to shake hands with his friend Hercules.

Ben, Jonathan's younger brother often slowed down his enemies' ambitions with a handshake. His famous father told him once he wouldn't have to run very often and he was right. But for Hercules, on top of using a handshake, he could just jump a few times pretending to be scared of his enemies. To be afraid yes, but to be afraid to hurt them too badly. He can this way though scare them enough to send them on their way.

The question is, could he one day propel himself the way his dad does it from one end to the other of the world and this in only a few seconds? One thing is that Hercules doesn't know yet about his father's achievements. I am under the impression though that this is about to change and the Hercules' learning experiences are just at the beginning.

It is fine to be able to jump up high in the air, but one has to know how to land as well and there is not always some mats or hay to receive a person. One has to know how to slow down and to stop as well, when he flies at a vertiginous speed. I am very curious to find out how Superhuman has learned how to do all of this. I would most likely learn it at the same time than everybody else and this is when Superhuman will teach his son how to do it.

Then Jeannine went home with her little Justine and Just installed them both comfortably in a great big bed, but Justine, even though she is just five days old was already as curious as a young teenage girl and she was disappearing and reappearing in every single room of this castle. She came back in her upset mother's arms after a grand tour of the house.

Just realized then that things were going to go wrong between the baby and her mother and he decided to bring Justine one more time into the future. He brought her then ten yours farther, so she knows and understands well the concern she causes her mother to be in.

"If you continue this way; you will drive your mother crazy and this is something I wouldn't allow you to do." "And what are you going to do about it?" "Your mother cannot follow you, but I can and this no matter where you go." "To follow me everywhere I go; you would have to read my mind and I'll bet you that you can't." "And I will bet you that I can and that I can even change your mind." "Alright, tell me what I'm thinking about now?" "Paris, Montreal, Carina, your school friend. Don't be this mean Justine; this is not right and you can only hurt yourself." "You can read my thoughts even if I am thinking about my boyfriend?" "I can read all of your thoughts if I want to, but there are times when I prefer not to. I can even, if I ask God, take your power away from you, make you lose it and this is what I'll have to do if you keep on challenging me and your mother the way you do." "I don't believe this, just try to see." "Well, you've asked for it and you'll have to live with it."

"O God, my Father in heaven; I'm asking You to take away from my daughter her extraordinary power, even if this is only for a few minutes; to teach her first not to challenge her father anymore and also for her to understand once and for all that everything is temporary here on this earth and all of this as You know my God is for the wellbeing of her mother. Thank You Lord."

"How do you feel now?" "I feel fine, but I don't have my power anymore and this is making me feel funny. I liked it, but I won't cry if I don't get it anymore." "This is because you don't realize yet the luck you had." "I don't understand either how you could take it away from me." "It is not me who took it away from you, but this was done by the Father who is in heaven and He did it because I asked Him to do it." "And He listens to you, just like that?" "It is true that He listens to me better than you do, but you must know what is written in James 5, 16. 'The prayer of a righteous man is powerful and effective.'"

"And of course, you are Just and just." "Not only I am Just, but I am Just Just." "How could I have ever forgotten this?" "You do as you wish my little darling, but if you keep it on with this attitude; you are going to lose a lot of happiness; I can assure you this. I'm leaving you now, because I must return to your mother who is worrying right now. She is my first and the most important love too. Goodbye!" "Dad, don't leave me here alone?" "If you're coming back to your mother; you'll have to change your attitude, because there is no way I will leave you hurting her." "Alright, I got the message; let me go back to her now." "I cannot take you along with me and if I was to try this; I would be killing you, because you cannot survive such a speed, no one can but me." "What else to do then?" "You'll have to pray God to get your power back; this is the only and the unique way." "But I am not as just as you are." "You are Justine Just, so yes, you are Just. Then pray to God and if you are sincere; He will listen to you. You can be sure of this."

It is at the age of ten that Justine learned the power of the prayer and the power of God. Ho, she heard about it many of times before that day, but to really see it and to really believe in it, it was that day. She knew from this day on that everything she would ask from God in the name of the Messiah and if it is something that is also the will of God, the Father in heaven; she would obtain it. See Matthew 21, 22. 'If you believe, you will receive whatever you ask for in prayer.'

Many may have thought they didn't have enough faith. They might have prayed for the will of God to be done on earth as it is in heaven also. So they cannot be granted if they're asking for something else than what is the will of God.

After being granted, Justine returned in the arms of her mother having in mind not to play her little games anymore. She stopped disappearing for all kind of reasons from that day on and if she did it; her mom wasn't aware of it. Having a husband who disappears at any moment of the day is one thing, but to see her little baby of a few days old doing this is rather scary. She went to lie down between her two parents a few times and this was when there was a thunder storm outside, but that was all and this was very understandable too. I'm pretty sure too that if all the kids could do it, they would. She is more than happy to be in her own little bed otherwise. Her mother put on a soft music every night, so she can go to sleep happily and when her father has the time for it, he sings her a little song of his own and it goes like this:

The Smell of Roses

Thank You my Lord, thank You my Lord, thank You my Lord

Thank You my Lord for this wonderful smell of roses
Thank You my Lord for giving me so many things
Is it for You time of the apotheoses
It's time for me to say thank You for everything

I know You are the Almighty
You have made this beautiful flower just for me
She is faded, what have we done?
Only You can bring her back to what she used to be

We are the seed, the garden of your kingdom
Your creation made by your hand, your ambition
Your enemy, this despicable phantom
He has faded my nice flower, my companion

God You blessed us and You told us
To be fruitful, to multiply, fill up the earth
To lead over the animals, fish in the sea
And all the birds upon the earth

Thank You my Lord for this wonderful smell of roses
Thank You my Lord for giving me so many things
Is it for You time of the apotheoses
It's time for me to say thank You for everything
Thank You my Lord for making me in your likeness.

When Just is seeing her smiling and curling up to herself with a little breath of satisfaction; he knows then that she is happy to be left alone for the night and she knows he will be there for her again tomorrow. This is happiness that doesn't cost much, but it is priceless.

When Just returned near Jeannine; he asked her; "Would you like me to sing you a song too?" "A little later, if you don't mind; my favourite show is about to start now and it will be on for an hour." "Are we already entered into a routine for you to choose a show over my singing? And what is the name of this show?" "It is called; 'The Unknown.' This is a series about the deeds of the superheroes or aliens who have done some out of the ordinary things. I think that without knowing it they are talking about you and our friend Superhuman." "Interesting, let's watch this to see what they have to say about it. I can always sing later on, can't I?"

"Good evening ladies and gentlemen. We would like to present to you tonight a series of strange facts that were witnessed by a number of people. To start with, I would like to ask you, the public a simple question. Do you believe that we, people of the earth on our planet are visited by aliens? If so, do you think they are good or bad? Our receptionists will take your calls between nine and nine-thirty tonight. You will see our phone numbers at the bottom of your screen in a few minutes and also our Email address. We also have to introduce to you many people, eye witnesses who have seen and heard some very strange stories. I have to say that many of them are sceptical, because most of them have been mocked and accused of being erratic by telling what they have seen and heard."

"Good evening Mrs.! Can you tell me your name please?" "My name is Gisele." "What can you tell us about your own strange experience?" "I can tell you that I had experienced the fright of my life when I was on board of this passenger train that was travelling from Montreal to Quebec City the other day. We have been saved by some aliens apparently, according to many witnesses, but no matter who they are, I thank them from the bottom of my heart, because without them, no doubt, we would all be dead by now." "This means then that you believe in aliens?" "I don't really know who they are, but to me they are heroes, because they have saved my life." "Thanks very much Gisele for your testimony; I appreciate this a lot."

"There were at least twenty passengers of that train who were basically saying the very same thing, but hundreds of them refused to say anything, because they were afraid to be ridiculed and afraid that others might think they are retarded.

Here is a man now who is courageous enough to talk to us about his adventure."

"Good evening sir! Would you mind repeating in front of the camera what you've told me earlier?" "I don't mind at all sir. We were at least one hundred clandestine passengers on a very old leaking boat that was travelling from my country to Japan when we were all rescued by an unknown individual, but what is the hardest thing to believe, even for us who lived through it, is the fact that five minutes later we were all sound and saved at the Montreal arbour. I still don't know by what kind of miracle we could travel this far in such a short time. We were all a bit daisy when we arrived there, but healthy otherwise. The Canadian Government took charge of all of us and let me tell you that for us; this is another miracle." "And there are so many people who don't even believe in miracles. Do you think there are other people who could corroborate this story?" "We are at least one hundred and twenty-three people who will tell you the exact same thing and we are not afraid of being ridiculed." "Thank you very much for your testimony sir; this is the most interesting."

"We have one more witness to introduce tonight dear viewers, but he is asking for complete anonymity and we also had to mask his voice in a way to make it completely unrecognizable to satisfy him. I have to say too that this is very reasonable and we understand why.

"What is your name sir?" "Hey, hey you, come down to earth please?" "I am very sorry sir; I didn't mean it this way and I beg you to believe that I just did this as I usually do. I assure you that I didn't mean to embarrass you in any way, shape or form or to be mean to you. I have way too much respect for all the people who dare

come forward like you do to betray them in any way."
"You are forgiven, but don't you do this again, because
you almost caught me identifying myself and this after all
I went through to avoid it." "Now that all the emotions are
settled down, tell me, what is your motive for testifying
about this?" "I heard from my own ears a ghost man
speaking to me without being able to see him. I can
tell you today that he is a very wise man and if I had
followed his advices; maybe I wouldn't be in jail for the
rest of my life. I just want to tell everybody that if he
ever is on your way, listen to him; you will be nothing
else than better off. Then there was another very fast
and strong man, who made me travel through time like
this is not possible. In just a few seconds, he made me
travelled from Windigo to Ottawa. I thought I would die,
but he protected me from the wind. I can assure you too
that he has a good grip. I don't know if they are from
this world or from elsewhere, but I can assure you that
they are good people. They are people who deserve our
admiration and I want the population to know about it.
I also want to use the occasion to ask this ghost man
to come to visit me as soon as he can, because I have
a charity mission for him to perform, if he wants to of
course. I have nothing else to say, thank you." "Thank
you very much sir and again, forgive my mistake." "It's
alright sir, no harm was done."

"I would like to tell our viewers that this last interview
was performed directly from the maximum security

prison of Donnacouna. We received 444 calls and the result of these is this; 161 people said they don't believe in aliens and 283 said they believe in them. On the other hand, almost all of the respondents said believing in superheroes. They say that the majority of the family fathers who raise their children until they are grown up are heroes. This is quite interesting. Thanks for your attention ladies and gentlemen. We will be back next week with some new testimonies. Have a good week until then."

"It is hard to believe the way this James has changed and this for the better. He actually went from being a real beast to a kind of gentleman. I just wonder what he wants from me now." "Be careful anyway; we never know what is going to happen with a wild beast." "Don't worry sweetheart; I can defend myself." "Now you know why I didn't want to miss this show." "Yes and I understand this very well as well. I knew this had to be something important for you to postpone one of my songs." "I hope that you didn't change your mind about it; it is just an hour later. Come, come and put me to bed too; I love your voice more than anything." "And yet, they were saying I had no ear for music when I was a child." "Maybe this was true then." "Mmmm, maybe you are right. Come to bed and I'll sing you the romance." "What's the name of this one?" "It is called;

The Last Romantic Lover

I will sing you the romance, like were doing our parents
It is no longer the tendency like it was then
I will sing under your window with my guitar in solo
You must be the only one to whom I'll sing this one

The great lovers and the mistresses, where are they all today?
And what about gentleness; is it also gone away?
According to the last statistics, I could be one of the few
The last lover romantic just like my mother knew

Will someone talk about our story? I will say it in my songs
Will they believe in it today? That we could have a love so strong
To me this is not important that they believe in it or not
As long as I have the chance to hold you, this means to me a lot.

I just sang to you the romance like they did in the old days
Even though it is not like it was, I love you more anyways
But this is the true story of two romantic lovers
Who love each other more than any others.

'This is great,' was saying Jeannine with applause. "You are the most wonderful romantic lover on this earth, as far as I know anyway, but you are the only one I know. How lucky I am!" "Stop this; you'll bring red colours to my face." "That's nothing; I'm the only one to look at it." Laughs.....

"We still have to wait thirty-four days, might as well sing and laugh about it." "Wait???" "Don't make me talk about it; it's hard enough as it is." "Poor you, what would you do without me?" "Right, laugh at me now. Kiss me good night and go to sleep; this will be best for both of us before she wakes up again."

The next morning at around ten o'clock, Just was at the prison to meet with James, the prisoner-guard to answer his request.

"First thing, I would like to thank you for you good words. This is something I could not expect from you at all and I appreciate it a lot." "And I thank you for answering me so quickly." "What can I do for you?" "Since I was promoted to my new post as an assistant guardian I make quite a bit of money and as you most likely know already; here is not a place where we can spend much money. Then I would like, if this is possible to you to find the families of the men who died at the Lake Windigo because of me and see if they need financial help. If this is the case, I would like this money to be given discreetly to them. If this is not the case, then

I have another charitable plan, but just as good I think."
"This is very gracious from you and I think it is worth for me to get involved. I'll see what I can find and I'll get back to you soon."

Just quickly went to all the families concerned and he went back to the prison to report what he found.

"Hi James! I can tell you that two of the widows are sorry for their children, who have to grow up without their father, but not sorry at all for themselves, because they are remarried to wealthy men and they say being very happy. They also say haven learned from their first mistakes of being married before to men who were married to fishing and hunting and who ignored the wife and kids most of the time. They also say not being mad at you anymore and they forgive what you have done. These two are saying not being in need of anything and not to worry about them at all. When comes to the third one though; this is a different story. She said she will never forgive you, but it is mainly because of her children that she feels this way, because she too is remarried to someone nice and she too is not in need of anything. I told her to go read carefully Matthew 6, 12, 'Father forgive my sins as I forgive who ever sins against me.'

I also told her to read Matthew 6, 14-15. 'For if you forgive men when they sin against you; your heavenly Father will also forgive you. But if you do not forgive men their sins, your Father will not forgive your sins.'

I told her also to look at what is written in Matthew 18, 35. 'This is how my heavenly Father will treat each of you unless you forgive your brother from your heart.'

Some people will say; 'Yes, but this one is not my brother or my sister.'

I got little news for those. People who do evil are all brothers and sisters among themselves, a very huge family. They all are sons and daughters of the devil. The ones who are righteous and do good are also united among themselves. They all are brothers and sisters, a smaller family and they are sons and daughters of God. To be surer of what I am saying; they have to read 1 John 3, 1-10, Jesus' brother. They will see that there are really two families and to which family they belong to.

As far as I am concerned; I think you should look somewhere else to find a place to spend this money." "This is done already. I would like this money to be used for the education of some of the First Nation children, so they can get the chance I didn't have. My father was drinking all of his money instead of sending us to school and he forced me to hunt to feed the rest of the family, but he was doing nothing at all but drinking." "We don't choose our parents and parents don't choose their children, but we have to put up with them. We all have, the parents as well as the children to be on the look for help and hope to find it in time. I know very well that this is not easy for everybody, but if I can give one advice to everyone; this would be for youngsters as well as the adults to pay attention and try to help the poor instead of mocking them." "I personally couldn't complain to anyone and neither cry out without receiving a slap behind the head or a kick in the ass and sometime both. This was the way until I was tall enough to survive by myself in the deep forest. If I had stayed another year; I would have ended up killing him and my mom wasn't much better. I sold ten dollars worth of fish one day and when I came home with this money; my mom pulled it out of my hand and she went to buy a gallon of wine with it. They both drank it until they were both passed out." "I can tell now that you weren't spoiled at home." "It is kind of funny to say this, but I am treated better here than I ever was and I have more money than I ever had." "What are your parents doing now?" "I have no idea and really; I don't care either. To me they are not worth a thought. I take this back; they are not worth a bad thought." "Maybe you should write the story of your life." "I already started it." "And what is the title?" "This will be: 'From Being The Wild Beast To Being James.'

I think this will be good. If you ever have the right to an outside journey and you need to have company, just let me know; maybe we could go fishing together." "This would just be wonderful." "Then pick a time when the moon is at its best, just a quarter moon." "Don't worry; I know." "I warn you right now though; I am not for illegal fishing at all." "We will do it the way you want it sir." "Now I would like to know the name of your village and the name of your family. I just want to make sure none other of your family is going through what you went through." "I don't think you will be welcomed if you want to tell them how to live their live." "This I absolutely don't care of what they think or not or what they say. I am distractedly not concerned about it." "Distractedly, what is this mean?" "This means I won't be disturbed or distracted by what they think or say." "Ho, I see." "You didn't receive any education at all?" "The only education I received, I received it here. I mainly concentrate on the French language, so I can write my stories properly and I certainly don't need mathematics to count the years I still have to spend in prison." "I understand this very well and I don't blame you at all, because I think you're right. Well then, continue, because I truly admire the progress you have made. Tell me how much you have to give at this point in time?" "I do have seven thousand dollars sleeping in my bank account." "I will see that you can make it multiply for you. See you later." "Hey, thanks for coming over." "That's nothing."

Following this conversation, Just went North of La Tuque in northern Quebec in a little village called, 'Westtimouche.' He found there nothing else than desolation. Dozens of parents half drunk and children who were dragging in the street bare feet and half way dressed. There was a little girl of seven maybe eight who had her face stained with a blue substance. She had gone in a tiller and filled up her stomach with blueberries.

Then Just went in a sort of a building that had an inscription on its front, 'Town Office.' A young woman indicated to him a man who is the chief of the band and who fell asleep in his office chair with a bottle still in his hand. This man woke up when Just tried to pull this bottle out of his hand.

"Hey you, what are you doing here? This is mine." "This is all you do, drinking with our government's money? Where are the nice houses that we built for you? I saw an outside wall wide opened at the bathtub level to allow the horse to drink. Your children are walking bare feet in the gravel." "This is not of your damn business what we are doing with our money." "I am going to show you something that is some of my business."

At the same time Just grabbed this man and dragged him outside this building and he ran to the lake with this guy under his arm. Then he threw him a couple of hundred feet away in the water and waited till he came back to do it again. After four times of this exercise, the chief seemed to understand what was going on. A small audience was gathered around them by that time with a certain fear, not knowing what will happen to them. 'What will he do with us?' Everyone of them was saying to himself. But they all smiled when Just smiled at them.

"Now we can return to your office and discuss like two civilized men. Can you walk or I should carry you out again?" "I can walk and I'll be fine." "Let's go, but I'll keep an eye on you and don't try to run away, because I'll get you back anyway."

Once in the office, Just asked for two grown men to stay in with them inside the building as witnesses and to all of the others to wait outside.

"Do you have a school in this lost area?" "The government gave us enough money to build the frame, but for the rest; we are still waiting." "What are you missing to finish it?" "I would say roughly around one hundred thousand." "Is there someone in this village who can teach?" "My secretary is the most educated person in this village. She can surely teach all the children until they are ready for high school, if they want to learn of course." "All of the children under sixteen are obligated to go to school without any exception in the province of Quebec. But they need a school, this is for sure."

"What is your name Miss?" "My name is Monica." "Would you please show me the book of the finances for this village?"

"He, he!" "No chief, you'll have your turn again later on. I want to see your expenses before continuing anything else."

"Here it is sir, but there is nothing shining in there. I did the best I could with what I got, but I have to say that

I was forced to write some errors in there." "Thank you Monica; I will look at it quickly."

"You've received three hundred thousand for this school and all you have is the frame? Where went the other two hundred and fifty thousands?" "We have to feed everybody in this little community." "You mean feed and drink, don't you? I have a suggestion for all of you."

"Would you ask everyone to come in Monica, please?" "Yes sir, right away."

"Come in everybody; we need all of you."

"How many are you in this village?" "We are nine families and there are thirty-three children of school age. The ones who are a bit older are either gone hunting or fishing and a few of them are also gone to work in the bush to bring money home." "Is there one or more who is sober, at least most of the time?" "Our chief is the one the most sober." "Wow, no wonder there is so much of a mess in this place. Alright then; we will proceed to a new election, a vote to elect a new chief and I want that all of you who are six years old and older to be able to vote for the candidate of your choice. I would like that the actual chief runs again. I would also like that Monica here present apply for the post as well."

"But a woman cannot be elected chief of an Indian band." "And why not? If a woman can be elected to be Premier of the province of Quebec; I don't see why she cannot be elected chief of a little band like this one here and especially if she doesn't drink and she knows how to count."

"What do you say Monica? Do you want to apply for this post?" "If you think I have a chance to win, why not? But what will happen when you're not around anymore? Everything will be just like it was before." "What would you say if I promise you not to let you down?" "I say that I think I can trust you." "Then go ahead and put your name on the voting sheet. And I put mine too."

"You're not allowed to do that; you're not a member of this band." "If the majority is voting for me freely, then I will be elected legally and democratically.

Before this vote takes place in one hour from now; I'm asking all the candidates to tell this audience what they plan to do for the good of this community, starting with the actual chief."

"Well for me, I don't see what else I can do other than everything I have already done. 'No money, no candy;' this is something known in the whole world." "Do you have something else to add?" "There is nothing else to say." "Do you really think this is enough to win this election?" "I doubt very much that anyone can do better than what I have done with what we have here." "Fine, but I'm dying to hear what Monica has to say and especially what she has to offer you."

"I want that all of us standing here today can live in peace, learning and helping each other. The one and only reason why we don't have a decent school in our village is simply because of the lack of willingness from the direction. It is time to change for the better. I have seen from my own eyes way too much corruption and this is absolutely not acceptable. I will do everything in my power to bring this change. I want that all of these children could have the hope of a better life. If I am elected; I will make a new rule that forbids any man to beat his wife or a child and if he does after all this; this man or woman will be beaten too in front of the whole community. There is no point to put such individual in jail, because this wouldn't do any good to him or to his family. I will also make sure that the help we get from the Canadian Government is distributed equally and fairly for all of us. I will create a monetary found to help those who want to continue their schooling can do it without worries. Is there any point saying that my very first goal is to finish our school as soon as this is possible? I will also make a strict control about liquor and drugs that is circulating around here. Let me tell you too that full mouth liquor and this every day of the week will be over also." "How do you think you can impose such a rule?" Laughs.....

"Alright smart ass; didn't you see how I brought back to soberness your actual chief? If Monica is elected; she will be able to count on me at all time and if she is not elected also. Is this clear enough?"

"Keep it on Monica; I am impressed by you."

"I only have one more thing to say before letting this man speak. Here too in this village, school will be obligated to the age of sixteen for all the children."

"Congratulation Monica, I never heard such a nice speech in a long time."

"Come on everybody, this deserves a good hand of applause.

I agree to everything this woman said and I will only add a few things. If I am elected, I will make sure this school is terminated and ready for the students at the beginning of September of this year and this with or without the help of our government. I'm pretty sure that if the government has already paid for this school; it is not likely to pay another dollar for it. We'll have to find a different way anyway and the government's procedures are way too long to be ready for the beginning of the classes. Are there any trade people in this village, like carpenters, plumbers and so on?" "We have helpers, but no material." "I will take care of the materials. Where are they usually come from?" "They come from the Saguenay, but they are very expensive and the transportation too." "I will go around with the actual chief after this election to see what is missing and to evaluate the cost.

"Do you want to count all the participants Monica and make the voting sheets accordingly, please?" "Let's see, there are thirty-three children of reasonable age, seven teenagers and twenty-two adults and this includes

you and me. This makes sixty-two people all together."
"Then distribute the sheets immediately and I will help
you out. We also need a box to deposit the voting sheets
afterwards and this will have to be in a discreet corner."
"Why not using both washrooms; I cleaned them out this
morning?" "This is great and it will go faster this way too."
"I need your name sir to put on these voting sheets."
"Just write, Mister Just; this should be sufficient."

An hour later the whole count was terminated and
here is the final result.

There was one vote for the actual chief. Even his wife
and his son didn't vote for him. I think he only received
his own vote. At least this is what I think.

Monica received 23 votes and Just received 38 votes.
So, Just was elected with a majority. He then thanked
everybody for their participation and to have put their
trust in him. Following this he went out to make a tour of
the whole village. He also asked Monica to be his main
assistant and also his substitute in chief for when he is
out of town and he started immediately to make a list of
whatever is missing in this village.

"I don't only want a school in this place, but I also
want a little restaurant for people to meet, in which there
will be a bar open only on the Friday night and Saturday
night and this with a severely control flow. The liquor
will be prohibited every other day of the week and this
with heavy consequences for the cheaters. This will be
the same for all drugs and at all times. There is a huge

need for a grocery store in this village as well. We also need a community center that includes a gymnasium and it should be connected with the school; so kids can spend their energy somewhere else than on their temper. We'll make an example to be followed out of this Native village for all the other villages of this country. We will reduce this way the suicides and the suicide attempts and also the delinquency on children. We will create a joy to live that will become contagious for everyone. This will become a village where everyone will become one for all and all for one. The ones who like fishing will be fishing, the ones who like hunting will hunt, the ones who like to work will work and the ones who like to be lazy will be out of all those things that work brings and this includes a good cold glass of beer on the Friday night. Some will leave and others will come to live here, but the rules will never change for the worse."

Then Just left with a long list of materials. He first went home to pay a visit to his little family. Then he went in three huge material suppliers and asked for quotes in a way to get the best possible estimation. Before he left the village though, he asked Monica, his official assistant to file an official demand for assistance from the Federal Government and this for their immediate needs. But Just already knows that the government prefers to move them around to a community where everything is already more accessible instead of coming to their help by supplying their needs. The government never asked itself how it would like to be moved around like a garbage can. It is sad to say, but we seem to be still ignoring the culture and the roots of the Native communities and we wonder why they rebel against us and block the roads and the railroads. A bit of justice on their way wouldn't be too much to ask.

Then Just went back to spend the evening with Jeannine and Justine. His in-laws were there also wondering why their son-in-law was spending so much time away from his family.

CHAPTER 7

"Welcome finally to your own home Just." "Hey, father-in-law; someone has to take care of the poor Natives of this country, who live in total misery, because our government doesn't do much or at least enough to help them." "Our government did and does a lot for them, but they want to govern themselves and we have to admit it, most of them don't know how to do this properly." "I don't want to look like a dictator, but their monetary help should come with a competent administrator for those who can't do it and this way the government could make sure the contribution of all the Canadians is spent rightly. I saw something today in the Northern Quebec that is not much better than what is happening in the third world and maybe even worse. And we collect money for the elsewhere poor. What did the Lord say? Oh yes; 'First take the plank out of your own eye.'

I think this means to take care of your own first. There are Indian band chiefs in this country who make more money than our Prime Minister and this money is coming from all of us. Does this make really good sense? Especially if the inhabitants of these reserves have a hard time to survive? You already know James that I love justice and I don't see Justice in those cases; so someone will have to readjust their sights soon or later. I must tell you that I became an Indian Band chief myself today and my income will be split among all the members of the community."

"You became a chief of an Indian Band?" "Yes darling." "And it is for them that you neglected your family today?" "If you really think you are neglected; I'll bring you pay a visit to them as soon as you feel strong enough, then you can judge for yourself and tell me again that you are neglected. We need nothing; they have nothing, not even enough food. Is it their own fault? I don't know, but one thing is sure; it remains that they need help."

"What is the name of this village?" "It's Westimouche, but you don't have to worry about it James; I'm taking care of it." "I will nevertheless make some verification for my own curiosity, because as far as I know; all the villages and all the Indian reserves of this country received help from our government." "Ho, this village received help too, but this help wasn't distributed equally and fairly and this is why I got involved."

"Well, I'm sorry, but I'm not in favour of helping the Natives like the ones who tried to kill us all." "Can you blame this crime on a little six years old girl though? Can you blame this on a little girl who has nothing to wear, no shoes for her feet and who has to feed in a blueberry tiller to survive, because she has nothing else to eat?" "Of course not; you know me better than this." "Well. I wouldn't either. There are thirty-three school age children in that village and no school and no teacher. Would you like them to become killers like the ones we know?" "Not at all and I leave all this into your own hands. I'm also sorry for complaining; you deserve better than this. It is true that we have everything we need."

"Can you supply me with a list of everything that is needed in this village Just?" "Yes I can James, but they cannot wait from eight months to three years for help and for that reason I take onto myself to help them as soon as tomorrow. I am the chief of that band and I will take my responsibilities." "I don't think the government would want to pay for some work that is already done." "How many the government will let die from hunger before acting?" "I am sorry, but these are the normal procedures." "I know this and this is why I cannot wait and neither do they, because I gave them my word and I will stick to it." "Give me that list anyway and the approximate cost of them the sooner you can and I'll see what I can do. There is a reason why I am a minister." "Don't get yourself in trouble for this; just do what you possibly can do with honesty. If you can obtain retroactivity; this would be something."

Everyone went to bed after some long discussions, but at three o'clock in the morning, Just went to Paris with the idea of selling a few of his pearls or a few of his precious stones with the purpose to get enough money to buy what he needs for the village.

"Hi sir, how are you today?" "Well, I'm fine sir." "Did you by any chance make an evaluation of all my pearls and stones sitting in your store?" "No, but this can be done in a short time. With your permission this can be done within an hour." "How much will you take me for this task sir?" "I will do it for the pleasure of looking at them sir. It is the chance of a lifetime to be able to admire such collection. I must close the store though, because the risk is too high and if this was known to the thieves; my life would be in danger. They are of very high value, but my life is too, to me anyway." "I understand this very well, but if you ever are in danger, you know how to call me, don't you?" "Yes, I remember mister Just and this makes me feel a lot better." "Well then, can you choose the two most valuable of these stones and tell me how much do you think they are worth?" "This diamond here is of 51 carats and it is worth at least 50 millions and this one is of 43 and it is worth around 40 millions." "Would you know someone who could buy them at this price?" "Pieces of this value are usually sold at an auction where a great number of collectors are present. The biggest pink diamond known in this world was sold for 83 millions not this long ago." "I'm taking these two along with me and I should be back within an hour, alright?" "They're yours sir; you do what you like with them, but be careful." "Don't you worry for me, see you in a bit."

Just took these two diamonds with him and he crossed the English Channel to go meet with the Duke of Cambridge, having in mind to show him these two wonderful pieces.

"Hi Duke, I don't want to disturb you for too long, but I would like to give you the unique opportunity to acquire two diamonds that are very, very rare." "What a joy to see you again Just! How are you and how is your charming wife? I will never forget the way she sent me on my way with my two first offers for her jewels. We don't see this every day, a person refusing three and five millions dollars." "For sure, she has a head over her shoulders this one." "Show me these and I'll let you know what I think." "Here!" "Wow, these are worth a few millions, that's for sure." "The biggest is of 51 carats and the other one is of 43. What do you say?" "I make you an offer of ten millions for both."

Just burst out laughing.

"I'm sorry Duke, but I just learned that they are worth at least a million for each carat, so you are very far from the count, aren't you?" "Yes, I know, but a guy must try, isn't it?" "Just try to fool someone else, would you? I thought you were a friend of mine." "I'm sorry for offending you my friend and to help you forgiving me; I will introduce you and your precious stones to my grand-mother, the Queen of England. How's that? She is a much better expert than me and she loves jewels. What do you say to this?" "Let's waste no more time; let's go. I must be back in Paris in thirty minutes." "Make sure not to rush her; you would lose all of your chances to make a deal with her. Come along; we are only three minutes away."

When the two men were on their way to the Royal Palace; they were attacked by a herd of photographs, but Just seeing the panic in the eyes of his friend took immediately over the situation. In less than thirty seconds there were at least twenty photographs without camera and this without them understanding what was going on. All of them could write a story, but without a picture to back it up. So this means their story will be more or less worthless. There were many witnesses though who could corroborate the facts. Just who likes to work anonymously acted as much for himself as he did it for the Duke. He didn't damage the cameras, but he unloaded them all before putting them in a container near by. Then he joined the Duke again and they both continued peacefully on their way.

The Duke didn't understand everything that went through and neither why he was spared from being seen with a strange individual, but he hurried introducing him to his grand-mother, the Queen, who is a great admirer of precious stones.

"Majesty, this man is my friend from Canada. His name is Just Just. He is the man from whom we bought the jewels that you envy so much. This is said with all the respect I have for you. If he is here today, it is because he wants to give you the exclusivity to buy two magnificent pieces of pure diamond. I am pretty sure he could get a nice amount of money in an auction, but I think that if he is here right now; this is because he is in a hurry to get the money he needs and I don't exactly know why."

"Show me what you have sir." "Here they are, Majesty."

The Queen looked at those two pieces of diamond with not even the least reaction on her face. Just like an expert buyer in this field; she was playing the game of lack of concern or interest and she stayed rather cold and Just for the first time in the day thought that for sure he wasted all of that time. But the Queen rang the bell, calling for her servant, the one who is in charge of buying all of her jewellery. He is a man who is even a greater expert than she is herself. The man came with his set of fine tools and after a few seconds of discussions with her; she turned to Just and made him an offer of 70 millions dollars.

"But Majesty, they are worth at least 94 millions." "This is my final offer sir; take it or leave it, this is your choice." "Majesty, this money will be use to save a village of your Native subjects in Canada who are starving to death." "You say Natives who are starving to death in

Canada?" "Yes Majesty." "I'll have to speak to Stephen again, because I don't accept this situation at all. And you sir, you are ready to sacrifice these two very precious stones to save Natives?" "Yes Majesty!" "This reminds me of a certain Princess Diana, the mother of your friend, the Duke of Cambridge." "I was one of her greatest admirers, Majesty."

At that moment the Queen had to clear her throat a little.

"Good then sir, I'll sign you a bank draft of 94 millions dollars and I hope to live long enough to see what you have done with it. Besides, if you ever have another one of these to sell; I want to be the first one informed." "We never know; I might need money again some day." Laughs....

Just picked up this bank draft and he went back to see the jeweller in Paris, there where another huge surprise was awaiting him. The jeweller found among Just's precious stones another pink diamond of 58.1 carats weighting 11.2 grams and it is worth approximately 80 millions dollars. It is apparently the second biggest diamond in the world and its value is equivalent.

"The value of all your pieces is a bit better than half a billion dollars sir. This makes you a man quite rich sir." "I got 94 millions for the two pieces I left with an hour ago, but I had to negotiate quite a bit." "It was worth it, isn't it?" "I guess we can say that. Well, I think I should make you work a little more. I would like you to make me a diamond ring for my wife." "Well, we are not short of diamond over here. You choose the stone and I will do the rest. What is her date of birth and the size of her ring finger?" "Oups, Just wait five or six seconds and I'll be back with one of her rings.......Here it is." "And what is her month of birth?" "She was born on March the 13." "Then I suggest you this clear-blue one here. It is beautiful for one thing and besides, it is the perfect symbol of fidelity between two spouses and it is the warranty for a happy marriage. This is perfectly what I want for her and it is very pretty. When will it be ready?" "If you give me an hour; I'll make it right away. Of course, you want it on gold?" "Of course, I want nothing less for a golden woman. Alright then, I'll be back in one hour with what it takes to pay for it. How much will that be?" "Gold is now very expensive and the work of a jeweller expert also. Take this ring for example; it has a gold value of two thousands dollars and the work was one thousand." "I hope you trust me for the time being?" "I'm not worrying; I have a lot of collateral." Laughs.....

Just went to deposit the bank draft in the mean time and he asked for a cheque book. From there he went to Rona-re to get the first quote for the material he intents to buy. This comes up to four hundred and twenty-one thousand and a few dollars. Then he went to a second supplier to see what they had to say. There was nothing at all done over there, simply because the manager didn't believe in Just's buying power. Considering the net profit of such industry is around 25 per cent, so this means this supplier is losing around $114,000.00. What was he risking if he made a quote? Maybe a couple of hours at forty dollars an hour; which would have been $80.00. Then Just went to a third one. There the total was $391,000.00, but all the windows weren't included and no one bothered requiring about them either. The outside and interior doors were included though. So Just returned to Rona-re to order the materials.

"When can you deliver these materials?" "This depends mainly where they will have to be delivered." "They will have to be delivered right here in your yard inside some semi-trailers." "I don't understand what you mean." "I mean I will take care myself to deliver these where they have to go." "Then I can give you a one per cent cash back, which makes a total of $417,017.70. Bring me $417,000.00 and in two days all the materials will be ready to leave with you." "How would you like to be paid, a cheque, a bank draft or straight cash?" "Cash Really? Laughs.......

A certified cheque or a bank draft would be just fine. I don't really like to be in a possession of so much cash." "Fine then, I will be back in about ten minutes with it and get a receipt ready in the name of the village of Westimouche, please." "It will be ready when you return sir."

From there Just returned to Paris to pick up the ring for his wife and it was already all professionally rapped up. He paid without even looking at it, which proves how much he trusts this man and then he went back to his bank to get his cheque certified before returning to the supplier. After this he went to lie down near his wife who was peacefully sleeping.

When the morning came, at the day break of that day, Just brought to Jeannine breakfast on a silver plate in the bed and in the middle of it there was a little box with a card wishing her a happy first anniversary.

"Ho my love, this wasn't necessary at all. The nicest gift of all is there beside us and you are better than any gift; you are my life." "Take a look at it anyway, would you?" "How beautiful this thing is! I am really cherished with you, am I not? But how can you find such beautiful things?" "I am inspired by the most beautiful woman in the world." "And who is she?" "You don't really know her just yet, but she is not only the prettiest, she is also the most charming, the most loving and she looks like you as two drops of water look alike." "And I have nothing for you. If only I could travel like you do in the future, even if this was only for ten days ahead; I would make love to you the whole day long." "And what would you do with Justine?" "I would leave her with my mom." "Ten more days to wait. I will need to keep busy and this is news I must tell you now, because I have a village to rebuild and this will take a lot of my time soon." "You know what and you do what you have to do my love." "If you want to darling, like you say, leave Justine with your mother for a couple of hours; I would take you this afternoon to see the Paris Opera. We will take place in the Queen's lodge, because we are invited to it. The Duke and his wife will also be there. Don't forget to put on your jewels that will make a few jealous ones. I will go in a few hours shop for a new suit for the occasion." "You don't think that you are spoiling me a little bit too much?" "If you don't think you deserve it; I will cancel everything and return this ring." "You have a special way to convince me, don't you?" "This is my way to tell you that I love you with all of my heart. So, is it yes or no?" "It's yes of course, but how are we getting there?" "In a taxi, this is the cheapest and the fastest way."

"Superhuman, do you have a few seconds?" "Always, for you Just; nothing has changed for me." "Nothing has changed for me either, my friend and this is why I still need you. At one o'clock this afternoon, I would like to take Jeannine to Paris in a limousine to watch the Paris Opera. This is what I want to offer her for our first anniversary." "Has it been a year already?" "This is a dream she has been cherishing for quite some time already." "It doesn't mean anything to me, but I can understand some people could like this." "Tell me, have you found the work you were looking for?" "I found a part time job, but this is good enough for me and it is well paid too." "Don't you ever be shy to ask me if you ever need something, no matter what it is! Don't forget too that I am your friend and this is what friends are for. I have to go now; I must shop for a new suit." "I don't think you will find an adjusted suit in one day." "Ho yes, at Mooreles, they have tailors continually and I can even rent a smoking for the day, if I want to." "That's interesting; I will remember this. Okey then, I will be at your door at one o'clock sharp." "Ho, I wanted to tell you too that I will need you for a job in two days, if it is alright with you, but this one you will get paid for it and this is one of the main conditions." "And what is this for?" "I need you to take a few semi-trailers loaded with construction materials up north of Quebec." "Laughs....." "What's so funny?" "This is the kind of work I'm doing lately. I take them from British Columbia to the province of Quebec and to Ontario. I carry construction lumber. I do it at night, because I don't want to scare anyone and as you know, I don't need the tractor to do it. I could most likely take more, but I take two at the time and this brings me $10,000.00 for each trip plus one thousand for the fuel. The boss is satisfied with my work, because his customers are always served in time. Only once I had to leave the load in the middle of a parking lot of a shopping mall, but this wasn't for too long. I had to rescue a man who was lost in the forest and I could finish my job in time anyway." "Then I'll pay you the same amount for our load." "No way my friend; your load had to go a tenth of the distance I normally travel and you'll have to pay a tenth of what I usually take. I too can be as fair as possible." "And I appreciate it my friend. See you later on this afternoon."

Then Just went to Mooreles and the tailor started taking his measurements when Just raised his voice suddenly.

"Wow, what a piece of a man you are." "You touch me there one more time and you will receive a slap you will always remember, if you don't lose your memory."

The middle age man started shaking and Just asked the manager if there were someone else to take his measurements.

"What's happening here?" "There is only one who has the right to touch my family jewels and this is my wife. If you have no one else, I'll go somewhere else."

"Out of here you stupid bitch; I told you to be careful with that."

"Hold your jewels aside sir; I will measure up your leg. I beg you to forgive this idiot and I assure you that he will be reprimanded." "He just misjudged me for another kind of clients, that's all." "Your suit will be ready within two hours sir. Do you need anything else? We do have shirts, neckties, socks and belts for half price for whoever buys a suit right now sir." "Can you assure me that your prices weren't raised up double before sir?" "We run a serious business sir." "Yes, I saw that. How much do I woe you?

I can pay you with cash if you want me to, even though I was happier to shop before." "We only take cheques and credit cards sir." "I definitely saw a better place than here to shop. Tell me, is it because the direction doesn't trust you that you cannot take any cash?" "Not at all sir; it is because we were too often the target of the thieves, who love the cash and our life was at risk every day." "That, I can understand. I will take two shirts, four pairs of blue socks and one belt and you already know my measurements. Tell me how much I woe you, please. The total is $819.00 sir." "While I think of it; don't you advertize two suits for the price of one?" "Give me two seconds here; I'll look at the ad. You're right sir; the ad runs until the end of the day." "And you didn't know this earlier? If I wasn't so much in a hurry, I would go somewhere else. Here is your cheque and I will be back in two hours. For the second suit, I want a light grey." "Come sir; come to choose what you like." "I'll take this one here; my wife will like it."

Certain people who are fast thinkers will say that Just couldn't have been in Paris at a jeweller one morning and in Quebec the same morning and around the same hours to shop for clothes and do banking with all of the hours differences.

It is just that to follow Just, one has to think even faster. If Just can go ten years into the future with his baby Justine and this with no problem at all; there is no problem at all for him to shop the present day, the next day and the previous day either. This is for the ones who think faster than others.

But the first thing Just did as soon as he was in possession of all of his money was to get a truck full of groceries delivered to his village in the name of Monica, his assistant.

All of these people who didn't believe in Santa Claus anymore, even on December 25th had to reconsider and believe that this year; he came in summertime. All of them who didn't believe that a woman, especially a young one couldn't accomplish some great things had to reconsider too and believe in it. No point saying that for many of these people; this was the nicest day of their life. This was not the only surprise that was coming their way though.

At one o'clock of that afternoon, a limousine was in front of the house-castle of Jeannine and Superhuman wasn't far behind. Just the time to sit in it and they were both on their way to Paris, the city of lights. The chauffeur didn't understand anything, but he was nevertheless happy of the invitation to participate at an opera for the very first time of his life and to be paid on top of all. It took more time for Superhuman to find a parking lot than to travel from Gatineau to Paris. It also cost more for the parking lot than it cost for the trip as well. But when a man sold for 94 million dollars of diamonds in one day; he doesn't care about the cost of a parking lot, even if he is thrifty.

The usual salutations and introductions took place and then it was complete silence until the intermission. The queen was cordial, but nothing more and her husband; well, I rather not talk about him. A man who didn't like Princess Diana, doesn't deserve to be mentioned at all. Maybe he wasn't happy that his wife spends so much money in only one day, but in their home we know who wears the pants. Fortunately for them, the young Duke and his wife were there, otherwise this intermission would have been extremely boring.

Jeannine came back home happy and anxious at the same time. Happy for haven seen her first opera in her life, but anxious for haven left her baby daughter behind for the first time. She was mainly concerned because of her disappearances. Was she going to stay in her cradle or going after her mother? We might just never know, unless she says it herself, because this little one can, if she wants to, leave and come back without anyone noticing it. Her grand-mother was taking a look at her though every ten minutes or so, which was exasperating the grand-father.

Two days later at the day light, when all the children started yelling of joy seeing the three semi-trailers and dozens of men who were busy emptying them. There were also four ready-mix ready to unload their content as soon as the forms were installed. They were for the footings of the gymnasium, the restaurant and for the new grocery store. All this to say that there is sometime something good to come out of something bad and James, the ex beast is a living proof.

Superhuman was quite happy with the change also, because there is a lot more fun working for the good of a community than to chase and to fight criminals. Although, a huge battle was awaiting him, something I will talk about later on.

Then Just, remembering the little girl who had her face covered with blueberries went for a little tour in the field to find out that there were a lot of them around. He then asked Monica to organize the blueberries picking with all of the children and all the adults available. Two things, this would for one thing bring a good income to the village and keep them away from the dangerous construction sights for their own security. Just reminded Monica how to call him if she needs him.

This was not very long. One of the employees, who likes Monica a bit too much, got into his head that he could take advantage of her if he wanted to. Two minutes later though, he was bound to the passenger seat of a ready-mix and ready to be delivered to the police authorities for sexual harassment and sexual assault.

"This village is destined to happiness. They have known their share of misfortunes and it is not you who will change their destiny now. I will see you in a couple of days at the queen's bench, young bastard."

But even though this guy acted like a real bastard, he was not the most aggressive one; because two hours later Monica was screaming again for help. This time it was a huge brown bear that kind of thought that children were more appetizing than blueberries. But a punch in its forehead quickly put an end to his ambitions. Just brought it to the village to be bled and butchered. The Natives love bear meat and the fir makes nice and warm clothes. But the war burst out among the men to find out who would keep the fur.

"Fix it up the way it should be and later on tonight we'll make a draw to find the winner. This way it will be fair for everyone. The winner will be happy and all of the others will have to be happy with the meat of the animal, is that understood from everybody?" "Yes chief!"

"Yes chief!"

Each one of them was babbling to himself, but the problem was solved.

Then Just went to Lac-St-Jean to find out how much the blueberries pickers were getting for their work, but one little problem came up. All of the pickers of this village had put their blueberries in the same basket, sort of speak.

"This is not a very big problem; I will distribute the total amount evenly to everyone." "I am strongly against that solution sir." "And why is that, Monica?" "Because one of the boys picked up almost nothing, sir." "Then this one will get almost nothing, that's all. This will teach him a lesson. 'Whoever picks nothing has nothing.' This is something known from everybody, isn't it?"

When the evening came, all of them, but mainly the children were amazed to see what was done in only one day. They were even more amazed to see the sixty dollars that each one of them earned the same day; all of them but one of course. The lesson was hard on him, but beneficial for his apprenticeship.

"Now, if you want to, Monica, I would like you to organize a bank system for all the ones who want to see their money grow and also be secured against the predators. Maybe there is none, but again, maybe there are some and we cannot take any risk with this." "Truly sir, I am way too tired tonight to do anymore." "What would you say everyone, if I would keep your money until the picking is done?"

All but a few accepted this deal, but the next morning the same few girls had already lost their money to a young thief. They went to see Monica, crying to complain about it. When this news came to the ears of Just, he simply told them not to worry about it, that the one or the ones who are guilty won't be picking blueberries today. Sure enough, the one who didn't pick many blueberries the previous day wasn't picking at all the next day. Just surprised him while he was burying the money that he put inside a tobacco can.

Just left him finishing his job and he waited for the young boy to go away. Then he got the can out, took out the money and he put the can back where it was. He then waited for the boy to go back to his treasure and as he heard the boy yelled out; Just was with him like a blow of the wind:

"Do you need help, young boy?" "No, no, I, I!" "So, it is true then that laziness is the root of all evil. If you want to stay a member of our community young boy; you will have to change your manners, because I won't tolerate this kind of actions in this village. I make superhuman efforts to make this village a better place to live and I don't deserve some punk of your kind."

"Did you call me Just?" "No, I'm sorry my friend; I was talking about my efforts, but while you are here, might as well take a few of these ready-mix down and deliver this employee to the police. He is accused of sexual assault on a young woman and there are many witnesses."

"As far as you are concerned young man; I suggest you go pick blueberries right away and do it right, otherwise I will sent you somewhere else. You will also have to admit your crime tonight in front of everybody and ask for forgiveness from your two victims, even though one of them is your sister. Go, I have seen enough of you."

Then one day the young James received the right to an outing with an escort and Just offered him two choices for fishing, either at the Lake Windigo, a lake that he knows quite well or the lake near the village of his childhood; there where still lives his family he didn't see for the last seven or eight years. A person changes a lot from the age of fourteen to twenty-two.

"I'm not ready to return to Windigo just yet. There are there a lot of bad memories for me." "Then we'll go near your village that you won't recognize anyway and where hardly anyone could recognize you."

Something happened a week earlier though between Just and Monica, the young woman who is Just's assistant. She fell in love with Just and she admitted it to him. But Just is Just for a reason and he told her that he was well married to the best woman on this earth and that he wouldn't change her for nothing and no one of this world. He told her too that he was not worried for her and that she will find one day soon a young man who will make her happy. He told her that a young woman who is as pretty as she is and with a head over her shoulders as she has, cannot do otherwise than to find someone suitable.

Monica turned around very sad, but at the same time knowing she wouldn't want someone who is not as honest as Just. She knew too from then on that she will have to look somewhere else, because a man like the one she loves wouldn't change his way of living this easily. She is young maybe, but she knows what she wants in life.

"Do we make a contest to see who could take the most and the biggest?" "If you want to, but I cannot compete against you." "How's that?" "I am only allowed to catch six pickerels and there is no limit for you." "Ho no, I am limited too, unless it is to feed the people of my family." "Well, people of your family need to feed and fish is very good for them. We have to agree about using one way of fishing and I suggest the fishing rod. I don't know any other way anyway, so this is settled." "Most of the people of my nation are using nets." "I know and I am strongly against this method." "And why is that?" "Because they kill more fish than they keep." "The dead fish feeds the biggest predators." "The biggest predators are big enough to hunt on their own, no?" "We could argue for a long time about this, but I prefer and by far that the biggest pike eats the useless dead fish thrown back in the water than eating the nice pickerel like the one that just bit at my lure." "Well then, you caught the first one." "Do they hunt or fish for their prey?" "They hunt, because they have nothing to lure them. The bigger ones run after the smaller ones." "Do they run or swim?" "They run after. A race could be on foot, in cars and at swimming as well. Do you try to learn something from me or you are teasing me?" "I am learning, of course." "Before we get going again, I would like you to choose three lures of your choice for the day and I will do the same, but we'll have to stick with them. Do you agree?" "This is fine with me." "You chose yours, now here are mine." "You took three of the same, why?" "I like better to have three of the best one than to have two that are not as good. Now I am not allowed to do what you do and you're not allowed to do what I'm doing. Do you still agree?" "Of course, I do." "I will drive the boat for an hour and you will for the next hour, so we have the same opportunity." "I still agree." "You will do your best to help me getting my fish out of the water and I will do the same for you." "I still agree." "If I catch some nice pickerel in one spot; you wouldn't go somewhere else for your own advantage?" "I will be as honest as you are." "Good then, I have worms and you?" "Maybe not so, but I have a fish and I can use the eyes from it and all the other parts that are not good for human's consummation." "Good then, the contest begins now."

In thirty minutes Just had already taken his limit of six pickerel and James had one more pickerel and a thirty-two inches pike.

"I will use now a non barbed hook to avoid hurting the fish before putting it back in the water, but I keep fishing and I think we should stop at around four o'clock. This way we will have time to make filets for everyone in the village. Pickerel filets and fried potatoes; nothing beats that." "I agree with you there. What adventure and I thank you for such opportunity. You don't mind if I allow myself some familiarities with you, do you?" "Not for as long as you don't forget that I am still your escort." "Don't you worry about that one; I am rather grateful for this beautiful day." "How far are you in with your book?" "I'm starting my fifth chapter." "I will have to talk it over with Monica first, the secretary of the village, she is also the one who will teach the children, but if she agrees with me and you too; next time you have an outing; I would like you to come to tell them what led you there where you are now. I think this will help a few from ending the way you did. Don't make the mistake to talk about this wonderful day and the luck you have to get instruction behind bars, because this would do the exact opposite of what we want them to see." "I will make them understand that life without instruction can easily lead to drunkenness, drugs, thief and jail, but mainly to be ripped off by everyone and mainly by the church. I have started another book, but I'm missing some information to finish it." "What is the title of that one and what it is all about?" "It is called: 'Worse Trader Than Judas!'" "Then I'll bring you a book called: 'The True Face of The Antichrist,' from James Prince, the author. You will find all the information that you need inside of that one; I am sure of it." "He is my favourite author and I carry his name because of it. I don't dare say he is my idol anymore, because apparently this is not right, according to the ten God's commandments anyway." "What is not right is to make some idols and to consider them as gods, thinking they can save us and grant us anything. This is a position that only the true God can occupy. Many Christians and other pagans believe the Virgin Mary and all the false saints can grant anyone something, but this is idolatry, a very grave sin and an insult to God, the Father of heaven and earth." "I'm glad that you made this clear to me, because he is really my idol as an author." "Well, I like him a lot too, but you don't beg him to light you up, do you?" "No, he lights me up without me praying to him." "Well, in this case there is no wrong for him to be your idol, especially if he leads you to God, the true One.

Well then, it is time to quit and to count our fish. I caught thirty-eight pickerel, seven pike and twelve perch." "You caught the most and I caught the biggest one. A forty-two inches pike weighting twenty pounds and three ounces. I caught 27 pickerel and eight pike; this should be enough to feed everybody in this village." "Let's go, I've got a sore back. I'm not used to sit this long, but I like fishing and I am happy with my day."

When the people of this village saw the two men coming with this load of fish; they all got together and applauded their success. Many of them started yelling; 'Barbecue, barbecue and potatoes and hurry.'

Yes, there was a lot of fish. There was enough for everybody and some left for the next day. This though gave another great idea to Just to make life better for the people of this village. This will be something to make them proud of themselves at the same time, because they will be able to bring a good living for everyone of them.

Monica insisted for Just to introduce his guest to everyone, but this took him by surprise, because they haven't discussed it before and Just would lie for any reason.

"Well, this young man is named James, James the Second. He is at the same time a prison guardian and a writer. He is a man to become a famous writer. I can also say that he is an excellent fisherman and you have the proof of that today."

Neither his parents nor his brother or sister recognized him, but James had his throat very dry when he saw his mom and dad. He almost gave up his identity when he recognized his young sister and his younger brother, who is almost a man now. Just was telling himself that he will question them later on about their older brother.

As far back as James could go into his memories; he could not remember a day when his parents weren't drunk and neither his grand-parents. In fact, the lake is one of the rare things that didn't really change in and around his natal place of birth. This is mainly why Just wanted to bring him there on the lake before he sees his village and the people of his village. He thought that otherwise James wouldn't believe this was his village.

To tell you the truth, I too wouldn't have believed all the changes that happened in the village where I grew up, if I didn't see it from time to time. There were only gravel roads and the whole place was mainly bush like when we arrived there in the village of Omerville in 1948 and now it is basically a big city joined to the town of Magog. I had to go get some wood to keep us warm in the winter and this as far as half a mile away and all the way to the red creek with Beaver, my faithful dog and best friend of my childhood. Him and I were making a very good team. I could lie down on my sleigh and tell him; 'Let's go home,' and he would take me home, there where my fun was ending and his too.

"Did by any chance anyone made a good blueberry pie? If there is enough for everybody, then bring it over. I like mine when it is coming out of the oven."

A woman brought him a big piece of pie the size of half of a plate.

'But this is cold.' He said. "Yes, I keep all of my pies in the oven."

Everybody was laughing, thinking this was a very good joke to play, but another piece of pie came up that was quite hot this time.

"All of what is best for our loved chief."

When hearing this, Just noticed that the ex-chief of the band put his head down with shame and he knew from that time on that he will have to have a talk with him and the sooner the better. Just knows very well that it is better to have an ounce of prevention than a pound of cure.

But a few of them got their native drums out and made them echoed until midnight, time when a fight almost broke out to find out who will keep Just and James for the night.

"There is no point fighting about this, Just yelled out loud; James and I will spend the night in the school dormitory and we don't want to be disturbed before nine in the morning. It is time now for everyone to go to bed."

A few of them were babbling a little, but they all knew there was no point arguing with their new chief. There are new rules now in this village and this is a turn for the better.

James could hardly believe his own ears, but he who just spent a few years under the discipline of the jail and who has to impose it now to others knows to well that authority is necessary so order can prevail.

In the morning the grocery truck was gone and the food was stored in the new store and James too was gone to everyone deception. James could easily use more than one day of this, but he was quite satisfied with what he got and all the villagers wanted to know more about him, especially Monica who looked at him with a good eye. She could remember a young boy that she knew before and disappeared suddenly and who some how looks a little like this James.

Just went to spend the night with his wife, whom he cherishes more than anything in this world, more than his power and more than his own life. But on his return in this village, even though all of them think he spent the whole night over there; many of them had a lot of questions about his mysterious guest.

"Are we going to see this charming young man again?" "Are you already interested in somebody else?" "I sure don't want to spend the rest of my life alone and I am not interested by any other one in this village either. They all are lacking maturity and a lot of other things as well, to my taste anyway." "What makes you question me about this young man? He is not at all like me and yet, you were saying not very long ago that you were in love with me. Don't you look for a man no matter what and how he is?" "Do you really think this is what I'm doing?" "This seems to me very obvious, yes. I will get you a book that will help you find the right man, because you seem to me being confused on this subject. I'm going to try getting it before the end of the day, if this is alright with you." "If you think this can help me in this far away from everybody corner of the world; I sure agree with that."

For a woman as well as for a man, the sexual desire and the need to have sex is a source of confusion when it comes to choose the right partner and the fact of having many sexual partners doesn't help at all. On the contrary, this causes more confusion in the mind of many. The woman who gives herself to any good-for-nothing guy is no better than a good-for-nothing girl.

"Here Monica, I have three books for you: 'How to find the right partner, how to find the man who is made for you and how to choose a husband.' I hope you'll find answers in those that are necessary to you." "But this young man, this young James; is he single?" "As far as I know he is, but don't you forget that there are two worlds between the two of you." "It's true that he is far from here, but love does bring two loving hearts together, isn't it?" "He would most likely never be able to quit his job. And you, could you ever leave your village, everyone that you know, all of these children for a man who lives far way?" "I should be reading in these books, shouldn't I?" "This is my sincere advice to you."

Then Just opened up another business for the people of his village in the two largest cities of the province of Quebec. The new business is called' 'Blueberries and Fish of The North.' All of the children who can walk and hold a fishing rod can participate and receive royalties.

A safe the same size as the one they have in banks was installed in the office building and the only one who has a combination for it is Just. They had to open a complete outside wall to get it in, but all of them who participate in the village income have their own deposit box and receive their due in full. A great part of Just income as a chief is also deposited in this safe.

Such a safe is worth its share of gold and iron in this case. An ingenious alarm system was also installed on it and it is different than any other system invented so far. When someone else than Just tries to open it, a voice comes out of it saying; 'Just, Just.'

This gives everyone the will to run away, but not the time to do it, because if just is not saving someone at the time; he is there before anyone can cross the door again to get out.

The first one who got caught was the ex-chief.

"Aren't you ashamed to lower yourself this way? Even if you would blow up this office completely; you wouldn't succeed in opening this safe. But this is a good timing in a way, because I wanted to talk to you since the evening we all had fish together. You seem to me the more and more distressed. What are you looking for exactly? Maybe I can help you with your plan." "I want to have enough money to go install myself somewhere else, because life became unbearable for me over here. Everything I look at is hurting me." "Not that I would like you to go away, but tell me how much you need." "I already have a thousand, but a few more thousands would help. I was planning giving back this money later on, but I don't know when. Are you wife and son agree to leave with you?" "They are both waiting and ready to leave, but they both disagreed with what I was about to do tonight." "You all are ready to leave in the middle of the night like thieves?" "They don't have the choice; my squaw is following me and my son is following his parents. All of this is perfectly normal." "What is not normal is travelling at night in the wild forest." "I have done it hundreds of times already." "I have a different suggestion for you, if you don't mind. You go to bed tonight with your family and tomorrow morning you come back over here. I'll make you then the loan that you need to go set up yourself and your family somewhere else." "You would do this for us? I sure don't deserve you to do this for me." "I must tell you though that you will never find anywhere else all the opportunities that we'll have here before long. I must tell you too that my job here as a chief is only temporary; just the time to put everything back in order. How long were you the chief of this band?" "I don't know exactly, eleven and maybe twelve years." "This is the reason why the books were so, so kept?" "It was for sure pathetically kept, no doubt and I am the only one to blame. What you're doing is very good and this hurts me knowing I couldn't do as much for my own people." "Everyone does what he can. Go now, go and come back in the morning. Bring your family along with you, so it knows that you didn't steal it."

The ex-chief listened to Just and he went to sleep with his family, happy not to have been sermonized more than this for his attempt. Fortunately for him, he was sober even if it is said that liquor is no excuse.

At around nine o'clock the next morning, Just was waiting for them in the office with an envelope ready and papers to be signed.

'I, Jos Marteleau agree conscientiously and accept the amount of twelve thousand dollars as a departure bonus for services rendered to the Village of Westimouche, and I signed this fifteenth day of August of the year 2015.

I signed this in the presence of the actual chief, Just Just and his secretary, Monica St-Clair, Treasurer of the village this 15th of August 2015.'

Jos couldn't believe a thing about what he was reading, so he passed this piece of paper to his wife in a way she can read it out loud in its entirety. She did it too, but she couldn't believe a thing of what was written on this paper either and she just threw it on the desk in front of her.

"Monica will be here any minute now and she will read it to you too. She has to be in anyway to witness your signature and this is a must to be legal. The whole process would be worthless without her presence.

Two minutes later, Monica too couldn't believe what she was looking at on this document that is to be the most important of her young career.

Jos got up as mad as one could be and he yelled out loud: 'This is all BS, I'm not allowed to this money." "This is not for you to decide."

Just told him even louder, so much that Monica got really scared.

"Sit down and sign this document, so we can finish with that once and for all." "Does this force me to leave this village?" "Not at all, you are home over here and we need everybody to grow as a community."

"Sign this document and pick up this envelope dad; I don't want to leave this village."

"Is there really twelve thousand in there?" "Just know Jos that I never cheat, but you still have to sign this to have the right to it." "Give me this here that I sign; tell me where." "As soon as Monica and I have signed it too; this envelope and whatever is in it will be totally yours. Although, if you can allow me an advice to you; you shouldn't carry this much cash for too long. There are people out there who kill for a lot less and not only in the Native communities." "You're right; I will look at it, count it and open an account immediately, if this is possible." "Monica will set that up for you in a few minutes. You should also make plans to fix up your house a little while the carpenters are still around here. This way you won't have to pay for their trip up here and there will be also some materials left and I don't want to return any." "This is a good idea, thank you."

And this is how Just made a few more happy people and all of this by exchanging evil for goodness. This reminds me a message from the Messiah and it is written in Matthew 5, 44-45. 'Love your enemies and pray for those who persecute you, that you may be sons of your Father in heaven. He causes his sun to rise on the evil and the good, and sends rain on the righteous and the unrighteous.'

This message from the Messiah is totally the opposite of the message that is written in Psalm 83.

The day I got baptized, I mean the one where I was conscious of it; I chose the Psalm 104, 33-34 and I sing songs to my Lord since. 'I will sing to the Lord all my life; I will sing praises to my God as long as I live. May my meditation be pleasing to Him, as I rejoice in the Lord'

But the next verse is rather hypocritical I think and it is totally contrary to the Messiah's message, just like the Psalm 83, as far as I know anyway. See Psalm 104, 35. 'But may sinners vanish from the earth and the wicked be no more. Praise the Lord, O my soul. Praise the Lord.'

Maybe the man who said such a thing didn't know the Messiah and his messages, but this was rather mean to say things like that, I think. Although, if this man was granted from God; maybe he too disappeared from the earth.

According to many Bibles I read, the only place in them where the writer used the name of the Lord in vain, just like the Witnesses do in the face of the world, it is in the Psalm 83. The Witnesses do it thousands of times in their own Bible.

I do have a Bible from A. J. Holman & Co., dated from 1882, 133 years old, in Roman numerals. I had to relearn these numbers to find out where I was in there. I am not used at all to these numbers by letters. This must be a Bible like the one that was read by Louis Riel and this could even be his. One thing is sure; this Bible is in Saskatchewan, Canada, there where walked, lived and fight a war Louis Riel; there where he was executed unfairly. I think this was a crime and it is one of the worse shames of our country. But the name of the Lord is written in this Bible, in the Psalm 83, 19.

I also have another Bible dated 1976 and in it too the name of the Lord is written in the Psalm 83, 19.

But in the other Bibles, like the Louis Second, in the New International and in the Gideons; the name of the Lord in Psalm 83, 19 is replaced by: 'The Most High,' in English and by: 'Très-Haut' in French.

All this to say that, if the Witnesses chose Psalm 83 to build the foundation of their religion; they have chosen an author who has a policy or a teaching that is completely contrary to the teaching of the Messiah.

Did you know that in all of his teaching; Jesus has never say the name of God? He rather referred to Him by saying: 'My Father who is in heaven.'

Some people will say; 'This is normal, God is his Father.'

Yes, God is his Father and He is mine as well and this is why I don't dare use his name in vain, just like his commandments ask us not to do it.

Did I need to write the name of the Lord to make myself understood here? Not at all. Then this was unnecessary for me to write his name to make myself understood. Then why the Witnesses are doing it all the time? I don't want to judge them, but the word of God does it.

I said a bit earlier singing to the Lord every day of my life and in case I can't sing anymore one day; I composed many songs and hymns that others might be able to sing for me and here are a few of them. This one is called;

Praises to My Lord

I want to sing praises to my Lord with the angels, with the angels of heaven
And I want to be happy up there with the angels and Adam, Eve and Abel
I want to sing praises to my Lord with the angels, with the angels of heaven
And I want to be happy up there with the angels and with all of his children

1-6
Listening to Jesus, to Jesus and Moses,
This is how I have known the Father as my own
And because they told me, this is why I can see
Yes now I can see through and I believe the truth

2
I'll be able to meet the great Job and Jacob
Shake hands with Abraham, I am one of his fans
I don't need Cadillac to meet with Isaac
I'll sing with the angels, Daniel and Ezekiel

3
I will seal with Noah and walk with Jeremiah
I'll fish with Hosea also with Isaiah
I will build some mentions with David and Samson
Be with the apostles and Jesus' disciples

4

My heart is with Joseph who in prison was kept
Was like me a dreamer didn't want to be sinner
So my God was with him, kept him away from sin
I'll meet him when ever there at the Lord's Supper

5

Now's the great gathering, will you be there to sing
With all of us one day in the heavens to pray?
The Lord is powerful; He's with whom is faithful
He will not let you down, come join us in the round.

I want to sing praises to my Lord with the angels, with the angels of heaven
And I want to be happy up there with the angels and Adam, Eve and Abel
I want to sing praises to my Lord with the angels, with the angels of heaven
And I want to be happy up there with the angels and with all of his children

Only God can control everything in the universe, but many still are obstinate and try to prove the opposite. If only they knew that even their own thoughts don't belong to them. If only they knew that the Almighty could in only one instant make them as useless as the most useless one on earth and maybe this is even what happens sometime. Just think at what happened at the tower of Babel.

Here is one more you might like:

You Told Me Lord

You told me oh my Lord; You brought to us the word
The kingdom of heaven belongs to your children
You made beautiful things, for You I'll be pleading
I found You amazing and for You I will sing

You are the Father of the heavens and the earth
You know all the secrets of the earth and the sea
Some want to take over what you created first
Only You know how to control the universe

Only You know how to change our hearth and our thoughts
What can I do for You? For You I love so much
From your word came my faith, now I do know my fate
For You I want to sing, the Master of all things

You are the Father of the heavens and the earth
You know all the secrets of the earth and the sea
Some want to take over what you created first
Only You know how to control the universe

You showed me oh my Lord that life is not a game
Many mock you my Lord, everywhere is the shame
Everything goes down hill, enough to make me ill
Sing is my destiny for the eternity

You are the Father of the heavens and the earth
You know all the secrets of the earth and the sea
Some want to take over what you created first
Only You know how to control the universe
Only You know how to control the universe.

I like the next one too

The Final Warning

Listen to this one great news sent to you today
To me it's the greatest: the Lord is on his way
He has made the universe, the earth and heavens
And all that you can see has been made by his hands
'Many times I have showed you the mighty power
I have flooded the earth but I have saved Noah
When Abram the good man has pleaded for his friends
They got out of the towns Sodom and Gomorrah
2
Do you remember Joseph I sent to exile?
He was sold by his brothers, he was put in jail
He was to save my people from the starvation
Of a deadly famine seven years duration
And what to say of Moses drew out of water?
To guide you through the crises and lots of danger
I told him all I wanted as for you to know
He carried all my commands down to you below
3
The wisdom of Solomon, the strength of Samson
Can just not save your soul from the lake of fire
Only Jesus the Saviour with his compassion
Left his beautiful home, they took him for ransom
I sent you my loved Son for the sacrifice
He has done nothing wrong yet he has paid the price
Now if you are telling Me this is not for you
Just one more thing to say I've done all I can do
Instrumental

4

Now you are out of time and I am out of blood
Too many of my children have died for their God
Many of Jesus' good friends and his apostles
And so many others died as his disciples
Now it is time to crown my own Beloved Son
He's going back to run everything that I've done
Will you be lost forever or will you be saved?
That is what you should know before you hit the grave!'
5

Listen to this one great news sent to you today
To me it's the greatest: the Lord is on his way
He has made the universe, the earth and heavens
And all that you can see has been made by his hands
And all that you can see has been made by his hands.

CHAPTER 8

Nowadays we see a race as who is going to build the highest tower in the world. We will see them fall down soon and this might be ironic to say, but then men will come down to earth too. It is the same for those who are looking in the space for another place than the earth to live. What are they thinking about really? Maybe they are thinking about blowing up the planet and settle down on another one and set up a transportation business and bring on the billionaires who can afford to pay for the trip. What is the low price of the barrel of fuel means? Does it mean the warehouses are all full and there is no room for anymore? This wouldn't surprise me one bit, but this would also mean the world is getting ready for another world war. A war where the world will finally understand that God is the Almighty and this war will be directed the way He wants it to go. We only have to read Ezekiel 38 in its entirety to understand.

There is also a good reference in Deuteronomy 3, 21-22. 'You have seen with your own eyes all that the Lord your God has done to these two kings. The Lord will do the same to all the kingdoms over there where you are going. Do not be afraid of them; the Lord your God Himself will fight for you.'

What a reassurance, what guarantee this gives to the children of God who rely on Him!

Then came the time when James the Second was to give a lecture to the students at the school of his village. Any point saying that he was very nervous about it? This was the very first time of his life he was going to do such a thing. He knew though that he could count on Just, his friend and escort for support. It was at one of these lectures that the life of many people in this village would be overturned. His own life will be first, then the life of his parents and grand-parents, the life of his sister and brother, the life of Monica and surprisingly too, the life of Just and Jeannine. The whole population of the village was present for such event and Just even brought his wife Jeannine over for the occasion. She too was to be overturned by the story and have a very hard time to believe what she heard.

James was applauded like a Premier when he entered the hall. Never in its entire existence, had this village lived through such an honour. A sound system was installed for the occasion and James started with a trembling voice. Everyone could hear a fly suddenly and this made everyone laughed a lot, which kind of released the tension that the whole crowd could feel.

"I will start tonight by telling you the story of a young Native like you, who grew up like you, but didn't have a chance like you to have someone who cares for him.

He was a very hard worker, fishing and hunting and picking all the little wild fruits in the summer and the firewood in the winter. There was no school in his time like you are very lucky to have one today. He was quite brilliant even though he never set foot in a classroom.

He knew the woods and the deep forest better then anyone and hunting was for him a chance to get away from everything, especially the hardship with his family. He never went hunting a single day without coming back to the camp with a prey of some kind for his family and for the rest of the band, but he was lucky if he could get a bite out of it. His parents and all the others who were stronger than him were tearing apart his prey and when he asked for some of it; he received a slap behind the head and a kick in the ass.

Fleeing became his only goal then, his only hope for a better life. But where is better and how to get there? Leaving without knowing where to go is kind of stupid, isn't it? There was no one in his village to tell him where to go and asking for directions would have created suspicions. This would just have made things worse for him.

It was after receiving a slap behind the head and a kick in the ass from his father that he got the courage and he decided to go in the deep forest and to never go back again. Anywhere he could go couldn't be worse than returning in this village, was he telling himself. Then anywhere could only be better for him.

He walked days and nights, moons and more moons. He crossed lakes and more lakes and fortunately for him; he knew how to survive in the forest and he also knew how to catch fish and this since he was two or three years old.

The only regrets he had all of that time was the fact he left behind his young sister and his young brother who were going most likely to inherit the sad destiny he was in before with his parents who were drinking every single day of their life. One more regret he had was a young girlfriend with whom he got along pretty good. The only good times he had in his entire measurable childhood; he had them with her.

He crossed many Native's bands from different nationalities, but he didn't seem to be more welcomed there than he was at home. So he continued walking until he decided it was time to settle somewhere and he thought he had no other choice than to settle in the forest.

He finally set his camp around the Lake Windigo."

When Jeannine heard these words, she straightened up on her chair immediately. She just understood then that the men who attempted to their lives was just there in front of her and telling others the story of his life. But she didn't say a word about it and Just knew that she just understood the situation. James kept telling the story all of that time.

"This was for him a permanent place to live finally, thinking that a little bit more, a little bit farther will bring nothing new and nothing more. This was a good hunting territory and this was also very good for fishing. What else and what more to ask for, really? But some poachers, some white men began chasing him around, so he became the hunted hunter.

During more than five years long these none scrupulous men got together to make a search trying to catch the one who was destroying their illegal and exaggerated poaching traps. But this young wild Native knew the wild life better than anyone and hiding was just for him a kid's game. One day though, he had enough to be chased this way and he decided to move from defensive to the attack.

He saw three of these poachers who were fishing at a couple of hundred feet from shore on the Lake Windigo. It's there that he took the matter into his own hands. A little bit like Tarzan would have done it; he dived and he swam under the water and he went to cut the nets these poachers were using illegally. But when the three men started shooting guns at him in the water; he went under their fishing boat and he pierced it many times with his knife and then he went back to shore.

The boat was quickly full of water and in a few minutes, it was down in the bottom of the lake. The three men didn't seem to know how to swim and none of them had a life jacket either. So he swam back there to help them out, but two of them were drowned already. When he arrived at the third one, a fight broke out, so he had to leave him to his own destiny and return to shore.

Then the real panic got to him and he didn't know what to think anymore. Then he got into his mind it was best for him to get rid of all traces of these men. So he went back to them with a sort of a creeper plant and a stone that he attached to the leg of one of them, so he can be pulled down to the bottom. He repeated this action two more times and there was nothing showing anymore. If he wasn't betrayed by his ex-companion; these three would still be resting in the bottom of the lake.

Excuse me now; I must take a glass of water and a few minutes of rest, if you allow me."

Just just realized then that a huge injustice was committed and that he is guilty of it as much as the justice system is. It was easier for him to understand too now the reason why the attempt on the bus that was supposed to carry the poachers only and this was what James was thinking. These were some poachers who were destroying his territory, chasing him around and threatening his life continually. No one should take justice into his own hands, but when and where there is no justice around, who should take over this dirty job?

While he was thinking all this over in his head, Just was promising to himself to restore justice one way or the other and this as soon as possible.

"Following the young boy's departure from his village, a ferocious war broke out between his parents and his grand-parents over his younger brother, because neither one wanted to see him go away like the oldest did. The mother told her husband that if he beats him the way he did the other, he would go away for sure and from this time on the father's attitude changed completely. He had to start hunting again himself to feed his family. The departure of the oldest one was kind of a wake up call for the parents, but they were still wondering if their oldest son was still alive. Eight long years went by since he left."

Many listeners had tears in their eyes, especially the parents and the grand-parents, thinking that this could very well be the story of their son. They knew very well that many of the facts were corresponding with their own story, but they couldn't recognize their own son. The father did search his son in a circle of a hundred miles around his camp, but he couldn't find a single foot print of him.

Monica too could remember many details of her childhood, but she couldn't make the connection between James and the young Ryan of her village she knew years ago. She was in love with him and she was very upset with him for leaving without a single word or a good bye. She understood over the years that the life of the young boy became intolerable and this despite the good times they had together. When she thinks about him some times, she realizes that she is still in love with him, but also that this is hopeless. Her most memorable souvenirs, the ones she cherishes the most are on the little beach where they swam both of them naked before kissing and apparently this beach was known from no one else. Ryan discovered it one day when he was fishing. He too has never forgotten this little beach and neither the young girl who kept haunting his craziest dreams and still does.

Monica went back there a couple of other times, but this was heartbreaking for her and she stop going. James was thinking that night that he would like to go see it one last time before returning behind his walls that keep him prisoner, but he would need first to get the permission from his escort agent.

James had a very hard time controlling his emotions when he recognized her the first time and this was the very first time he was allowed an outing with escort. He has a very hard time controlling his emotions tonight as well, being before all these people that he recognizes without being recognized. In reality, he doesn't know what to expect and how to react, if he is ever recognized by his people. It was with a lot of courage that he went back to the microphone to continue his lecture.

"I must say to start with that we are lucky to be on a Friday night, otherwise the children would have to go to bed. Since they can sleep in in the morning; they can stay up later tonight. But tell me, what do you think about my lecture?"

Everybody stood up all at once and applauded him.

"This means then that you want to know more about the story of this adventurer?"

They applauded even more and this until James put his arms up in the air to stop them.

"Well then, I don't think I have any choice; I have to keep it up. Laughs.....Where was I?"

A young boy stood up and yelled out; 'Three dirty poachers in the bottom of the lake.'

"Thanks you young man, thanks a lot. Maybe it is because I am trying to forget completely about those three. But they weren't alone and this young Native a bit wild thought that maybe it was time to put an end to this poaching network and being hunted by them once and for all. This wasn't for him an easy problem to get rid of. There was no one around either who could help him with this challenge. This was one against all, all against one before his friend joined him.

He knew though that a big number of these poachers had to take the bus the same night. So, with the help of a friend, he managed to get inside a huge garage where the bus was stored until the time of the departure. They found there all the tools they needed to do the work. So they pierced a very small hole at a brake line with the help of a drill for the fluid to leak only slowly until the need of pushing on the brakes harder was necessary.

Unfortunately for them, a different bus was used to carry the poachers with all of their catches to their destination and the damaged bus was used to carry many innocent people the next morning. Fortunately for these two young men and for twenty some other travellers, an unknown hero, by I don't know what kind of miracle saved them all from a certain death. Another hero took these two young Natives down to a police station to be prosecuted and haven been found guilty as charged, they are both to this day serving their prison sentence.

This is where I stop for the day. I thank you very much for your attention, children, Miss; ladies and gentlemen, goodnight."

This was under the applause that James got out of the school. Just excused himself to his wife and he went out too and the two men waked for a few minutes outside.

"I wanted to personally congratulate you for holding your composure; you did this like a real professional in the field. This must have been very hard on you." "I was even more nervous here tonight than I was at my trial. If you would allow me; I would like to go recollect myself on this little beach for a few minutes." "Only if you promise me not to run away." "You know and I know that I can't do that, but I don't want it either." "Then go and take your time; I will go join my wife now."

James borrowed a fishing boat on the side of the lake and he went to look at the very best sight of his memories and this under the very bright moon and the sky was lighted up by billions of stars. All of them who were at the assembly, young and older were discussing the evening, when Just noticed that Monica got out too to walk under the stars. James hided first behind a group of people and then he disappeared. Monica was only a few hundred feet away when he reached and asked her.

"This is a nice evening, isn't it?" "It is absolutely majestic and I think that something else also majestic is about to happen. This is him, isn't it?" "Him.....?" "You know exactly what I'm talking about." "Yes, but I'm not too sure if this is a good thing in itself." "What are you afraid of exactly?" "I'm afraid that this might be possibly impossible for the two of you." "And why is that?" "Didn't you hear what he said? He is not only a guardian at the prison; he is also a prisoner and he is in for seventy-five years. He earns a bit of money, but he is still there for another seventy-three years. This is not little to say and if he is here tonight, it is because he received the right to an outing with an escort and I am the one responsible for him. I can tell you though that the idea of making it possible for all the children of this village to receive an education is his and part of the money too. He is no longer the young boy you knew years ago." "I think I know where he is gone; do you mind if I go talk to him?" "Don't promise each other anything, other than to keep his identity secret, not yet anyway." "I promise you." "Go, but don't get lost on the way and come back here; the kids need you." "Don't you worry, I know my way there and my way back."

"This place reminds you someone?" "Miss Monica, you became a very pretty young lady. I was wondering how you would look like if I ever see you again." "I couldn't recognize you, even though I could see some hints, some points that remind me of the young Ryan I have known years ago. You are the first and the only one who saw my breasts and this happened on this little beach, but I never regretted it, because I was deeply in love with you." "They were quite small then." "They were mine anyway." "I dreamt about them during hundreds of moons, because this was the very best of my souvenirs left behind." "I was mad at you for leaving without me, but mainly for leaving without letting me know about it." "You couldn't have survived where I went through and you would have most likely got pregnant and life would have became a nightmare and you would have ended up hating me. It was best for you to stay over here and become who you are, the magnificent young lady that you are. Do you think my parents recognized me too?" "Certainly not; they wouldn't have been able to hide their emotions. I watched them during your lecture and I could feel they were very emotional as they listened to you." "Tell me about my sister and my brother; how are they?" "They had a much better luck than you had with your parents. Your departure turned them a lot more responsible and mainly sober and we could sense their attachment to the two of them. If you want me to; I will question them about you, just to test the ground. They might have been mad at you too for leaving the way you did. It is always hard to see someone we love leaving, no matter how it is done. I am extremely surprised to see how you are educated and with the ease you can speak in public. I could never think this about you, the boy of the forest. We should go in now though, before someone thinks you kidnapped me. What do you think about all of the changes in our village?" "Beside you, the only thing I recognized at first is the lake. Laughs…..Tie out your boat to mine and sit with me, would you?" "Sure, it's been a long time since we did this. Can we keep in touch by letters?" "Do you know how to write? Laughs….Times have changed and so did we. Thanks for joining me; this was very beneficial to me." "To me too!"

As usual, it was Superhuman who brought the three of them down, Just, Jeannine and James who had to show up at his post for eight o'clock the next morning. Jeannine can hardly leave Justine behind for too long. She is as many say; 'A mother hen.' She wouldn't be as much after more than twelve kids like my mother had, but this is not the case yet.

Jeannine didn't know what to think anymore about the one or the two men who damaged the bus in which her and her husband took place. But Just quickly told her their actions were rather self-defence and aiming at the criminals, not at innocent people. He told her too that the actions of the poachers who tried to kill him were just as bad or even worse and they were free as birds and he had to take care of this business before long. But it was not that night that he was going to solve all of the injustices in this world and they went to bed.

In the morning, James was back on his job at the penitentiary and he received one more mark of confidence to be added to his file.

Then the young Hercules and his friend Charlie were questioning themselves a lot about their instructor, trying to find out why he was sleeping at the dojo when he has a home and a family to go to.

"You have a family, mister Prince, why don't you go sleep at home after work?" "This is a question of security my boy. When a man lives a life like I live mine and his solving hundreds of cases of injustice; he doesn't have only friends out there; he has a lot of enemies also. If the address of my family becomes known to my enemies; its security would be at high risk. Not all the members of my family can defend themselves the way I do. Is this a good enough answer to satisfy your curiosity?" "Yes sir and forgive me please." "I hope you will remember this when you'll have a family too." "I will never forget this, sir."

The next morning, Superhuman decided it was time for him to spend a few hours with his son and to see how far he is with his abilities.

"What do you think about going to the sea and see how high you can jump? Coming back down on the ground can hurt, but it is not so bad in the water. You took some swimming lessons, so you know how to swim, don't you?" "I could even win some swimming contests, if I participate." "All the contests could possibly make you famous, but at the same time; you would show them your powers, which is not really a very good thing to do." "I know this; my instructor told me." "So, we understand each other?" "Yes dad!"

I have to say here that Hercules is not aware of all the extent of the power his father has and vice versa. He had a little suspicion the night his father delivered a paedophile to the police station, but otherwise, he knows nothing at all.

"Jump in the air and let yourself fall down in the water farther out and come back swimming to shore; this way you will know how far you can go and also gain knowledge of your capabilities."

The first jump was only some twenty feet high and Hecules fell down in about five to six feet deep of water.

His return swimming to shore was done quickly. But Hercules kind of like this little game and this reminded Superhuman of his own childhood. His second jump was a couple of hundred feet high and his coming down seemed even faster than his ascent. Seeing him swimming back to shore this fast; Superhuman realized then that it was true his son could easily win some swimming contests. There was no more doubt in his mind; the son inherited his father's powers. But attention now, on Hercules third jump Superhuman lost sight of him completely. He was so far away that without the help of his father; the child, no matter how powerful he is would have died out of exhaustion before getting back where he left.

Superhuman jumped too in the same direction, but not wanting yet that his son discovers his powers; he dived under the water about half a mile before and he swam all the way to Hercules, who was fighting for his life just like a mouse in a pail of water. It was then that Hercules learned how to get out of such situation.

"I can see that you began panicking. You should never panic my son. First of all because it is a sign of weakness and you are not weak. You proved this a number of times already and also because it is a huge and useless lost of energy. You have to stay calm. Too many men lost their life because they lost their calm. Think about it for two seconds, what can you do from here; knowing your strength and your abilities?" "How far are we from shore?" "We are at about fifty miles. Two things you have to consider. First, you have to make sure in which direction you have to go and from which direction you came from. On which side of you was the sun when you left the shore?" "The sun was on my right when I was facing the sea." "Then to return in the same direction you came from, on which side of you the sun has to be?" "On my left, I think." "It is true, but you also have to consider the time, because the planet keeps turning." "What do you do when there is no sunshine?" "It is a good thing to learn the celestial body in relation to the time of the day." "Hey dad, mom wants me to be in before nine o'clock at night." "There will be some exceptions, don't worry about that and besides; you're not going to remain at eight years old either. There will be some evenings when you'll be able to come out with me and we'll be able to learn them together. There is also the wind that blows 99% of the time and 99% of the time it blows coming from the West. This can also help you find your direction. The waves, even if they are very small can also show you the wind direction.

Now that you know which direction to take to go back to shore and approximately what strength to use to get there, what can you do to get out of here?" "Really dad, if I knew it; I wouldn't be here and neither would you." "Can you float on top of the water to save your strength?" "This yes, but in my excitement I didn't think of it." "This is why that keeping our calm allows us to better think and this is true in all situations. Now, if you go under the water, what can you find over here?" "I would think there is some fish." "Yes and some big fish. Now, what can you do to a big fish?" "I can kill it I think, if I want to." "It is not necessary to kill it, but you can knock it out with a punch in the head. This fish then would float for a certain link of time...." "And I could climb on it and jump from it to my destination." "All this has to be done without forgetting your direction. Do you see another solution, in case there is no shark or whale around?" "I don't see, but I am under the impression that you have another idea." "Yes son and this would help you out more than once and it is one of my favourite ways." "And what is it?" "I would go all the way to the bottom, from where I can push as hard as I want to and get to my destination." "I personally don't need this today." "And why is that?" "Because you are here to serve as a big fish for me."

At the same time, Hercules who was standing up on his father's shoulders propelled himself in the direction of the shore, but luckily for him, his father is faster than he is, otherwise he would have smashed his head against rocks that are two miles off the shore.

"You acted in a very unsafe manner my boy and you will have to learn to control all of your powers before risking your life the way you just did it." "How did you manage to get here this fast?" "I too could win swimming races if I want to and on foot too. If I suggested you to jump towards the sea; this was for you to avoid dangerous landings the way you were about to do. This is what I'm going to try inculcating in you next time." "Inculcating, I don't know this word, what does it mean?" "It means that I will get it into your head next time. Do you understand it now?" "Yes dad." Laughs......

The young boy got home with his dad happier than ever and he was promising himself secretly to show his friend all of his new achievements. When we're young we think, but not very far, even if we can jump very high. Hercules already knows that his friend Charlie is very courageous. He knows too that he is a very good swimmer, because they often swam together. They also took their swimming lessons at the same time. You see this coming, don't you? Well yes, this is exactly what they did at the first occasion. Hercules was throwing Charlie as far as he could and in my opinion, this was way too far. They played that game until Charlie was completely exhausted and even though he is a very good swimmer; the last time was one time too many and Charlie wasn't coming back anymore.

At first Hercules thought that his friend was playing games with him, but he didn't think this was funny at all. Fortunately for both of them, Hercules remembered his dad last advice about not panicking and to stay calm no matter what. If only Hercules went away to get help; his friend would have died drowning. Instead Hercules swam quickly towards his friend, found him and brought him back to shore and he practiced on him what they both learned during their training and this is the artificial respiration. They both thought this was funny then and saying they could never put their lips against the other one's lips. But the laughing time was over then and he had to act quickly. This was not a question of a mouth against a mouth anymore, but a question of life and death and this was about the life of his best friend, no longer a play. Hercules managed to save his friend's life that day, but he aged a couple of years at the same time.

Hercules told the whole story to Jonathan, his trainer, but he asked him not to tell his father about it.

"Why don't you want your father to know about this?" "Because I still have a lot to learn from him and I don't want him to think that every time he'll show me something; I will turn around and show it to my friend. My friend is very courageous, but he is not made like I am." "Was that courage or carelessness? There is a similarity in both of them." "It might have been a bit of both, but one thing is sure; I will never throw him anymore, unless this is to save his life or to protect him some how." "I can see that you have learnt a good lesson from that experience. Is Charlie better now?" "He told me he will be here next time." "Good then, let's get to work; it's getting late."

The day the trial of the captain of the old tub and his crew came up. Just found him the best existing international lawyer. He is very expensive, but there is no price on the years in jail. Twenty thousand dollars paid in advance; otherwise he doesn't even look at the case or at the circumstances, either they are extenuating or not. This racket is a real little gold mine and he has not much to extract other than a little bit of the truth and a few lies here and there. It is like the one who impresses the judge the most has a much better chance to win and money means everything most of the time.

I remember taking to court a car dealer for swindle in a case of a mechanic problem. He billed me for a timing gear and a timing chain and this without either one of them needed to be replaced or repaired. Before the trial I brought the two parts to an expert mechanic of the consumer protection affairs who confirmed that neither of the parts needed to be replaced. When my turn to speak came up, the judge asked me if I took my vehicle over there to be repaired. I said yes. He then hit his desk with his little hammer that I find ridicules by the way and he said; 'You must pay.'

For me and my witness to be listened to; I would have had to spend more money on lawyer's fee than on the car repair. We have to feed this diabolic system to be heard by it. The car dealer pays for a licence that gives him the right to rob people and the justice system say it is alright. Neither I nor my witness could add another word. The sentence was declared and there was nothing else to do or to say. And then they are wondering why so many people don't believe in the justice system anymore.

Besides, if I had insisted a little more; I would have been charged with contempt of court. Be nice and quiet or watch out. And from there without a lawyer it is jail for sure and a criminal record.

There is a reason why the Messiah said what is written in Matthew 5, 40. 'And if someone wants to sue you and take your tunic, let him have your cloak as well.'

If you listen to the Messiah, you will save money and time, because most of the cloaks are a lot cheaper than any lawyer and without a lawyer, you're not listened to and you are wasting your time. A judge told me this once.

In those days I didn't know the Messiah as much I know him today; at least I was not listening to him as I do now, otherwise I would have saved money and time. But I could never stand for the injustice, so I had to fight, even if this was only to prove how wrong they were. This happened to me many of times during the last fifty years. On the other hand, I could always remember Matthew 5, 6. 'Blessed are those who hunger and thirst for righteousness, for they will be filled.'

So, I am kind of caught between two dilemmas here, do I have to give to the one who wants to rob me or fight to obtain justice? I prefer and by far fighting for Justice, at least if I have a chance to win and to give to the one who needs when I can; instead of giving to the crooks who want to rip me off.

Coming back to the captain's trial and his crew, his lawyer pleaded the indifference and the lack of initiative from the governments of many countries, who leave these poor people to their sad destiny, instead of giving them a chance to reach the country of their choice.

I don't understand the whole immigration system, but it seems to me that it is much easier for the North American people to move to a different country than it is for other people.

"These people have no other choice than to get in touch with crooks to get what they want and hundreds, if not thousands of them lose their life in the process. It was just by a kind of miracle if the passengers of my client didn't lose their life. The man who is on the accused seat his Honour might be just an outlaw for the justice system, but he is a real hero for those who want to go to exile and this even if they have to pay a lot and also to risk a lot.

I call as a witness, his Honour, one of the main witnesses of the miraculous rescue of one hundred and nineteen passengers of this expedition. His name is Just Just, but I must tell you immediately his Honour that this man doesn't swear for any consideration like thousands of blind people do it." "And why doesn't he swear like everybody else does? Counselor, I would like the man to answer me himself; if this is alright with you." "No problem, his Honour."

"I don't swear, your Honour, because the Great Master asked me not to do it." "And who is your Great Master, if you don't mind me asking?" "Don't you know the Great Master is Jesus, the Messiah himself?" "Ho, you are one of those who still believe in these stories?" "If you don't believe in them, your Honour, why then are your insisting for people to swear on the Bible?"

"Counselor, your witness should know that it is us who question others in my courtroom." "It seemed to me, his Honour that this was more of a discussion between two men than an interrogation." "Your witness can always give his testimony, Counselor, but I don't think I can retain it as evidence." "Can you be a little more precise, his Honour?" "Well Counselor, if he cannot back up his testimony with an oath, what is it worth?" "Isn't it the truth more important than an oath to lie, his Honour?" "I'm not the one on the bench of the accused, Counselor." "I can tell you that this is not my witness either, his Honour." "Well then Counselor, let him say what he has to say and I'll see afterwards what I can retain out of it."

"Would you mind coming to sit on the lying bench mister Just, please?" "Of course, this is why I'm here for, but I'll tell you right now; I don't lie and I will tell only the truth, either it is pleasing or not to certain people." "Do you know the accused in this business of illegal people trafficking, mister Just?" "Yes Counselor; I am the one who delivered him to the authorities."

"Excuse me for interrupting, Counselor, but I would like to know how he proceeded." "This is not a problem, his Honour."

"Mister Just. But where is he?"

When the judge looked towards Just on the witness stand on his left to question him; Just was sitting on his right and when he looked again on his right, Just was back on the bench on his left. When he wanted to question him again, Just was on his right again and again when the judge opened his mouth one more time, Just was on his left.

"Is something wrong, his Honour?" "Something is very odd over here today." "Should we adjourn this trial? One thing though; this is very costly to my client." "This session is adjourned to two o'clock this afternoon." Bang....

Everybody was there at two o'clock except the judge, who was not oriented well enough to find his seat back, so he sent a cop to instruct the audience that for health reasons he couldn't continue on that day.

The very experienced lawyer then asked for a judge substitute, arguing he would not accept a second adjournment in one day.

Just knew very well this judge was bought in advance, meaning before hearing all of the witnesses, all of the facts and all of the extenuating circumstances.

This judge was a little troubled and thinking he had a vision problem; he quickly went to get a sight test. He too should have known that God moves in mysterious ways.

The trial continued then with an impartial judge who was willing to hear all the witnesses assigned to this case. Three days later the captain was found guilty of manslaughter and sentenced to two years less one day of incarceration and all of his crew was cleared of all charges, because all they did is doing their job and this despite terrible work conditions. The captain had only two more weeks to serve, because he was jailed already for more than half of his time. He had his eyes wide opened though when he got out of jail and Just gave him his own money, which was one point two million dollars. Even before the old tub was in the hands of the Montreal police authorities; Just found that money and hided it until the outcome of this trial. Just told the captain at the same time that if he plans to do business securely in the future and be more reasonable with his clients; he would consider helping him getting back to business. Recognizing all the help Just brought to him and to his crew; he could only trust him one more time and the deal was concluded with a strong handshake. Illegal or not, when the cause is fair; Just wants to be part of it.

Then Just satisfied with the work of this attorney retained his services for the reopening of James the Second's new trial. This lawyer makes good money, but at least he allows good people to be proved innocent and to be judged fairly. He is not for the poor though; unless the poor have friends who have money, are generous and love justice.

James got the surprise of his life when he received a court order that invites him to show up at the queen bench for a review of the murder case of three men at Lake Windigo. The crown attorney did everything in his power to object it, but one judge decided there were enough extenuating circumstances to authorize a new trial. James' lawyer demanded a detail report of the autopsy of the three men involved. The report was very clear; the cause of death of the three men was by drowning. So it became evident that a little man the size of James couldn't by himself drown three big and tough men. The legal aid lawyer who represented James during his two previous trials was very negligent by not demanding this very important report for his defence. It was evident also that this report could have changed the course of the trial and James was way too upset to see through the system; he who had no education at all. Besides, everything he has done was only justice in his mind; justice he couldn't find anywhere else. The self-defence was also for him the most natural, the most normal thing to do. It is a sure thing too that if James would have been reasonable the day of his arrest; things would have turned out differently, but no one can redo what was done; we can just try to pick up the pieces. On top of being very upset that day; he was also terrified, even though he might never want to admit it.

There was also the declaration of his friend and accomplice to consider, but this man never saw a thing; he just recounted what he heard or thought he heard from the other one. He knew some details, like the stones attached to the legs of the three men, but this couldn't prove that James killed these men. When it comes to give a decent burial to those three poachers at the bottom of the lake; isn't it what all the boat captains do at high sea?

James talked to Gilles about it, his immediate superior, but he didn't know anymore about the trial than James knew. But as a jail director he was allowed to find out about the situation, because James wasn't only his prisoner, but he was also his employee. Gilles could give to the court a report of good behaviour concerning James; something that couldn't hurt his cause, but the only thought of losing his guardian in chief was not pleasing to him at all. He knew though that if his sentence could even be cut by a half; this would be a very good and encouraging thing for his friend.

Gilles received the news that an internationally renowned attorney was hired and paid by a rich individual to represent James at a new trial and that there were enough attenuating circumstances to allow it. James didn't know what to think about it too much, because he likes his job now and his imprisonment allowed him to get education and also to acquire the formation of a Masked Defender. He can also write in peace; this is one thing he would have a hard time to find anywhere else.

A hot letter from Monica though, his flame from his childhood came to torment him even more. If there was one little chance in this world to love and to be loved by one woman; she was the one.

Some people would go as far as saying that he is a lucky man. Ironic, isn't it?

When the passengers of the bus heard about this new trial; they were all madly furious, particularly the driver. But Just had the intention to give each and everyone of them a copy of James' manuscript; which would explain the biggest part about the incident. This he thought will no doubt attenuate their madness and maybe change their mind about seeing James condemned. The story that got Just and a band of Natives emotional, some of them with a cold heart could for sure get a few more people emotional too. But Just was concerned by a question of legality about James' book and he went to meet with him at the penitentiary. Gilles too, the new director of this jail was happy to see him again. He too knows that he owes him a lot.

"I must warn you about something James." "And what is this all about?" "It is about your book and its publication." "Do you really believe it will be published?" "Chances are extremely good, because I'll do everything in my power for this to happen, not only for you, but for all the readers." "When will you have done enough for me?" "Maybe when justice will be done, but I don't do all of this only for you. There are many people who really need to know all of the truth about you and your story.

There is one thing though that you must know and this is that a prisoner cannot profit from his crime if he is sentenced to jail. So I suggest you to say it is fiction and to use a pen name, a pseudonym to avoid losing it. Maybe you deserve a lot of things, but certainly not to lose your creation. Your story should belong to you and to you alone. I am not aware about all of your activities of the pass and present, but I want you to keep this one. I will go around and find out what is going on." "I too do have something important to tell you though; I received a letter from Monica, your secretary." "I know, I am the one who brought it here." "There is nothing I can hide from you." "Better not, for your own good. I don't know what she is telling you and neither what she expects from you, but my advice to you would be not to give her too much hope. Now, if you want to give her an answer; I would be pleased to bring your letter to her." "Can you wait fifteen minutes for me?" "No problem, I need to talk with your director anyway."

"I would like our conversation to stay private, if this is possible." "Don't you worry, I can be discreet." "You already know that James is getting a new trial, don't you? I don't want him to get too much hope, but I do think he will be found not guilty this time of the three murder convictions against him and when this trial will be over, I will see that his conviction for attempt murder be reviewed as well." "He is an exemplary prisoner and the same when it comes to his job as a guardian too and I would hate to lose him." "Not to the point to be harmful to his freedom, I hope?" "No, I would never do such a thing, especially not to a friend, but nevertheless, I would like him to keep his job, no matter what happens. He seems to like it a lot too." "If he comes out of this trial cleaned and completely free; you will have to pay him his full salary." "He is worth it and this to the last penny." "Well then, can you come to testify in his favour, if you are invited to?" "Of course I will; he is a good friend of mine. I am even under the impression that I am the one who gave him his new life." "When it comes to his job; he will have to decide for himself." "Sure he will, if he is a free man; he will be free." "Then we understand each other correctly. There is one thing that might make a difference to him; he might have a chance to love and to be loved and also to create a family, but this will be far away from here and I can see him becoming the chief of his band, if this was offered to him." "Don't tell me now that he has a band of bandits." "No, no, don't you know he is an Amerindian?" "Ho, this is the band you are talking about?" "This band I believe will become the most prosperous in this country one day." "And I could bet that you have something to do with this?" "Me, very little, but James, a lot." "A rich individual paid for his attorney, who is apparently internationally renowned. I just wonder who this can be." "I am held to the professional secret; I cannot tell you anything about that one. I can only tell you that he is excellent and this is what James needs to obtain justice."

Just was just finishing saying these words when James entered the director's office and he gave his letter straight to James' hand right away. The other two were wondering what it might contain. Gilles as a director of the prison had full rights to open it, but he didn't do it; respecting this way James' privacy. The temptation was very high though, because he knew very well the future of his friend had a lot to do with the answer that was in this letter to this woman he might be in love with.

For Gilles, the chance to keep his friend as a guardian in chief of his institution was getting pretty thin. A woman he is attracted to on one side and the possibility to become the chief of his band on the same side; these were two very tempting offers to say the least. But Gilles was not born from the last rain. 'Happens what happens,' he said. One thing he knew for sure; he didn't want to force his friend's destiny. The meeting between the three men ended with a handshake.

Fortunately and unfortunately at the same time, the James' new trial was to come before his book was finished and published and Just knew very well that all of the passengers of the bus would want to come to testify again. When this news came to the knowledge of his lawyer; he simply said: 'This is not an alarming problem at all; you only have to print twenty some copies of this manuscript and give them to these people. They will be forced some how to better understand what really happened. Don't forget though, they will be invited only to the attempt murder trial, not to the murder trial. So there is no reason to get excited for now.'

"What we need as we speak is the report of the investigation on poaching of that region. If it is possible to ensure the security for Jack, the ex-chief of the organized crime, who was involved with the ex-leader of the opposition, who was in direct connection at the head of the poaching network, then we'll be in business. His testimony could possibly supply the attenuating circumstances that we need, maybe not to win this case completely, but maybe enough to reduce his sentence considerably. After all, this Native was just defending himself against a human killing machine. If he wasn't an expert of the woods like he is; he would have been dead and disappeared longtime ago. I can almost say that his surviving is more or less miraculous and so is the way he escaped his aggressors like he did.

I cannot imagine how I could escape, if twenty some hunters were chasing me in the deep forest armed with guns. This was worse than a war zone, where at least both sides have a chance to fight back. I just can't wait to have a chance to read the rest of his story to find out how he got away from it." "I personally can ensure Jack's protection and to tell you everything; he owes me one or two." "Well then, I leave this up to you." "We cannot trust the police force of this region to ensure the security of all the witnesses for this trial, because too many of them were involved in this scandal and I don't think they were all arrested. You are also aware of this fraternity; we help each other among brothers. I even think that you yourself will need protection in this case." "I am not really worrying about my personal security, but I do think that James' life will be at risk during his trial, mainly because of the job he is on now." "You are defending him; this means you are just as guilty as he is; according too many misinformed people anyway." "Well then, I will ask the national defence to ensure the security of the law court, but this is very expensive." "Give me the bill when you'll get it. There wouldn't be so much fuss if you were defending a real criminal." "I know, but there is nothing we can do about this." "While I think of it; me and a few sure friends of mine can assure the security of everyone." "Are you sure of this?" "My best friend, Superhuman won a war by himself and with bare hands against forty snipers armed with machine guns and bazookas. Nothing and no one can reach him." "This is what we'll need and at both trials." "How long do you think it will last?" "This depends mainly on the judge. If he is corrupted; we will need some very solid and convincing proofs. I will know within a half hour weather he or she is or not, depending on who presides." "Make sure to let me know as soon as you know, even if you have to adjourn the trial for this and I will make sure that he is fair and impartial." "I don't want him to be intimidated in any way shape or form, because then, our victory could be annulled." "No, not at all, but if there is a need, I will make him understand that I don't accept injustice from anyone. Then he will give us justice fairly; I am sure of it. I only ask for justice, nothing else." "If I ever need you to investigate or to win a trial; I will remember you." "And I will remember your fees then too."

This kind of gave him a forced laugh......,but the message was out for this lawyer too.

James' letter was delivered to Monica the next morning at the seventh hour and Just didn't have to read it to get an idea of what was in it. He knew very well that it would be either sad tears or a beautiful smile from the young lady. Ho yes, this was a flood of tears.

Just thought that for Monica this story was simply a flirt of a youth, but he found out then that this was way more serious than he previously thought.

"Are the news this bad for you to react this way?" "He said he has affection for me, but nothing more and to look somewhere else if I was looking for a husband. He also said he is not the type of men to get married." "I don't believe this at all. He is maybe in an unenviable situation, but I wouldn't say that his situation is disparate. On the other hand, I can assure you with sincerity that he is not in the most attractive position for a husband or for a family father and there is also a long distance between the two of you. He wouldn't be honest if he gives you any hope about what so ever." "But I know now that I have never ceased loving him. He also became a much better man that I could ever hope for. If you can find a better Amerindian in the whole country; please introduce him to me, would you?" "Can I also look in the United States? Laughs.....

I will try to find more about the way he really feels about you and if he loves you, even if this is a little, then I'll see what I can do, what do you say?" "I say this is wonderful, because you are the only connection I have to get to him from now on and my only hope too. He asked me not to write to him anymore." "I asked him not to give you any false hope, not to discourage you completely. You can count on me; I will go to the bottom of this story, but I am sure that if he wanted to see your little beach again, the place where you both have known happiness in your childhood; this is because he still feels something for you. But this man has a very turbulent pass and he just can't ignore it and you either. He knows too that his future is badly mortgaged and you do know this too.

Nothing is sure anymore, even though he obtained the review of his first trial that has strong chances to be fairer than the first one." "Is that true? Ho, I'm so glad. I know and I feel it will be better for him this time. It cannot be otherwise. But why didn't you tell me this sooner; secretive man that you are?" "Just one thing at the time; as they say!

How are the kids?" "They have never been this happy before. I see joy shining in their eyes and in the eyes of their parents also. Everybody is happier since you are our new chief, even the ex-chief came to terms with the situation." "If everything goes the way I wish; the next chief will be good for you too." "Tell me now; you're not thinking about let us down, do you?" "As soon as I found another good chief for you; I will leave this position, but trust me, I will never let you down. Every time you will need me; I promise that I will be here." "Keep me informed, would you? I can't wait to know how he feels about me, but I am sure that he loves me too." "Then you have nothing to fear, because love always joins two loving hearts, one way or the other."

Just has never thought about himself being a heart connection messenger, but the circumstances were very exceptional and if he could help joining two loving people, why not? And this especially when two human beings have always been made to be together. I know for example that it is a lot harder to get mad at a childhood friend we always loved than at anyone else. And this is why it is written in proverbs 5, 18 to 5, 20. 'May your fountain be blessed, and may you rejoice in the wife of your youth. A loving doe, a graceful deer—may her breast satisfy you always, may you ever be captivated by her love. Why be captivated, my son, by an adulteress? Why embrace the bosom of another man's wife?'

And here we are; wisdom has spoken and it really means something. Just knew very well that their destiny depends a lot on the result of James' second trial for murder. He knew too that if James wanted to keep his job at the prison, the only one he has known in his entire life; he would be torn apart between his job, his village and his close ones, including the one he loves, Monica.

Just knew as well that James, if he had the opportunity would be the best possible chief for his tribe. A chief who would make it progress, a chief who would protect it against any attack, no matter where it is from. He would be a chief on whom everybody could rely on at all time. Just was wishing nothing less for the people of the village he saved, but he knew too that what we wish and what happens is not always the same and for him at least, no one can ever say he didn't try.

CHAPTER 9

Then the so much expected day of the trial finally arrived. Just made sure that all of the critical seats were taken by his friends and these were Jonathan and many of his Defenders. There were some on the left, some on the right, some in front and some at the back of the room that was bigger than usual, for the simple reason that never before a court case received this much publicity. For the same reason this case had to be heard by judge alone.

Just's best friend, Superhuman was sitting on the roof of the court house for the time of the procedures. He is also the one who went to get Jack, one of the most important witnesses in this case. The deal was concluded earlier between Jack and Just. Never before a court case needed this much security. There was in front of the court house a squad of policemen just to make sure the court was not invaded by too many people. But to Just and to Superhuman this squad was the one to fear, because all of its members were legally armed.

James who was the accused in this trial was completely defenceless, because he had his hands and his legs chained. He was still the accused of three first degree murders. Just kept a very close watch on the two policemen who were holding him, one on each side and he was ready to intervene at any time with the speed that is faster than light. An army battalion could never be as efficient as the crew who was keeping an eye on James that day. I even think that never in the history a man accused of murder had this many friends ready to protect him this way. When I think of it, maybe Louis Riel has, but he didn't have the luck to know Just and Superhuman as friends and this was just too bad.

'Quiet everyone, stand up and take your hat off,' a policeman was saying when the judge appeared in the doorway of the room. Just immediately thought this was one of the most critical moment, because everyone had their mind busy with something else than James' security at that precise moment. They had their mind set on the judge then.

Then Just started thinking about who could easily enter this room without being searched or even look suspicious. There was the stenographer, the Counselor, James' attorney, the police officers and the judge himself. Just knew too that all of the witnesses without any exception will be searched before entering this courtroom, but who was in charge of searching everybody? Then Just went out and he asked a Masked Defender to replace the officer who was searching people before entering this room. He then came back quickly to his seat right away.

James' accomplice in the attempt affair against the bus came to testify that he never really saw James kill the poachers, but that he heard him say he got rid of them and that they were in the bottom of the lake with stones attached to their leg. He also said that this attempt against the bus was directed only to the poachers who tried to eliminate James in many man's hunting sessions in the forest. This was in a self-defence manner this man who was hunted like a wild beast acted, name that stuck to him for some times afterwards.

"This is why I decided to help him, because this man was desperate and he didn't want to flee anymore and he was saying he has done enough of it." "Didn't you testify before under oath that you help him under threat?" "The threat didn't come from James sir, but I too had death threats from these poachers. I too had to hide from them to save my life." "How do you explain then that both of you escaped from them." "I strongly believe this is because of James' high experiences in the forest that both of us are still alive today." "Can you tell us how both of you escaped from their hands?" "I would rather not tell this detail sir; we might need to flee again some day." "Aren't you still in jail for another twelve years or so?"

"Objection, his Honour; this man is not here as an accused, but as a witness." "Objection retained."

"Counselor, keep your questions concerning the accused and the accused only, would you?" "Yes, your Honour."

This last question from the crown attorney was very suspicious to Just. Why this man wanted to know how James escaped his pursuers?

Just who can change the mind of people, immediately put in the mind of this judge the idea of asking this Counselor if he was searched before entering this room. The Counselor offended got very mad, pointing his finger at the judge, telling him; 'You wouldn't get out of it this easy, you S.O.A.B.'

The judge in turn got very upset and he gave the order to a police officer to search this man immediately. The Counselor then lifted up his court gown even before the cop reached him and pulled out a 38 pistol fully loaded. While one cop was executing the order from the judge the other cop near James took him in a headlock grip at the same time with his arm installed under James' shin and directly at his throat. This was just a question of a second or two before James pass away. While on his way to James, Just made it to this Counselor and with a good kick at his gun, made it fly away from him, way up to the ceiling and with the palm of his hand; he knocked down the cop who was choking James to death.

Of course, the judge who didn't realize everything that happened suspended the course of this trial until further notice. He saw in fact a cop and a lawyer at fault, but he couldn't understand how they were controlled. Everything happened so fast, just like a blow of the wind. The officer who received the order to search the Counselor put him immediately under arrest by reading him his rights, but the other one told him that he already knows totally and perfectly all of his rights.

"Good for you then, because it is as an accused that you will enter this room next time around and I hope you will be facing the same judge." "This is impossible idiot, because it would be conflict of interest." "Maybe so imbecile, but the fraternity among them is very strong. If you can take my opinion; you are done, banished for life. I hope for yourself that you are well paid for this ridicules gesture." "I have friends who are way more powerful than you and this judge and you will hear about them very soon." "You make threats on top of everything and in front of witnesses on top of all. You should shut up, because you make your situation worse as you keep talking. Not surprising that so many criminals got away from justice this easy with a crown representative as mediocre as you are. I suppose they were your friends too." "Maybe you're not so much of an idiot after all." "You are the idiot over here. Let's go, there is a room that is awaiting you behind bars." "My bail will be paid within an hour." "For this you'll have to find a judge who will allow it and let me tell you that your chances are very thin." "But!" "Shut up; you're pissing me off."

Then this cop rushed the new criminal to the police station and he was accused of mistreating him, but the officer pleaded the lawyer resisted his arrest.

The connection was made a little later and it was discovered this crown attorney was also a legal member of the mafia. What is better than an ally at the courtroom to make a trial of these experts in crimes fail?

But then James' trial was dragging on and his lawyer became the more and more demanding. But money is not what scares Just the most anymore, especially when a fair cause is at stake. He wanted another ten thousand to continue defending James. Just gave it to him, but he told him too that he has a very good memory. He told him also how to reach him if he ever needs someone to defend him, to protect him or just to help him out. We never know who needs help in this field. Just knew very well that sooner or later, such a man gets some how trapped in some corners.

Then James' trial got going again and not only James needed protection, but the judge too. This time though, everyone without exception got to be searched, even the judge and the crown attorney.

Gilles, the director of the prison where resides James came to court and he gave one of the most favourable testimony and so did the ex-director. In the mind of many people these personalities are still very important.

But I believe the most important testimony came out of the mouth of Jack, the ex-leader of the organized crime. He came to tell the court how the ex-leader of the opposition was bragging about having set up the most sophisticated poaching network of this country with the intention to involve as many members of the government as possible who have a fishing camp in the same region. He actually explained how his accomplice had police officers and conservation agents involved in his network and also how they managed to chased even the Amerindians out of this territory. He told the court how this man was bragging about being untouchable and how he was informed about anything that happens on this territory as well. Then James' lawyer interrupted him to ask:

"Did he ever mention to you something about this man here sitting on the accused bench?" "I don't know if he was talking about this man here or someone else, but he mentioned many times haven made many hunt searches and this with twenty some men in a hope to capture a Native he called; 'The bastard.' He was saying this man was a smart fox; this Native was costing him a lot of money and that he was the only one they couldn't chase away from this region." "Were you worried about coming to testify in this trial here today, sir?" "Let's just say sir that before this my life was holding just by a thin tread and now this tread is stretched to the maximum." "So then, you're worrying for you own life?" "One could say that, yes." "What made you come to testify anyway, sir?" "Let's just say that I changed my life around since and I don't like injustice this much anymore. And if I can add this sir; let's say that a trusted friend promised me his protection and I have every possible reason to believe in him." "Could you name him, sir?" "I prefer not doing this, sir."

"I am done with this witness for now, his Honour. If my colleague wants to interrogate him; it is up to him."

"I have no question for this man for the time being, your Honour."

The crown attorney couldn't see any possible question at that point that could help him create a doubt in the mind of the judge from a man who risked his life by testifying for justice to be done. To do it would have only contributed in demolishing his own credibility; something he couldn't afford to do.

"Counselor Gerard, do you have more witnesses to be heard?" "Yes, his Honour!"

"I call as a witness Mister James Ste-Jolie, Minister of the external affairs of your government."

Everyone one in the courtroom was looking at each other, wondering what such minister could had to do with such a cause and such accused. All of them were going to find out in a few seconds though. Even the judge was fronting when he heard this name. Just too was completely out of the scoop and the surprise was greater for him than for anyone else in this room. But how this name came to the knowledge of James' attorney; he who is not even from the region? It was a bit later that everyone learned this lawyer never enters in a cause to defend without an expert crew of investigators who get their noses in everything possible. Then the interrogation started as soon as James, Just's father-in-law took place in the witnesses' box.

"Minister, can you tell the court if you know the accused and if yes since when, please?" "I know him for the last four years, sir; I mean for two years before his incarceration." "And how did you come to know him?" "He was my fishing and hunting guide during these two years and I can assure you that he is highly qualified for this job." "Did he ever reveal any secrets to you, Minister?" "He told me that he was from a far away region and that he left his village because he was mistreated by his parents." "Did he tell you something else during these two years, sir?" "He told me that he was chased around by a number of people and that he didn't quite understand why. I told him to contact the police about this matter, but he was afraid this could make the matter worse. I'm afraid today that if he had listened to me and succeeded in contacting them; he would have called death on himself." "What make you say such a thing, Minister?" "Well, he told me haven escaped death many times by a narrow margin and if this wasn't for our government fishing camp that is situated in the region of Windigo Lake; he wouldn't be of this world anymore. I asked him how he managed to enter in our camp and he told me that a fox always finds a way and like a fox, he made himself a tunnel that led him under our camp house." "Did he tell you how many times he escaped them?" "When I asked him; he didn't know how to count, but he showed me his ten fingers three times. I understood then that he meant about thirty times." "I have one last question for you, Minister. What do you think about this young man sitting on the accused bench today?" "I sincerely think he is the victim of a huge justice mistake that has to be repaired as soon as possible." "Thank you, Minister, thank you very much."

"I have no further question for now, his Honour. I leave the room to my colleague. This witness is all his."

"Minister, Mister Ste-Jolie, tell me, how many times in a year do you go to this camp of yours?" "I usually go there three times a year, sir. I go there twice a year for fishing and once a year for hunting in the falls. I can also say that I missed my guide a lot in the last two years." "This is not what I asked you, sir. Try please to just answer the question. You don't miss him enough to say anything to get him back, do you, Minister?"

"Objection, his Honour! We are talking to an honourable man here and this insinuation is totally out of line." "Objection retained. You are absolutely right Counselor; I agree."

"It's up to you Counselor Ducharme, but if you keep it up; you're going to lose points with me. Proceed carefully now." "Thank you, your Honour."

"You said knowing the enemies of this young man accused of three first degree murders, Minister; can you tell the court how you came about to know them?" "I don't know, sir." "You don't know what, Minister?" "I don't know how this happened." "But you know them?" "Yes!" "Who do you know exactly?" "I know Paul and Timothy, his right arm." "How did you happen to know him?" "Well, he was the leader of our opposition." "Then we can almost say that he is your enemy too?" "I guess we can say that." "You won't be here by any chance for revenge, are you?"

"Objection, his Honour. This witness is not an accused." "Objection retained."

"Counselor, make sure to question the witness, not to accuse him, unless you have solid proofs for that, would you please?" "Yes, your Honour, but I was just trying to demonstrate this witness might have a reason for revenge."

"Excuse me, his Honour, but there is no reason for this witness to revenge at all, because the person we are talking about is already in jail for one part of his crimes. Besides, this man, this minister is not at all the type of man to hit someone already on the ground. Then we have to conclude the revenge is totally out of context here." "I am tempted to agree with you, Counselor Gérard and this is not something I usually do."

"Resume your interrogation, Counselor Ducharme and try to be a bit more charming, would you?"

"Yes, your Honour."

"Mister Ste-Jolie, can you tell the court when you met this Paul for the first time and what was the occasion?" "Of course I can; I met him the first time when he made his entry to the parliament and I can't remember the exact date right now." "And how many years ago was that?" "I think this was just after the 2008 election, sir." "Your answer seems to me a bit vague, Mister Ste-Jolie." "I can remember the exact day and the exact time I met my wife for the first time and this was twenty-four years ago, sir, but I must tell you; there is no comparison with the meeting of this Paul at all." Laughters.........

'Quiet, order!' The judge had to hit his desk many times with his little harmer before the silence was back again, but he himself had a hard time not to laugh too, just like everybody else in this room.

"Counselor Ducharme, I would like to know where you are getting at with this kind of questioning." "I just try to demonstrate the connection between this witness and this Paul to prove he has a grudge against him and this might be the real reason for him to testify in this cause." "But this wouldn't diminish at all the value of his testimony; even he has a grudge against this Paul. Anybody could have a grudge against this Paul; this won't forbid them to testify in this cause." "Then I don't have anymore question for this witness, your Honour."

"This session is adjourned until ten o'clock tomorrow morning." Bang....."Stand up everybody, please."

What Ducharme was trying to prove, is the minister could have been upset with Paul because of the poker game where he won a lot of money, but it is rather the other way around. It's Paul who had an extra reason to be mad at James for making him lose a pile of money. But the bottom line was that he tried to prove that even a minister could be caught in an illegal activity. What Ducharme didn't seem to know is the judge too likes one of these card games once in a while and I think he saw him coming with this interrogation that was not getting anywhere. But the biggest mistake of Ducharme was that again, he tried to prosecute a witness.

James' enemies wanted to make him pay for all the troubles he caused them, first in the forest near the Lake Windigo and now at the jail behind bars. Of course the minister is in the same category and if there was the least little chance to hurt his reputation; he had to grab it.

Then it was Gilles' turn, the director of the prison where James resides to testify, but he couldn't say anything at all about the so called murders at the Lake Windigo. He could only speak about James' good conduct since his incarceration and his evolution; then the risk for him to be free to live like everyone else.

"Put your right hand on the Bible and say; I swear to tell the truth, only the truth and nothing but the truth. Say I swear." "I am left-handed, sir." "Then change hand if you want to and say I swear." "I don't swear, sir." "What is the matter here; are you all crazy about Christ?" "Don't blaspheme sir; this could very well turn against you."

At the same time, Just who is faster than light, then faster than the eye can see gave him a slap behind the head that made him go forward three or four steps. The man shook his head and he asked:

"What was that?" "Surely a spirit. Don't say I didn't tell you." "Tell the court your name and occupation, please sir." "My name is Gilles Morency, director and principal of the Donnacouna Penitentiary." "Is it fair to say that you know this man sitting on the accused bench?" "Yes and if you want my opinion; you should take these ridicules chains off him, because he is less dangerous than anyone else in this room." "I'm asking you sir not to add anything than an answer to my questions during the course of this interrogation. How long have you known the accused?" "I first met him two years ago." "And what was the occasion?" "He was brought in handcuffed at the institution where I was working as a guardian at the time." "Please tell the court sir why he was handcuffed." "This is the usual way Miss Court." Laughs….

"Well, well, we have another funny guy here now."

"Objection, his Honour, this witness doesn't have to put up with insults from this Counselor for testifying in all sincerity." "Objection retained."

"Counselor Ducharme, can you just keep questioning this witness without insulting him? You can resume now."

"Mister Morency, can you tell us how was behaving the accused when he arrived?" "Can you be more specific with your question, sir? Do you want to know when he arrived at the police station, at the Lake Windigo or at our institution?" "I mean the arrival that you witnessed, mister Morency." "Then I cannot tell you anything, sir." "And why can't you say anything about this, sir?" "Simply because I was not there at his arrival sir; this was my day off." "Then how can you say he was handcuffed?" "Within guardians we communicate, sir." "In this case, let me ask this in a different way. Mister Morency, can you tell us how the accused behaved at the beginning of his incarceration?" "He was scared like a wild beast that was chased around for some times and I understood right away that he needed someone to reassure him and to make him understand the hunt was over." "And how did you know, mister Morency that he was chased around?" "We are informed ahead of time about the clients who are coming inside our walls, sir."

"I have no more questions for this witness for now, your Honour; I even have the impression to be wasting my time."

"We could have lived without this last comment, Counselor Ducharme." "I'm asking you to forgive my frustration, your Honour."

"Counselor Gérard, do you have any question for this witness." "No, his Honour, my colleague did it for me and he did a very good job too and I thank him."

The more the procedures were advancing, the more the crown attorney was getting impatient and this was exactly what James' lawyer was hoping for. He wanted to wear him down slowly but surely and the other one wasn't smart enough to see it and this is what was important for him and for his client.

This was a psychological war between two men and clearly, one wasn't measuring up with the other. Counselor Gérard is a specialist in this field and he knows it. He only waits for the opportunity and he takes advantage of the other one's mistakes.

The judge knew it very well and he could only admire such character and besides, he was not allowed to tell the crown attorney about it.

Finally, James was found not guilty for the death of the three poachers, but an accusation of manipulation of evidences and one count of obstruction of justice was retained against him. This got him a sentence of two years less one day of imprisonment. But Counselor Gérard, sure of his business was not going to leave this go without appealing the decision, even if this was only to earn another ten thousand dollars in few days.

His reasons were very simple; there was neither authority nor any justice in the region where this supposedly crime took place. Then no one could blame this man for acting as justice of peace himself and besides, the only police officers and conservation agents who were around were his immediate enemies who wanted him dead.

For the lack of sufficient proof and the lack of eye witness, James was cleared of that crime as well. The only ones who could possibly testify against him could not do it without accusing themselves in the process. But the judge could not tell James he was free to go, because he was still jailed for another crime. But nevertheless, fifty years of imprisonment strike out of one's life; this is something to celebrate.

Despite the exorbitant cost for the fees of this international renowned lawyer, Just could only admit that he was effective. But the question was; is he going to be just as good in the next cause of attempt murders against twenty some innocent people who had nothing to do with this big mess? Some people could easily say that this was just a big mistake, but nevertheless; this was a very serious mistake.

Again, another date for a new trial for attempt murder against all the passengers of a bus, including the driver travelling from the Lake Windigo to Ottawa was set. The same crown attorney who performed in the previous trial was assigned and he was not happy about it at all, but this made the day to Gérard who saw in it a fun game to come.

If it wasn't for Just and his super power; James would most likely have never been discovered and his crime, if there was a crime, would have stayed unpunished.

But now, Just would have to testify against his protected friend and this against his own will. Besides, he is the one who paid for this new trial. All the passengers of the bus on this trip will want to testify too about their terrifying experiences, just like they did in the first trial.

Just weighted it all, the for and the against, but because he is not the least selfish, he opted for giving his friend the best possible chance to reduce his sentence.

What he wanted to avoid at all cost is that his identity as a superhero was revealed to the population. He knew that if he is called to testify; the only fact to tell his complete name in public would most likely tell everyone who he helped and all of his enemies who he really is. Changing his identity is out of the question too, because lying is not part of his vocabulary. He even wonders if James made the connection between him and mister ghost who forced him to give himself up. They both have almost the same voice. One has a strange costume and the other one looks normal. One thing though, James was so upset that day that he might have never made the connection between the two of them. The Just, the superhero who escorted him to his village and went fishing with him a full day and met with him at the penitentiary has maybe the same voice than the one who pays for his lawyer, but they don't look alike at all.

The only thing then that could reveal his identity is his full name, if he testifies as a normal individual. But then if he testifies as the superhero or as mister ghost, then the risk disappears, just like only he can do it, if it is necessary.

But what to say then, if someone asks for his name? Just that he is mister ghost, that's all and he too doesn't swear.

It was then that Just suggested to James' lawyer to have a good and long conversation with his client and this before the new trial.

"Hi James! You talked in your book about a kind of a mister ghost, who forced you to give yourself up; do you know who he is exactly?" "Well yeah, he is my escort, when I get a permission to get out. He is also the chief of my tribe who was voted in lately and he does a wonderful job. He made everybody happy in my village." "I would like him to testify in your new trial; can you ask him to call me as soon as possible?" "I don't know if he would want to do this; he is a very busy man." "You also spoke in your book about another very strong and very fast man; do you know who he is?" "I don't have the slightest idea of who he is, but this one I don't ever want to see him again. He might be good, but I am scared of him. I wasn't very polite with him. I even told him that I'll have my revenge against him one day, when I'll be out of jail. I am sure he will be on his guard, if I am ever a free man again, but I am not upset at him anymore, because he was just doing his civic duties." "I can see that you are much wiser than you were once before your jail time."

"I learned to live, to read and to write since; I only knew how to flee before that." "You didn't have it too easy; this is for sure. What can you tell me about the bus?" "As you already know now; there were twenty some men who were chasing me and they were trying to kill me as well and this for several years and when I found out they were taking the bus to return that night; I thought this might be my only chance to escape them and to save my life. Then I made a little hold in the brake line and I cut a wire to the ignition contact, so they couldn't stop when they need it the most, but one thing I didn't know is that they had their own bus and their own driver. Then I almost caused the death of many innocent people by mistake. The next day a mister ghost came to torment me and my friend and I got caught without being able to flee once more. You know the rest." "Well, I can't promise you anything, except maybe that I'll do my very best to at least reduce your sentence that is way too high in my opinion anyway." "It is mainly because of my attitude of the time if it is this high. I must have driven everyone furious against me, even the judge and the one who tried to defend me. I am the only one to blame really." "If we have the smallest chance to reduce your sentence now; it is mainly due to your new attitude. To sincerely repent before a compassionate judge is very effective. I am not too sure yet, but it is very possible I make you testify this time around. If this is the case; you will have to answer the questions of the other Counselor as well and this will not be easy for you at all. Do not ever answer too quickly, even if you are mad, because he will certainly try to upset you as much as he can. To him this will be just a way to prove you are not fit to live among people. What ever he says and what ever he does; stay calm and this will turn against him. In another word; he is the one who will lose his temper, but this is only if you listen and do what I said. Well then, this is all I needed to know from you and all I had to tell you. I'll see you Monday morning at the court house by ten o'clock. In the mean time, try to reach your mister ghost, would you?" "Yes sir!"

A few minutes later Just was in a discussion with James about the day of his arrest.

"How fast can you write on your computer?" "Ho, I can write around twelve pages an hour, why?" "I would like you to change the forth chapter of your book about your arrest to help your cause at the trial." "What do you want me to do exactly?" "I want you to rewrite the forth chapter and to call it; 'The Arrest, The True Story.' I will deliver it myself to the crown attorney. He will be found ridicules when he'll try to make you look stupid. I have learned from a reliable source he doesn't believe anything about what you wrote on your story. I need you to make it look like it was some police officers from Ottawa who came to arrest you at the Lake Windigo and do what ever you want with the rest of the story; after all, you are a writer. Just make sure I can read it before Monday morning. I can just imagine the face the passengers of the bus will make when they'll hear this. Write it and let me take care of the rest. I contributed in parts to get you in this mess and I think it is mine to at least try to get you out of it. I also think it would be best if I can meet your lawyer to talk about strategy." "Good then, because he asked me to get you in touch with him as soon as possible." "Tell me something about the man who came to meet you here to talk about UFOs and aliens." "Ho, I hope you are not upset about this." "On the contrary, you were rather nice towards me in this interview. How did you contact him?" "He's the one who found me and I think this was through one of the passengers of the bus from Windigo, who might have told the story the way he saw it. He actually left his business card with me. You can have it, if you are interested." "This is exactly what I need; I want to talk to him. I got to go, but let me know as soon as you are done with this new chapter, even if it is three o'clock in the morning, would you?" "Of course; it is of my interest too, isn't it?" "I have a hard time believing the way you've progressed." "I owe it mainly to Gilles who believed in me. I was completely without any education, but I was not crazy." "I can see that." Laughs……

"Hi sir, I do have an alien story to tell you, if you want to be the first one to hear it, but this will have to be live, if it is possible." "I think this can be arranged; even though it is unusual." "Can we meet to discuss the details? I want our first meeting to be without microphone and without camera for this time. On Monday you will be able to do things your way, but today it is my way." "I might be able to agree with you; who am I talking to?" "Some people would tell you that I am an alien." "Would I be this lucky that this only happens to me?" "It is yours to decide, but I don't play games and I am very serious and it is also for a very serious cause." "It is rather dangerous for a journalist to venture on unknown ground these days; you know this, don't you? There are two of them who got cold blood and cowardly killed yesterday morning by a sort of an idiot who spent his rage on innocent people, because of a job he lost by his own fault. Just try to understand this world in which we live in." "Ho, I understand it very well, but this is not everybody's case." "Who are you to claim such a thing?" "Some people would tell you that I am...." "Yeah, yeah, an alien, I know." "You don't seem to believe in them very much?" "Just like hundreds of people; I'm waiting to have the proof before my eyes, I suppose." "Keep talking on the phone and I will answer you in person; what do you think of that?" "I say this is impossible."

Just sitting on a couch not far from this journalist told him suddenly:

"Impossible or not; I'm here." "Who are you?" "Some people would tell you that I am an alien." "And are you really?" "No, I am from the earth like everybody else, made out of flesh, of bones and blood, but I am what many people call a superhero, nothing more and nothing less." "If I hang up this phone; would you still be here to answer me?" "Of course I'll be here: I am the one who wants to talk to you." "Then let's talk, since this is why you're here. Tell me to begin with, how did you come in my house without opening a door?" "I can't and I don't want to reveal to you all of my secrets; this is not what I want to talk to you about." "Then tell me what brought you here."

The two men discussed for another hour to set up a strategy that Just imagined for the purpose of leading astray the crown attorney and at the same time to impress the judge who presides the case.

From there Just took off his outfit and he went to meet the lawyer he hired to defend James, the man he wants justice done for.

"Is there new evidence that came to light since I last talked to you; I mean something I can use for his defence?" "Is it possible to have a huge TV set installed by eleven o'clock sharp Monday morning in the court room?" "Just about anything is possible, if this help me make the life of my client better." "Then make sure this TV set is installed and functional for that time and you and everybody else will see something quite special and useful for our cause." "You don't want to tell me more about it?" "No and this is not necessary either, but I can assure you; this will be very good for the cause. I can only tell you the crown attorney, your colleague will be quite confused after seeing this show." "The poor man already has a hard time as it is." "Don't tell me now that you feel sorry for him; especially not before this trial is over?" "No, but I still can sympathize with the guy. After all he is a colleague of mine." "Yes, he is one of your colleagues, who does his very best to make an individual pay at least ten times the amount of time in jail he should be doing, is that fair?" "No, but this is his job and he does it to the best of his knowledge. We have to admit this too." "Alright then, let's admit it and let's do our work too and everything will be fine for everybody. This won't take anything away from him; except a bit of pride maybe, but he will recover quickly."

James got to work on his writing right away to change the fourth chapter as Just asked him to do and this was without even knowing the real reason for doing so. The only thing he knows in this matter is that he can trust Just with his eyes closed. This was to become a copy especially made for the crown attorney, who was going to put his foot in it. Just has foreseen that Ducharme wanted to embarrass James with, like he said; his cock-and-bull story, boring to death or to fall asleep on, but the reality will show that he will see something to keep him awake following up his next question period.

James took only a couple of hours to rewrite the fourth chapter completely and this was only twenty-two pages. This was a Friday night, only three days before

James' new trial took place on the following Monday morning. As soon as he was done, as Just asked him to do; James called Just right away. No surprise then, Just went to get this new copy and he started to read immediately.

"This is exactly what we need." "You don't want to tell me what you want to do with it?" "I'm going to simply deliver it to Ducharme tomorrow morning, even though I am not supposed to work on Saturday, the Sabbath day. I know this is for a good cause and that God will forgive me this time. Like the Messiah said it, see Matthew 12, 11-12. 'Jesus said to them. 'If any of you has a sheep and it falls into a pit on the Sabbath, will you not take hold of it and lift it out? How much more valuable is a man than a sheep! Therefore it is lawful to do good on the Sabbath.'"

Some people would say that Just has more than one sheep. He would answer you that he has none, but that every time he sees one in trouble; he does everything he can to get it out of it, either it is on the Sabbath or not and either it is a friend or an enemy.

Just as he has planed it, Just delivered the fourth chapter of James' manuscript to Ducharme the next morning and I just like Just had foreseen it, Ducharme would do anything in his power with this new information to find damning proofs against a man that, was he saying, doesn't deserve to live among people.

As soon as he was in possession of the new details of James' arrest, Ducharme went to the federal police station having in mind to find the two officers who according to James' new story would have escorted James to their quarters, along with the two conservation agents.

Those four officers who carry their badge proudly and swore to do their job with honesty, made themselves available to testify against James at his trial on Monday morning. The temptation for this opportunity to put a last nail in the coffin of this man was way too high to let it go by without any action. The man who pissed them off for more than five years was going to pay for all the times he didn't. They were coming to court with two false investigation reports of accusations of poaching and attempt murder against police officers and against conservation agents.

At James' first trial, no one wanted to believe his side of the story and the poor guy couldn't bring the least proof of what he was saying, but things will be different this time around and this thanks to Just new plan.

Ducharme was rubbing his hands with joy just at the thought of winning this last round. 'You've mocked me enough until now; we'll see who will laugh this time around.' He was telling himself.

I don't exactly know how James' lawyer managed this, but he obtained the right to bring to this trial a TV network with a high definition camera and a large screen too. All the judge knew is that this will show the innocence of the accused and the formal proof will be made live. In fact, this is all Gérard knew too. Just had to be very convincing, for the other man to trust him this blindly. Ho, I sometime forget that Just has among other things the power to change people's mind. His wife must not be thinking to often about arguing with him. If all men and all women had this power; there would be a lot more harmony within marriages and a lot less divorces in this world. This would be a perfect world, but this is not the case. Although, Just promised to himself to never use this power against his close ones and only in some exceptional cases against his opponents.

According to the writing of Matthew about the Messiah, Jesus too could read people's minds. See Matthew 12, 25. 'Jesus knew their thoughts and said to them, "Every kingdom divided against itself will be ruined, and every city or household divided against itself will not stand.'

The amount of divorces in this world proves this statement to be a great truth and not only within marriages; this is also true for the governments. Harper knew this.

After the usual salutations of the judge as it is normally done, at the time of the beginning of James' trial on Monday morning; everyone suddenly remained still and was kind of gasping for breath. No one wants to get a person who has the power to decide if you'll be free or not the next minute against him. And some people are saying the one who has the absolute power on earth is the pope.

'The session is opened.' The judge said hitting his desk with his little harmer. Let's call the first witness, please."

"Counselor Ducharme, you have the word." "Thank you, your Honour."

"I call to the stand the officer Réjean Normandin of the federal police force."

The one who took place on this stand more than once in the same circumstances didn't have any problem finding his way to the stand and neither for the swearing ceremony. This was the same for the other three agents who followed his steps.

"Officer Normandin, how long have you been in the police force?" "I have been a police officer for the last twenty-two years, sir." "Tell the court please where you were working two years ago in the case we are interested in." "I was and I am still working in the Lake Windigo region, sir." "Do you know the man sitting here on the accused bench, officer Normandin?" "Yes sir." "Would you sir tell the court in which circumstance you got to know him?" "Well, this was during the course of his arrest and this was a little more than two years ago, sir."

There were whispers to no end in the room and this to the point of getting the judge exasperated, he who didn't seem to have too much patience that morning.

"Quiet in this room or I'll have it evacuated." Bang....

"Keep going Counselor Ducharme." "Sure! Thank you, your Honour."

On top of the four agents who were testifying; there were six officers from the provincial police who were assigned as guardians of the peace.

The one who was at the witness stand didn't seem to be overly concerned about it, but he nevertheless found this unusual. He knew though that this was a trial on a very high tension. There were police officers everywhere inside and outside the building.

"Officer Normandin, how happened the arrest of the accused?" "It was rather rough sir, because he didn't want to cooperate with us at all; we had a hard time to control him." "And how many of you were there to arrest him?" "We were four officers, sir." "How did you travel from that region to your quarters with him, officer?" "This was the usual way, sir; in our cruiser with the accused handcuffed on the back seat." "Was he injured in any way?" "As far as I know sir, he was not hurt, at least not visibly." "What do you mean exactly, officer Normandin?" "I'm saying that we cannot see if a suspect has a stomach ache, a head ache or something else similar."

The three other officers have also testified in a very similar way. The whole situation looked strangely like a conspiracy to the eyes of the judge and to others too, but yet, if they all lived through the same experiences; it is about normal they all have the same thing to say in their own way.

"I have no more questions for this witness for now, your Honour and I gladly leave the stage to my colleague."

"Thank you, Counselor Ducharme."

"When ever you're ready, Counselor Gérard; this witness is yours." "Thank you, his Honour; I was anticipating this privilege."

"Officer Normandin, you realize, isn't it that you are still under oath?" "Yes sir." "Do you mind telling this court what an oath means to you?"

"Objection, your honour; this witness is not an accused for one thing and therefore, there is no reasonable reason to doubt his word."

"But I don't doubt his word, his Honour; I just want to hear from his own mouth what an oath means to him, that's all."

"Objection overruled, Counselor Ducharme; I too would like to hear his answer."

"Answer the question, officer Normandin." "Well then, an oath means to me that I am telling the truth and this oath should assure everyone around that I'm telling the truth and no one should doubt it."

"Continue on, Counselor Gérard." "Thank you, his Honour."

"This means then, officer Normandin that you know the exact consequences of a perjury in court?" "Fully and perfectly, sir!"

The man answered red with anger, but the judge quickly told him to calm down immediately.

"Forgive me, your Honour, but I don't like anyone to doubt my word." "This is very reasonable officer; for as long as you are telling the truth."

This, without being an official confirmation was in some ways telling Counselor Gérard that the judge too had knowledge of the real manuscript of the accused and that he had the tendency to believe James' version of the facts rather than the version of the officers; even though it is a hard to believe story.

"Officer Normandin, did you really say that you were four big and strong men to control such a little man like the accused is?"

The people in this room who heard that couldn't help but to laugh and even the judge had a hard time stifle his laughter.

"He might be a small man, but he is vigorous like I rarely saw before him." "Did you have to brutalize him for you to control him, officer?" "We don't have the right to brutalize anyone, sir." "Everybody knows that you have no right to brutalize anyone, officer. This was not the question at all. The question was; did you have to brutalize him for you to control him?" "The answer is no, sir." "Did you read his rights at the time of the arrest, officer?" "I can't remember which one of us did it, sir." "You are still saying under oath that the four of you arrested this man sitting here on the accused bench, officer Normandin?" "Yes sir!"

At the same time Superhuman dressed in his superhero costume entered this room. He went directly to James and he put him on his shoulder to the astonishment of everybody. The six peace officers put their hand to their gun, but the judge told them right away to back off. No point saying that Just kept a close eye on them. James' lawyer who wasn't aware of any of this stood there stunned and speechless.

"Objection, your Honour; he cannot leave with the accused this way." "What do you plan to do to stop him, Counselor Ducharme?" "E, e, e, e." "This is it." Laughs.....

The whole country could see what happened and it was going to see the rest as well. Seven seconds after the exit of James and Superhuman from this court room; the two of them were in Halifax in direct on a special TV show in a Radio-C-Canada Station.

"Here is your favourite host, Jacques Mars. Good day ladies and gentlemen. All of you will be witnessing today the strangest thing of all times. A man, an accused of attempt murder at the trial in the court room in Ottawa, from the National Capital of this country and this at the time I am speaking to you all and for security reasons travelled all the way from there to here with whom he calls a superhero. This is a distance of 1435 kilometres,

896 miles in five seconds and he says with all sincerity that it is the same superhero that brought him to a provincial police station in Ottawa, two years, one month, ten days, seven hours, twenty-two minutes and a few seconds ago. Hard to believe, but true. It took me longer to tell you this than it took then to travel this distance. I was told about it, but I didn't dare believe it. I now leave the word to the magistrates who preside this case immediately and we are listening to the conclusion of it."

"Do you want to go get him, Counselor Ducharme or to continue the procedures, even though the accused is away? The accused is present on this screen." "I prefer to continue, your Honour, but I think now that I put my foot in it badly."

"I ask for the last four witnesses to be put on close watch until the new order, because I do have good and reasonable reasons to doubt the sincerity of their testimony."

"Do you have any question for the accused, Counselor Ducharme?" "Not for now, your Honour."

"Would you like to precede, Counselor Gérard?" "Yes, his Honour!"

"Accused, James the Second, Ryan Demaison of his real name; do you have something to add for your defence?" "Yes, Counselor Gérard. The four last witnesses that you've heard are all accomplices in the man hunt they led against me during five long years. They hunted me down like a wild beast no stop, summers and winters and I must say that it is a kind of miracle if I escaped them the way I did. In fact, I didn't know it then, but my arrest by Mister Ghost and this superhero over here was for me the liberation and I am much safer now than I was then. I'm asking forgiveness from all the people I have hurt or scared while trying to escape these poachers and I admit committing a huge mistake when I damaged the wrong bus. I understand too now that it is thanks to these two superheroes that the damages were limited to a great fright for many people. I hope with all of my heart they recovered from it. This is about it, sir."

Everybody in the court room applauded, again and again, except the four despicable officers, who took advantage of this distraction to try to escape, but Just pushed and pinched them all with force against the wall.

The judge ordered them to be put under arrest immediately for perjury, an accusation that will be added to many others.

"Please provincial officers, read them their right, even though they know them already."

One of the four asked anyway: "Can we retain your services, Counselor Gérard?" "No, I'm sorry, but I am so pleased for defending an innocent man that I think I got the taste of it now. I always have a sour taste after defending and getting free a guilty bandit, especially a man who is guilty of murder. I will only defend the innocent people from now on; this is way more pleasant.

I know they don't always have the money for it, but my money is made now and I don't need anything else anyway, so life is great. The four that you are don't deserve my help. In my opinion, the four of you deserve to rot in jail for the rest of your life." "Then you'd be doing good to watch your ass from now on." "Threats on top of all you have done already and in front of many witnesses on top of all. I wish good luck to your next lawyer; this won't be easy for him at all. To me you are a lost cause in advance." "Go to hell dribbler." "Hell is your home, not mine. If I remember well the Scriptures; this was mainly Paul who handed people over to Satan and you are of the same gang. I believe this is what happens to all who don't have the true God in their life. See 1 Corinthians 5, 4-5. 'Hand this man over to Satan.'

You should read Proverbs 19, 5 too. 'A false witness will not go unpunished, and he who pours lies will not go free.'

So, there is no point defending you."

"Enough of this now; I have a sentence to announce within ten minutes."

"Officers, please get this vermin out of here, will you?" "This will be my pleasure, your Honour."

The judge retrieved himself just for the time to regain his composure. When he came back in the room a few minutes later he asked:

"Do you have something to add, Counselor Gérard?" "Because of the circumstances, his Honour, I demand the complete and immediate freedom for my client from the accusation of attempt murder." "You too can admit there was a very serious misconduct committed by the accused, can't you?" "You too can admit there were also some very serious extenuating circumstances, his Honour." "I admit it."

"Counselor Ducharme, do you have anything to add?" "I only want to say that all of this is a very big mess." "Do you have anything else, Counselor Ducharme?" "No, your Honour!"

"Then this is my verdict. Accused, please stand up to receive your sentence. I sentence you to two years less one day for damages cause to public property with the order also to pay for the damages you caused to the same property. You have already served more time than the sentence you've received; this means you are free to go right away. This trial is over." Bang....

There were some applause and applause and applause again to no end.

Before thousands of viewers, Superhuman with two fingers from each hand pulled apart the chains James had to his feet and hands and he put James on his shoulder again and as soon as he was out of the door; he brought James back to the court room in Ottawa. The court officer, the only one who has the key, then a few seconds later finished the work by freeing James from the rest of these chains. This was the very first time in the history that a seventy-five years sentence was reduce to next to nothing.

Monica, who came down from the North for the occasion began to cry from all of the emotion building up inside of her. James on his side was hoping it was not too late for him to change his version about his intentions and his feelings for her. He quickly asked Just if his letter was delivered to her, but Just who never waste any time told him he did, but not to worry, that if she really loves him; she'll be there for him. James replied:

"You know Just that now-a-days people are single yesterday, married today and divorced tomorrow." "Maybe so James, but not her!" "And me neither!" James answered.

In the mean time at the TV station, it was time to end the special show.

"Ladies and gentlemen; what else can I say about such event? If there are still some people who don't believe in superheroes after all of this; after such demonstration of power and speed, then I can't tell them anything anymore. It is well written that; 'To see it is to believe it!' Then what more to say? I leave you with these words and I say; good day and see you next time. Here is Jacques Mars on Radio-C-Canada with the show; Strange things.

The biggest surprise was for Hercules, who just discovered for the very first time that his father is a great superhero and maybe the greatest in the entire world.

But his mother who watched the show with him quickly warned him not to talk to anyone about this; not even to his best friend and this even if he trusts him fully and completely.

"The tongue is the organ that is the hardest to control and this is true basically with everybody in this world. Only God can help us to direct it in the right direction and wisdom too comes from Him. There are many biblical examples of what I say my boy. Read if you want Proverbs 18, 21." "'The tongue has the power of life and death, and those who love it will eat its fruit.'" "Read also James 3, 8." "'But no man can tame the tongue. It is a restless evil, full of deadly poison.'

No man mom, I'll bet you it is even worse for women. Do you think children are spared from it?" "Just listen to yourself, my boy and you'll get the answer. You also show a lack of respect for your mother. Go read the fourth God's commandment when you have the time." "Where do I find it mom?" "It is in Exodus 20, 12. If God is not in your life; if God is not with you; you will have a very hard time to follow God's commandments and this will be for you almost impossible, but with Him, everything is possible. Also, if you can take a good advice; read James 1, 19-21." "'My dear brothers, take note of this: Everyone should be quick to listen, slow to speak and slow to become angry, for man's anger does not bring about the righteous life that God desires. Therefore, get rid of all moral filth and evil that is so prevalent and humbly accept the word planted in you, which can save you.'"

I must admit it was with time and age that wisdom was given to me and allowed me to be slow to anger to accomplish God's justice and to be worthy of the Messiah. The truth, the word of God, which is in my opinion the most powerful strength in this world, is with me and I love it with my whole heart. It is the word of God that gives me the taste to write about it, the taste to make it known and the taste to share it with the biggest possible number of people. I strongly believe that without it; I wouldn't have much to say or to write about. There were days yet this year when I asked myself what changed me this much and I have no other answer than it is the word of God that did it. But this is absolutely wonderful. To live in the kingdom of heaven, to live in Jesus' kingdom is the most marvellous thing that could happen to a human being and this is what gives me the taste to invite people of all the nations to join me in it. I hope from the bottom of my heart this is what my books and my hymns to the Lord will do. This is the exact reason why the Messiah, Jesus gave his life for, that we could be all this happy. May he be blessed above all men who lived on this earth!

Talking about hymns; here is one you might like:

Only One is Good

Only, only, only, One is Holy, Holy, Holy, He is the Almighty
Funny, funny, funny, so many are called holy
When Jesus said that only One is good. See Matthew
19, 16
Part spoken
And then, he wasn't even talking about himself, but
about the
Father who is in heaven; the One he loved dearly and
served faithfully.
Part sang
Today, today, today, I know about what's holy
The truth revealed to me
The truth from Almighty! This was Jesus delivery
The true prophet, the one hanged on the wood
Spoken
He didn't do it for the money and neither for gold.
He didn't do it for a religion and neither for an empire.
He did it for the Father and for us, whom he loved more
than his own life. This was Jesus, the true prophet of
God, who was the King of the Jews in the years 30-
33 of our times. He was crowned with thorns, when
he deserved all the best of this world. Follow his word
and you will enter the kingdom of heaven while still on
earth, because if you do; you will never die. See Matthew
19, 17.
His word which means that God the Father will hold you
from falling into the abomination that causes spiritual

death. Be free from the slavery of sins and experience the total happiness. This was Jesus' and is my wish for you.

Sang

Only, only, only, One is Holy, Holy, Holy, He is the Almighty
Funny, funny, funny, so many are called holy
When Jesus said that only One is good
Yes Jesus said that only One is good. See Matthew 19, 16.

The ones who think the word of God is not inspiring; it is just because they don't know it. In any cases, I could print you at least twenty hymns and this out of my own compositions. And what is to say about my books? There are also twenty of them and all of them inspired by the word of God. This is to the point that even my own mother asked me if I will write about something else some day. To tell you the truth; I don't really know, so I didn't know what to tell her. No matter where the inspiration comes from; no one can order it. It comes to you or it doesn't come. If this was differently, maybe everyone could write. I'm not jealous and neither selfish; so if I can inspire someone, this would be a good thing. In fact, there is one writer who lives in British Columbia; a man who wrote is first book too in the same period of time I wrote my first one and he told me that I was inspiring him a lot. When I first met him; he asked me to translate one booklet of his in French about the life of Louis Riel and this is how I came to know Louis Riel a little more. This writer was talking mainly about the politic side of the life of Louis Riel and I talked mainly about the spiritual side of his life in a book called; Why I Have To Die Like Jesus and Louis Riel?

This writer also liked a song I made about Louis Riel and he told me he likes mine better than another twenty other songs made about him. Here it is:

He Was Only a Man

He was nothing, but he was fair, was nobody
Who did something, for his people, he was a man
Was elected, was evicted fought all the way
His victory, our history, the guy has won
A patriot, strong wills fighter, a Canadian
Gave his best shot as worker until the end
Recognition, form the nation is essential
Cause with his life, he paid the price, this was Riel
Course
Riel, you're a hero, now lot of people know
That you were innocent, for the crime you were sent
Riel, you're a hero, now lot of people know
You didn't deserve to die, this way under the sky
Riel, you're a hero, now lot of people know
That your cause is not lost, it's heard and it's a must
Riel, you're the hero, now lot of people know
I told many of them, your home is the heavens
See Matthew 5, 10.
2
And he had faith, this Canadian until the end
In his country who betrayed him and all his friends
Will he get paid, for all the aid he contributed?
For the rights of, Métis and whites, Native's disputes
He sacrificed most of his life for the settlers
It would be nice, to see his rights, for the others
It's not in vain; he fought the shame, it's our glory
His cause today, democracy, our victory.

Riel, you're a hero, now lot of people know
That you were innocent, for the crime you were sent
Riel, you're a hero, now lot of people know
You didn't deserve to die, this way under the sky
Riel, you're a hero, now lot of people know
That your cause is not lost, it's heard and it's a must
Riel, you're the hero, now lot of people know
I told many of them, your home is the heavens
I told many of them, your home is the heaven
See Matthew 5, 10.

As far as I know, the real reason for killing Louis Riel was because he was talking about the truth, the same truth I write about in all of my books and he was talking about it the same way I do. This displeased a lot the leaders of the Christian religions back then. He was talking about the truth, the presence of the devil in the Bible, about the devil's contradictions and lies. The leaders of these religions know very well that it is the truth that will destroy them and their businesses.

The truth, just like Jesus said it, is the sword and the sword slices between the truth and the lies, but the leaders of those religions were not going to leave a half white and half red from the bottom of the forest cut off their income this easily.

See Matthew 10, 34. 'Do not suppose that I have come to bring peace to the earth. I did not come to bring peace, but a sword.'

Long before killing him, they sure tried to make people believe Riel was retarded, but this was not enough. So they had to make him keep quiet for good, like their master told them to do. See Titus 1, 10-11. 'For there are many rebellious people, (Louis Riel and the Métis' rebellion, 1870 and 1885) mere talkers and deceivers, especially those of the <u>circumcision group</u>. <u>They must be silenced</u>, because they are ruining whole households by teaching things they ought not to teach.'

Which meant the truth. From there they got the idea to create the Canadian Indian residential school system.

A school to find out who knows the truth they've learned from Louis Riel, the Amerindians and Métis children of the West, so they can be silenced too. It is always much easier to make children talk than adults. It is also easier to make them disappeared.

Take notice too that the circumcision group was working hand in hand with the Jesus' apostles. Only Paul was against them as he was against everything that is from God; like his Law, his commandments, the circumcision, the reproduction with men and women relationship. There come so many nuns, friars and single priests. All of them are not fruitful and are useless to God. 'Be fruitful and increase in number.' God said to the people He crated. But God's enemy chose to say the opposite. See Paul in 1 Corinthians 7, 7. 'I (Paul) <u>wish</u> that all men were as I am.' (Single)

This, my friends is a wish that is totally opposite to God's wish, to God's will.

Some whole households who understood the messages of Louis Riel about the truth he was talking about were parts of this equation and many of their children were silenced for good too. More than four thousand children could never return home from these schools. Ho, they tried to make people believe the children were there to assimilate the canadian culture, but I just know better than this. This was more to assimilate the Christian religion, mainly the Catholicism and all the ones who didn't want to have anything to do with it were eliminated. They also tried to make people believe the children died from sicknesses, but these Métis and Native children were tough and they would have survived if they were left at home with their family. Why do you think the children disappeared and the parents weren't told? Why more kids died where there were wealth and better accommodations than those who stayed at home? I figured it out long time ago. This massacre remains, in my opinion, the biggest canadian scandal, just like the assassination of the Messiah remains the biggest roman scandal and the death of fifty million people during the last world war, including six million Jews remains the biggest scandal of Germany.

CHAPTER 10

For the very first time of his entire life, James, alias Ryan Demaison really felt free. Free to do what he wants to do, free to choose where and how to live his life, free to live as a single man or to get married, free to think for himself, free to be able to publish his writings, free to get out without an escort, free to go where ever he wants to go without any permission from anyone, but the very first thing he did was to ask Just to go with him to another nice fishing day. In the mean time though, he went to talk with his boss and friend Gilles for whom he also has a lot of recognition.

"We do have quite a few new pensioners and they all are men who ate me to death." "Are you afraid of them?" "Not necessarily, but I am not fool enough to ignore the danger they represent to me." "I do have a suggestion for you, but you are a free man now, so feel free to tell me freely what you think of it.

First of all, tell me how many men you think you can control at the time." "I don't really know exactly, six maybe seven I think." "What would you say if we organize a fight between you and the last four that came in, the same way we did it with Jonathan and the eight attackers? I sincerely think this would be the quickest way for you to obtain respect from these four crooks." "That's an idea to consider, but would it be legal?" "Would you have became the greatest follower of the laws now?" "Maybe not so, but I certainly do not want to find myself behind bars again." "There is no risk for this to happen; we will make them sign a responsibility discharge from all of them who are willing to participate. Everyone will participate at their own risks and fully conscientious and I am confident you can beat them all." "I even think that all of them will be happy to have a chance to give it to me once and for all. I agree to give them the lesson they deserve." "Alright then, I will organize everything; just be sure that your training and your physical condition is at the top." "Come on now boss; I practice every day by working here. I wanted to tell you too that it is very possible I quit this job in a year from today; especially if the one I love is willing to marry me." "I was expecting that some how, but I was hoping you stay here anyway. What do you plan to do for your living?" "I don't know yet, but I am sure I can catch enough fish to live on. I'm sure too to be able to find something to do in my village and I have a lot to catch on over there." "You must know that the lost time can't be recaptured, but time continues and now you can do it your way." "This is exactly what I plan to do."

"Hey father-in-law, do you have fresh news for my tribe?" "I am still working on this my boy, but I think I can get you a retroactivity concerning your demands. I simply pleaded the incompetency of the previous administration and I showed them the proofs of what is accomplished since you are there. I made them understand, especially to the Minister of Indian affairs that if the money was well administered and if the Indian bands could be self-sufficient afterwards; the government could save millions of dollars. I can assure you that he likes the idea." "We all know that if he can save money and keep these Indian bands quiet; he's got it made for a long haul." "You got it."

In the mean time, Counselor Gérard came to pay a visit to Ryan at his work.

"I tried by all means to find the man who paid for your defence and despite having a super team of experts at my service; I could not find him. I want to give him back his money, because just the joy I got out of this cause, the joy to defend an innocent person was greater to me than what this money could bring me. There are $50 thousands in this envelope and if you can't find him within a year; then this money will be yours." "But you've done your job anyway, didn't you?" "This was for me just a fun game and besides, the one who really won your cause is the one who trapped the four dirty officers so cleverly. I can only congratulate him. To use a crown attorney to do it; this is something I have never heard of.

I don't know him, but to me he is a superhero. I wish you all the best that you deserve young man."

It was after a warm and strong handshake this lawyer left the place prouder than he has been for many years about himself. He was breathing joy like he rarely did before.

But for Ryan this was perplexity. To find himself in front of an envelope loaded with fifty grants he has to hand over to someone he doesn't even know; this could be quite a challenge. This was more money than he saw in his entire life. 'How am I going to do this?' He was telling himself. He had not the smallest idea of who this could be; a person rich enough to pay this kind of money and more, a person who wanted to see him free.

One more time Ryan went to see his friend and boss, Gilles with the hope to get an answer.

"There are fifty thousands in this envelope and I need to find the person who paid for my defence, but there is a huge problem; I don't know who this could be." "I could tell you this was me, but I would be lying." "I cannot keep such an amount with me; do you think I can put it in your safe?" "You sure can, but I must ask you to turn around for a moment; this is the rule and it has to be respected." "Of course, I understand this. What about you, do you have an idea of who this could be?" "Not at all and this is a big amount. Not too many people can afford such generosity." "This is what I keep telling myself too. But who could want to see me free to this point? I also hope this is not a trap for revenge. Could this be Monica, the one who says loving me very much? But I don't see how she could have this kind of money in her possession. The lawyer talked about he, so this has to be a man. This can't be one of my enemies either; they did everything possible to keep me behind bars. I'll take a year to find out who this is and if I didn't find him by then; I will consider it my wedding gift, how's that?" "This is a very good idea and quit worrying for so little." Laughs........

In the mean time, Monica had a very good conversation with Ryan's parents and also with his sister and brother, but the meeting was rather cold from their part.

"Why are you talking about him now and after all of those years?" "Because I still love him and I often think about him. What about you; you don't think about him anymore?" "We think he is dead somewhere; otherwise he would have come back to his family since then." "Maybe he couldn't come back; there are so many hazards in life. Maybe he thinks his family doesn't want him around anymore." "I myself cried way too much when he left and I don't want to go through this again." "I cried a lot too, but this is not a good enough reason not to think about him anymore, on the contrary. What would you do if he ever comes back?"

"I don't think he will ever come back and I sure don't want false hope either." "I personally have the feeling he is still alive and that he is stronger than ever and who knows, maybe more handsome too."

"I have the feeling that you know something we don't?" "Mister Demaison, if Ryan ever comes back here; you will have to excuse yourself to him, a lot of things to ask forgiveness for." "Just know that I know this my girl. I am full of remorse since he left and this is killing me. We have been so unfair to him that it is almost unforgivable and if there is one who understands why he never came back; this got to be me." "You will have to learn to forgive yourself too, mister Demaison." "I might forgive myself the day I received forgiveness from him, but certainly not before that." "Then this will be very soon; I can just feel it." "You, you know something we don't?" "Yes, I saw him again and he is well, very well even." "Does he want to see us?" "I can assure you that he has never ceased loving you all, but he is not a young boy anymore. He became a very important man. Do you remember the young writer who came to talk to us the other day?"

"Of course I do; he is so handsome and manly on top of all. This is a man like I would like in my bed. I dream of him just about every night."

"Take your time honey; you are way too young to talk like this." "We can always dream, can't we?"

"He will come back soon to talk about this young Amerindian who has problems with the law. What do you say about this?" "Then this young writer will talk to us again about our son; I just know it." "But what makes you say that, mister Demaison?" "I just know it, that's all." "I will let you know when he's coming back."

"Don't dream too hard young girl, I like him too. Good night to all of you."

Jeannine, my love, the young writer, who as you know now is free to go as he pleases, invited me to go for another nice fishing day and I just couldn't refuse myself this pleasure. What would you say about coming to spend another day in my tribe? This is a day that will end with another lecture from him in the evening. I think it will be interesting to know more of his story. This is not like an opera in Paris, but nevertheless, this could be nice." "I will go, but under one condition only." "And what is it, please?" "This is at the condition I can give them a lecture too when you are fishing on the lake." "But what an idea this is! Where is it from?" "I noticed the last time I went that many of the young boys and girls don't know anything about live in general over there and I would like to do my share for them too. I have learned from the meetings of our foundation that many women ignore a lot of things. I am sure too that I could be helpful to them, that's all." "I am sure of that too and I know that you can talk to them about things I wouldn't even dare brush against." "Like what?" "Nevermind what; I understand myself. Just don't put them to sleep; I want them to be awake for the evening." "Don't worry about that. I observed them the last time and they could have listened the whole night long." "Good, but what will you do with Justine?" "I'll bring her with me; she is not cumbersome at all and all of them will fight to see who will keep an eye on her." "Alright then, I will tell you when will be the day."

The following week was the one when Ryan has a weekend off and he was anticipating some very nice things. Among them was the idea of visiting again the little beach of his dreams. He knew too that he wouldn't be able to hide his identity much longer to his family and friends. Evidently this was something he couldn't avoid at all, but he feared this moment a little. He who had to face all kind of rain storms, snow storms, all kind of enemies and adversity felt very small in his shoes when he was thinking about what he had to do that day. The fear to be rejected is probably the worse for a man who is a little timid, but he refused to believe that jail was for him the best place to be, the best welcoming place in this world. Then he said to himself; 'I can always go back, if I want to.'

Then as predicted, fishing in a nice day of September can be very good, if we know how to do it right. The lake was calm for this time of the year and the two men as they were picking up their catches were talking about the adventures of their life.

"My lawyer gave me an envelope with the fees that were paid to him for my defence and he asked me to give them back to the one who paid them. He also said that he cannot find him anymore. But I have no idea of who did it and I give myself one year to find him. After that time I will have to give up, if I didn't find him. What about you, mister ghost, do you have an idea about who this could be?" "You know Ryan, when I am fishing, the ideas, I like to leave them at home. The Messiah also left us an important message on the subject and is it written in Matthew 6, 3. 'But when you give to the needy, do not let your left hand know what your right hand is doing.'

Maybe the left hand of the man who paid these fees doesn't know what his right hand has done. There are not too many of those, but there are some people like this. If I were you, I wouldn't worry too much about who this could be and I am sure too that if he is able to pay this kind of money; he can also get it back if he wants to."

But this conversation was suddenly interrupted by a very special event. The little Justine found herself on her father's knees to the overwhelming amazement of Ryan.

"But what in the world is this?" "This, my dear friend is my little girl Justine, mister ghost's daughter. She has the same power I have, but she should be with her mom right now. She must have been afraid of something or of someone for coming to me this way. Wait for me for a few seconds; I will bring her back to her mother."

But even before Just got up to leave, Justine was already gone to where she left. She suddenly remembered that her father doesn't like for her to do this kind of things to her mother. But at the village there were young kids who were panicking.

"Lady, lady, lady, your baby is gone." "Don't you worry about it; she is probably with her father." "But we didn't see him around." "Maybe so, but she knows where he is; I'm sure of it. Let's go take a look in her cradle. This is what I thought; she is here and smiling too. She mocked you in a very good way kids. Is there anyone of you who scared her maybe?" "This is john; he acted like a bear above her to make her laugh." "I just wonder who laughed the most. This is not right at all and in turn she got her revenge on you." "But how did she do that? This is impossible." "Sure it is possible, she's done it, didn't she? No one ever talked to you about ghosts; the spirits who travel in time. If you listen very well to tonight lecture; you will learn more about this."

"Where were we at? Ho yes! I am under the impression that this lawyer wants you to keep this money; after all, he is the one who earned it." "This is true; I never thought of that. This weekend I have the intention to ask Monica to marry me; do you think it is too soon?" "Since when do you know her?" "Do you think this counts?" "It is written in Proverbs; 'May your fountain be blessed, and may you rejoice in the wife of your youth.'

I think this counts alright. Besides, none other can fall in your arms better than this one." "If you don't mind now; I would like to go on this little beach of my childhood to meditate and to reflect about all of this." "You are now completely free to do what ever you want to do." "This is not completely true. You are my guest and I don't really have the right to ask you to leave me alone, but I will appreciate it if you do." "And just like a good friend; I cannot refuse you this much. Alright then, I'll bring you to this little beach of yours and then I'll bring all the fish to the village. How much time do you think you need?" "One hour should be enough." "See you later then and have a good reflection."

Just then did things the way they were discussed and as soon as he was at the village; he asked a few men to empty the boat of all the fish and also the equipment and to prepare the meal just like it was done the last time.

Monica all worried was wondering where was the man she loves.

"He is on this little beach of yours and I believe he would be happy to see you there." "Do you really think so?" "Come on Monica, if I say so; it is because I think so." "Forgive me; where is my head today?" "You should take a different boat though, because this one smells like fish a little too much." "But I like fish." "There is better than that for a honeymoon. Make sure too that there is enough fuel in it and if you need anything; you know how to reach me. Don't you go forget that he also has a lecture at seven tonight and there will be many people waiting for him."

But even before Just had finished talking; Monica was already on her way to the beach to join the one she loves since her young years. She got out of the lake a couple of hundred feet before the beach for the only purpose of respecting his privacy. What a surprise she got for herself when she was close enough to see and mainly to hear what Ryan was saying.

Ryan was kneeling one leg in the sand and he was practising his marriage proposal.

"Miss Monica St-Clair, would you do me the honour to become my wife? Miss Monica St-Clair, would you marry me? Miss Monica St-Clair, would you be interested to make me happy by accepting to marry me?" "I will accept with the greatest pleasure, Mister Ryan Demaison."

This is what she said with the most beautiful smile in the world while approaching him.

Ryan, who was holding an engaging ring at the end of his arm kind of jumped a little from being surprised this way, but he managed to keep his composure anyway as the love of his life was smiling and advancing near him.

Monica kneeled down before him right away and without wasting any time, Ryan took her in his arms to kiss her. But it is not in a deep forest or behind bars that we learn to do these things properly. So, it was quite awkwardly he succeeded to do it while falling on the side with her. But then, when he began to undress her; she told him that maybe this was the perfect dream place for that, but certainly not the right time.

"You are right. I waited all of these years; I should be able to wait another few days." "It is not because I don't want it, but there is a huge crowd that is waiting for you at the village for your next lecture.

I had a talk with your family and your father is sure you are talking about his oldest son. And also, your sister has a crush on you; she might be very disappointed when she'll find out who you really are. Your parents have a lot of regrets about the way they treated you back then. Your brother thinks that if you were still alive; you would have come back home longtime ago." "What about my mother?" "Your mother kept crying without saying anything." "Well, thank you; this was very nice of you." "Ho, this was nothing and the very least I could do for the man I love. Let's go now; they are waiting for you. Are you going to tell them tonight who you really are?" "There is a great chance they discover it before the end of my lecture."

They both got on the boat and within ten minutes they were back at the village to the applause of just about everyone. Only the young Louise didn't have the heart to celebrate. Ryan's young sister, who loves him without really knowing who he is had from that time a violent dislike for the secretary of the village; the one she always considered as a friend before.

A few women had plates full of cooked fish and hot potatoes in their hands for them when they arrived.

"I thank you all for your warm welcome and if you would go now take your place in the hall and give me ten minutes to swallow this appetizing meal; I will be with you right after."

Just then took things over from that moment on and just like a good sheep dog gathers all the sheep; he invited his people to leave the couple of lovers finish to eat their meal without being under municipal observation.

About twelve minutes later, Ryan and Monica were applauded again when they entered the hall full of people. It seemed that there were more people there than there are inhabitants in this community. I mean more than the presence of Jeannine and her baby. Maybe some relatives and friends coming from the next tribe; people who heard about the event.

As soon as the applause ended; Ryan took place in front of the microphone and Monica sat beside Jeannine, who was holding Justine in her arms. Just was standing behind both of them.

"Good evening everyone."

Everyone in the hall said it out loud; 'Good evening!'

This didn't please Justine at all and she left her mother all at once to go in her father's arms.

"This will be fine my little sweetheart; stay with mommy, daddy is just behind you."

Just then put Justine back in her mom arms to the questioning look of everybody around, who couldn't believe what they saw. Most of the Amerindians of the

North America ceased believing in spirits for a while now, but in the minds of many yet; this is not completely gone.

"I will start tonight by asking you all if you heard of the trial that took place a week ago and received a lot of media coverage?" "We only get the news a month after the events over here. The news we got last week that we know about happened over here." "Thank you sir; this will make things easier for me and allow me to give you some that are quite fresh anyway.

Last time I was here, I was telling you that these two young Amerindians were still in jail. But lately, a very charitable man I don't know and I don't know why either paid the fees, up to fifty thousand dollars to a lawyer to defend one of these young adventurers.

The trial for murder took place a few weeks ago and this young Native man was cleared of all charges for these three deaths, for what he was not guilty anyway. His sentence of fifty years in jail was also reduced to no time at all.

The reopening of his second trial, the one for attempt murder against more than twenty people took place last week. Two out of these twenty people are present here tonight in this crowd."

At the same time; there were a lot of mutterings in the hall and everyone was looking at others trying to find out who this could be. But at the same time a strange noise came up to the ears of Just who reacted quickly to grab an arrow that was coming in Monica's direction. There were only a few inches left to go before Monica gets it directly in her heart. Just bent down behind the two women to leave there the arrow under their chairs and to disappear the time to go out and to see who tried to kill his secretary and why.

"Louise, but why?" "She stole from me the man I love, the damn bitch. I thought she was my friend." "But this is not the right way to solve a problem, no matter what the problem is. If I haven been there; you would be a murderer now and I would have to bring you to the police authorities. Fortunately for you; I am the only one who noticed this. You are going inside now with me and listen to the rest of this lecture. I advise you to listen attentively, because there is a huge surprise for you in there. We'll talk about all of this later on."

When they were near the door, Louise entered the hall and Just took his place back and he bent down behind the two women as if he never left. Monica has never noticed anything, but Just thought that maybe Jeannine did, because of Justine reaction. Then Ryan was continuing his lecture as if nothing happened.

"The young man's second trial unrolled to the eyes of millions of viewers. The mister ghost, who forced this young adventurer away from his home to surrender to the police, is the same mister ghost who helped him to clear his name of almost all the accusations that were held against him. This young Amerindian spent a little more than two years behind bars and he has now served his sentence entirely. He is now as free as any of you and this man is the one talking to you as I speak. I am Ryan Demaison; I am your blood brother."

Everybody without any exception stood up all at once. His mother fell in the arms of her husband crying and she passed out. Louise bit her lips until the blood poured out and Raymond, his brother showed him his fist with rage. He was very mad mainly for not showing his identity earlier. Louise came to kneel at Monica's feet and she asked her for forgiveness.

"Forgiveness, but what for?"

Louise looked at Just in the eyes and then put her head down.

"For hating you to death." "You hate me, why?" "For stealing the man that I dream about." "But you are only fifteen; you still have plenty of time to dream and this thousands of times yet. I will give you three books that will help you choose a husband, but you cannot marry your brother, that's for sure." "I didn't know that he was." "And I didn't want to betray his secret."

In the mean time Raymond was yelling at his older brother.

"Come outside and settle this like a real warier, if you're not too much of a chicken." "If it is the only thing that will make you happy; let's go, but I got to warn you; there is only one man here who can win over me and this is the chief." "Bla, bla, bla, words are free, but I got fists and I can make them speak for me." "Don't say I didn't warn you." "Shut up and follow me out there."

There were a few men in this crowd, who wanted to interfere as they were going out, but Ryan told them to let go and that his younger brother needed a good lesson.

"I will make you swallow your words, shitty brother, an outlaw who is just out of jail." "Ho yeah and how do you plan to do this?" "Like this." "You are still hungry enough to eat some dust? I thought I brought enough fish for everybody. Come on, get up and fight like a man, would you?"

Ryan just moved a couple of inches when Raymond jumped him and he just found himself on his belly with his nose in the dust. The same thing happened two more times, but instead of understanding what the true situation was like, Raymond got more and more furious. Then Ryan turned his back to him and he started to walk towards the hall again. Raymond went after him one more time, but when he was close enough, Ryan made a back flip above his brother's head. He then grabbed Raymond by his clothes, pulled him down the way he learned to do it from Jonathan and he got a submission grip to immobilize him completely.

"What does it take for you to understand that you can't do anything against me? Who showed you how to welcome your relatives?"

Ryan let go of the grip and he helped Raymond get up on his feet, but Raymond still tried to hit him. But then this time it was the chief who grabbed him by his neck, lifted him up with one arm above his head and he said:

"Do I have to lock you up for the night for you to understand? I won't tell you twice. I advise you to shake hands with your brother immediately; otherwise this is what I am going to do with you, do you get it?" "Yes chief!"

What Just didn't know at that moment is the fact that Raymond too is in love with Monica and it is when he saw the engaging ring on her finger that he began building up anger. People have to understand that there are not too many people in this tribe who has true civilized manners.

Monica was in a conversation inside the hall with Jeannine about her engagement to Ryan.

"His proposal to me was the most romantic, but the kiss that followed was, I don't know how to say this, but the word would be; I think catastrophic." "You know Monica; it is not in the deep forest and neither behind bars that a man can learn how to do these things properly, but he is an intelligent man and if you give him time; I am sure he can get better. And what stop you from showing him how to do these things?" "Well, I don't want to hurt his feelings; you know how proud are men, don't you? I teach class to the children, but I don't have enough experiences to teach sex, especially not to a man." "I will get you a book that will help you help him. It is called: 'The art to kiss and to make love.'

Just know that there is no shame in learning, even in this field. This will help you too." "I don't doubt it, I too have only very little experience about this." "Neither I nor my husband had experiences either, but we learned to know each other and everything fell into place quickly. The main thing is not to worry and to take the time to know each other and the rest will fall into place. Don't forget either that real love overcomes a lot of problems between two lovers. Don't skip steps; just live your life one day at the time. Your first steps are made now; the others will follow through." "Thank you very much Jeannine; you are better than a mother to me." "Talking about mothering; I better go hide somewhere now to feed my baby. I don't want to scandalize all the men and boys who are in this room." Laughs...

This statement made the little Justine smile.

Then Monica and Ryan went back to the microphone to tell the crowd they got engaged earlier that evening and they planned to celebrate Christmas with a marriage ceremony. Almost everyone got up to applaud. Only Louise and Raymond didn't have at heart the applause, but Just gave them both a dirty look that made them change their mind quickly. Just was just thinking he has not finished with those two yet.

Ryan's parents kind of recovered from their overwhelming emotions and they came to congratulate them. They were not too sure of what to expect from their prodigal son. Ryan didn't know where to put his hands when his father hugged him. This was one thing he has never experienced to that day. It felt really awkward to say the least. Then he said to himself: 'What if this was my son?'

No one had ever see this man, Ryan's father cry, not even his wife, but then, he was crying like a kid or like a woman and asking his son to forgive him for all the hurt he suffered because of him.

"Stop that dad; this was only a bad for a good. Take a look at me today and see whom I became. I could never ever be this man if I stayed here with you all." "Don't you ever congratulate me for all the wrong I have done to you? I must tell you though that I looked for you during two long years and then I thought you were dead somewhere. Do not ever do such a thing to your son, because the remorse is almost deadly. I even think I suffered more than you did all those years." "Well then, all of this is over now and I see the future with optimism. When I look at everything that was done in this village; there are reasons to rejoice and to dream about a nice future. I could never believe this possible in my wildest dreams. I will be happy to raise my family here in this village and this is something I couldn't even say a couple of weeks ago."

"All with me my dear friends; let's give a good hand of applause for our chief, who sacrificed some of his precious time for our village. We will have to make him proud of us and continue what he has started for us.

Just was applauded even more than Ryan was for his lecture. But Just put an end to it, first because it was getting late and he had better things to do yet. He thanked everyone and he told them it was time to go home. Then he got near Raymond and Louise to tell them:

"I want to see both of you in my office at nine o'clock sharp tomorrow morning."

Just said the same thing to Ryan and Monica, but they had some serious questions about it.

"What is wrong chief?" "There are just a few things I need to settle before I go away, that's all. This is not something extremely bad, but it has to be done for sure."

The next morning.

"Louise and Raymond; let me tell you that I am very disappointed with both of you. Your big brother just started to live through a bit of happiness and this after living through misery, not to say through hell for most of his life and the last thing he needed is this kind of savage reception from you. What both of you did last night is absolutely disgusting. But I am telling you now that if you can't get alone with him; you'll have to leave; this will be your turn to find out what exile is. Maybe this will allow you to understand what he went through. What he needs above all is warm and open arms, not shit like you did last night. Fortunately for Ryan; your father was more compassionate than the two of you; otherwise he would have done much better to go somewhere else. What can you tell me to justify what you've done?" "I will leave this place right away, because I cannot stand seeing another man with the one I love and this is not because he is my brother. If you allow me; I will go now get my shit ready." "And where do you plan to go?" "With all due respect chief; this is not of your business." "Well then, I appreciate your frankness and I wish you the best of luck, but I'm telling you anyway that you are home here, if you respect the rules." "The rules won't change anything about the way I feel or about the situation." "I have to agree with you there. Like I said it; best of luck to you."

"My young brother, I am sorry for hurting you this way without wanting to, but I must tell you that Monica and I are bound to be together since we are born I think and nothing and no one could change a thing about that." "I might get over it some day, but for now I can't." "Ho, you'll come back in a little while to introduce your cute and nice squaw to us; I am sure of this." "I'm sorry, but I don't feel like laughing." "This is too bad, because it would be a lot funnier. I must go back to work tomorrow morning; why don't you take the time to think about all of this calmly?" "I don't have to take any advice from you, brother."

"Raymond frankly, you're pissing me off. I had a bit of respect for you before, but now I have none left. Yes, you should go as far as possible, because you don't deserve any of the good things we have here in this village."

When earring these coming out of Monica's mouth; Raymond got really mad. He lifted his arm as if he was going to hit her, but Just grabbed his arm quickly and pulled it down heavily to his belly.

"This is the way you love her? Rule number one; it is strictly forbidden for a man to hit a woman in this community and even less the secretary of this village, my secretary. It is not her that you are in love with, but with her pretty face, her round breasts and her nice ass. You absolutely don't know what love is all about at all. When you have done somewhere what was done to this village; then you'll be able to talk about love. Now get out of here before I break you to pieces."

"Chief, chief, please, my brother is not this bad; he is just lost right now, but I am sure he will settle down soon. If it is necessary; me and Monica will go somewhere else. I didn't come here to create dissension, but to be reunited with my family."

"But Ryan, I don't want to go away from here; after all we built in this village." "Woman, who takes a man takes everything that comes with him; if I leave, you leave too."

"Monica is very capable to decide for herself and what ever she wants to do with her life. It is not true that I built all of this up to let it be ruined for everyone else by a selfish boy like Raymond." "He's almost a man now." "He'll be a man when he can act like one. Either he straights himself up or he has to go away and that's it." "Alright then chief, what if we give him up to my next return to think about all of this?" "You're not afraid he causes trouble while you are gone; he tried to hit her in front of us." "I don't think he would have done it. I think he just wanted to look mean." "This was an act of violence anyway." "I admit it, but what Monica thinks about this?"

"I say that if he ever touches me; I will cut his balls off and he will be the last of his family three. If he doesn't know what this means; I will draw a picture for him."

"Don't worry Ryan; she knows how to reach me if she needs and if I catch him again doing something wrong; he will be sorry for a long time. They say that a warned man is worth two; then this would be twice as bad for him.

Alright then, you can all go, except for Louise; I am not done with her just yet."

Louise started to cry and to shake out of fear. Raymond wanted to come to her defence and he lift up his voice, but Just showed him the door right away.

"Just the two of us now! Do you realize that instead of celebrating his engagement, your brother would be crying for the lost of his fiancée, if I haven been there to prevent you committing this awful crime?" "I'm so sorry about what I did." "I wish I could believe you, but

I can't and I doubt very much your sincerity." "I wasn't myself at all; I was blinded by rage." "Then I only see one solution to your problem. Either you spend time in a temper control and prevention of violence institution or I take you to the police authorities for your crime. This is a first degree attempt murder. I am sure too that you'll be prosecute as an adult and you will receive your sentence accordingly. On the other hand, if you choose the institution I suggested to you and follow the complete program, then I will keep this secret for ever between us. But if you ever and at any time and for any reason have another fit like the one you had last night; then this promise will be automatically cancelled. Do you understand the importance of this agreement?" "Yes chief, but how will I be able to explain my departure to the others without telling them the real reason?" "I will make them understand that it is time for you to go to high school; this is something you will do jointly with this program anyway. If you pull it out; you will come out of it as a winner and if you do things the right way; you will be able to come spend time at our place every month and I will invite your parents too. Does this suit you?" "Thanks chief; I don't deserve this much." "Now I will make you a special favour. If you ever are in trouble, no matter what this is, if you need help; the only thing you'll have to do is calling my name and surname and I will be with you. One thing though, don't you ever do it just for fun, because then you would lose from me the only chance you have to be rescued. Is this understood?" "Yes chief!" "Go now, go say goodbye to your relatives and friends; we are leaving tonight." "But what will I have to tell them to be accepted in this program?" "I will myself negotiate your entry and I will tell them that you almost kill someone out of madness. I will negotiate your entry at the high school as well. All you'll have to do is behaving like a normal person and everything will be fine for you." "If you say so."

Louise's parents couldn't understand a thing anymore. They just got the luck to get their oldest son back and this after many years. The son they thought was lost forever and now only after a few hours and for reasons they didn't quite understand yet; they were losing another son and the only daughter they have. Secrets are very often necessary, but they could be also very painful.

It was Ryan who went to explain the situation about Raymond to his parents and Monica was with him. They have a lot of respect for her and this for a very good reason; she always been frank.

"Raymond has never spoken to me about his feelings before. I surprised him a few times spying insidiously on me, but I have never paid too much attention to it. I know though that he knew about my feelings for Ryan when we were young, but this was so far behind us that I forgot about it. I hope now he won't go do some stupid things." "He has a few friends in the next tribe east of us. He most likely will go there for a while and I don't overly worry about him. He is no longer a child, but sometime I wonder about this."

I never thought that my return would cause this much disturbance and I didn't come here to take his place, but to take mine and nothing more." "You will take the place that you want; you are here at home." "Thanks dad, a good word is always nice to hear. I will work down below for another year, because I like this job for one thing and it is well paid too and then I plan to come back here in my village to raise my family. I believe in our ancestral values and in our culture, but our kids will also learn other cultures. As far as I know there is good and not so good in every culture." "I'm not worrying for you Ryan; your wisdom will lead you a long way, I am sure of it. And with a wife like Monica; you can't go wrong. All of us love her very much. Her parents are also our best friends."

"What about you mom; you don't say much." "My boy, I know my culture too and I know to keep my mouth shut when the man speaks." Laughs.....

"It will be necessary to bring a few changes to our culture then, because women too have the right to their opinions. I'll need to have a conversation in private with you one day then, if I really want to know what you really think." "This will be the only way my boy and don't you forget that no one can teach an old monkey how to make faces, either male or female." "You should have a much better opinion of yourself." "What I think about myself is not important, which is important is what your father thinks of me." "I will not try to change you mom and if you are happy the way you are, then good for you."

Ryan's father was not too happy about the turnout of this conversation, but he kept it to himself this time.

The newly engaged couple went to their little beach from there, question of saying goodbye in private before Ryan's departure. Louise too went around to see all of her friends pretending being happy to leave for a new life.

Jeannine on her side was getting bored and began to miss her home. There is rarely a better place to be than at home; especially when someone has a place like hers. It is good to get out of it from time to time, but it is even nicer to come back in our own personal things. When she could talk with Monica; this was fine, but then, when she found herself alone; this was a different story and rather boring for her.

The children saw her more like the Madonna, but what can the Amerindians children discuss with the Madonna? They can certainly not talk about their sins. Jeannine didn't feel qualified enough either to start instructing them about her knowledge of the Bible's messages and she was telling herself that the kids won't understand anything of it anyway.

But the inspiration came to her suddenly at that moment. Instead of trying to instruct them, was she thinking, why not trying to find out what they know?

"Do you kids know Jesus?" "Well yeah, the little Jesus cries when we are doing something wrong." "Do you know his mother?" "Well yeah, his mother is the Holy Virgin and she too cries when we are doing something wrong." "They both must be crying all the time then, don't you think?" "I guess so, because we are doing something wrong almost all the time."

"Not me, I am a good little girl; my mom told me." "Do you thing they will stop crying because of you?" "Of course not, the others keep doing something wrong and there are many, many people who do something wrong. This is why the water often comes down from heaven and his Father is very, very mad and He shout very, very loudly and then I get scared. He shouts so loudly that the sky gets lighted up all over from heaven to the earth. Sometimes He throws fire on the ground and the forest burns longtime, longtime and this is very dangerous for us." "And this is why you don't do anything wrong, isn't it?" "Yes, the little Jesus protects me." "Did anyone ever tell you what they did to the little Jesus?" "Yes, they crucified him on the cross." "Then he was not the little Jesus anymore, was he?" "This is true. Why then do they say the little Jesus cries, if he became a man? And if he died on the cross; then he doesn't cry anymore." "But I think he can still be sad, because he was resurrected." "What is that mean?" "This mean that he came back to life and this is what all of the good people can expect from his Father. If the Father in heaven, Jesus' spiritual

Father could resurrect the Messiah because he was good and just, then He can resurrect all of them who are good and just. This is common sense, don't you think? When this little Jesus became a man, he said that all of them who listen to what he says will never see death, because like he did, we will come back to life. I think this means that as soon as our body dies, our soul continues to live and will live forever. I also think this is worth being good and just; what do you think?"

"I too want to live forever." "Then I will get you the gospel of Matthew from the Bible. He wrote many, many recommendations he got from Jesus, the prophet God raised up to teach us his knowledge. From him you will learn what to do and not to do to please God. You will know who to pray to be heard and to be granted. You will also know the truth and no one will be able to fool you anymore with their lies and contradictions and this even if they are in the Holy Bible." "What does fool you means?" "It means cheat you, mislead you and it is not nice at all. But unfortunately, many people do it and very often also without realizing it." "You, you are like the Madonna." "Ho no, I'm not like her at all! Like her I had a child and like her I'm no longer a virgin at all anymore. And just like her probably; I wouldn't like to see or to hear millions and millions of people to pray me without being able to help or to answer them. She must have a hard time to rest the poor woman; unless God blocks up her ears." Laughs of the children....

"God only has to give her a Walkman with some nice songs." "This is a very good idea and I hope she'll get many cassettes too." Laughs.....

The seed is sown was she thinking and she made a little prayer for this seed to be in good soil. Then suddenly a thought gave her a shudder of fear that came to haunt her. Will people kill them too for having too much knowledge of the truth, just like what happened to all the children who have learned from what Louis Riel sown in his time and disappeared, the prophet of the new age? Then she calmed down thinking that Just and Superhuman won't let this kind of massacre happen again, especially not to these children who are under Just's protection and if they can prevent it. But was she thinking, the resemblance between the story of Louis Riel and the children of his time and the story of the children of Westimouche is evident and she will have to talk to her husband about it.

"Don't worry sweetheart; God entrusted me with the protection of the people of this village and this is not for the colour of their skin. The truth will be known in all the nations and this includes all the far away regions as well. Just like I said it before, the ways of the Lord are impenetrable, but they can penetrate everywhere the Lord Almighty wants too. His word just entered in this village and this is just the beginning. Let me tell you that it will go from here to all around the world. The days where and when the churches could choke the truth are gone, even though they are not too happy about it. Remember the message of the Messiah that we can read in Matthew 24, 14. 'And this gospel of the kingdom of heaven will be preached in the whole world as a testimony to all nations, and then the end will come.'

This message is the main reason why all the churches tried so hard to hide the truth. This is also a prophesy that came to fulfilment with this generation and see what the Messiah said about this generation in Matthew 24, 33-35. 'Even so, when you'll see all these things, you'll know that it is near, right at the door. I tell you the truth; this generation will certainly not pass away until all these things have happened. Heaven and earth will pass away, but my words will never pass away.'"

My books and what I am talking about in them are a solid proof of what the Messiah said back two thousand years ago.

And yet, the devil and his diabolic institutions did and still do everything in their power to hide the truth by still preaching the lies. And despite all of their desperate efforts to hide it, the truth continues to make its way throughout the world. People who will accept it will be saved and the others will be lost. It is as simple as the one who accept a life jacket in the middle of the sea to save his life.

"When it comes to the village of Westimouche, I keep an eye almost constantly on it and there are a number of people over there who know how to reach me quickly. Don't worry for it; it is most likely the village that has the best possible protection in this world. When I won't be here anymore; it is Justine and Justin who will take over my duties and the word of God will be spread out all over the North and beyond.

I plan to retire as a chief as soon as Ryan will be ready to take over the reins of power and to continue my work in this village. I even think he is the only one capable to do it the way I would like it to be and this to the end and he will also be well supported by Monica, his wife. I trust them both for that job. Did you talk to her about the way we got married?" "Do you think I should of?" "Of course, you should; these are women subjects." "You weren't a woman when you talked to me about it." "No, but no woman could have done it then; now there is one and it is you." "Ho, I see." "Don't waste too much time; they planned to get married around Christmas." "I have to bring her a book about the art of kissing as soon as possible. I will then use the occasion to talk to her at the same time." "There is no rush and at the same time there is. You yourself know to what could lead a good kiss. I remember your lost of control from my second kiss. You said you weren't yourself anymore." "It is still the same today." "Then you should tell them to be careful or to get married quickly." "I think he is more in a rush than she is for that." "You know as much as I do that the two of them have to be on the same wavelength to get along well." "I can look after her, but I think you should take care of him." "This is not a subject that I am the most at ease with." "And yet you are at ease with me." "Yes, but you are me; the two of us make one; this is not the same. I will see what I can do for him anyway."

"Do you prefer I still call you James or Ryan?" "Here is James and at the village it is Ryan; this way no one will be confused, what do you think?" "I think it makes sense. Another thing that would make sense for you too is that you get instructions about how to live with a woman, so your relationship last longer than the time of a honeymoon. I like both of you and I wish you both a lot of happiness and I don't want you to get in trouble for a question of misunderstanding." "What are you suggesting exactly?" "Do you have access to Internet?" "Of course I do; as much as I want, but outside of my working hours." "Then go look on this sight: 'Learn How To Make Love The First Time.' You will find on this sight as well many little secrets about men and women. Then you will find; 'Advises for successful preliminaries and many other things for a pleasant wedding night for both partners.'

And don't tell me that you have a lot of experiences, because I will tell you yes, in fishing and hunting. If what I learned in there was good for me; it should be good for you too." "You went on an Internet sight?" "Why not, we can learn a lot of interesting things on it, enjoy the reading." "Hey, thanks for having our happiness at heart."

"Ho, that's nothing. This is a bit early to talk about it, but I would like you to run for the next election at the village; I would like to see you as a chief over there. You have a year to think about it; this gives you a lot of time to prepare your speech." "I will never run against you, not in my lifetime." "And why not? Monica did it and I am the one who asked her to do it. But you won't have to run against me; I will retire when you are ready to become the new chief." "Do you really think I can be a good chief?" "Certainly the best one, beside me, of course." "Of course!" "No one can be a better chief and protect this people better than you, beside me of course." Laughs.......

Next to the village of Westimouche, in the village of Eastimouche, Raymond and thirty some other young men, all armed with lighted torches were discussing the way they will take over the village of Westimouche.

"We will try not to hurt anyone, unless they attack us, but I want to destroy this new damned school and to open this damned bar and help myself as much I want to." "What do we do if they do take arms against us then?" "There is only a dozen men over there and they can't do anything at all against all of us. Let's go, they must be all sleeping at this time of the night. These stupid people are all obeying to an imposed curfew and this even if the chief is leaving for the night. He faked sleeping in the school dormitory one time, but I found out that he wasn't there the whole night. Note that I don't blame him at all, with the beauty he is married to, but she sleeps in her home near Ottawa and he joins her every night. This village is completely out of protection at night. Let's go and don't make any noise."

A bad dream about her marriage to Ryan woke Monica up. She was all in sweats, but when she saw a glimmer of light from the fire coming from the school direction, she instinctively called her chief. Just, even though he was in a love making with his wife; he was there in no time at all. When Just saw the seriousness of the situation, he called Superhuman immediately. This superhero filled up a fishing boat with water and he dropped it on the corner of the school that was in flames.

Just grabbed these outlaws two at the time and he threw them in the lake at a distance of a couple of hundred feet away from shore. Is it necessary to say that the water up North is quite cold at the end of September? When the fire was out; Superhuman too started to throw them in the lake, but he was throwing them a bit too far off the land and he had to go get some of them, so they don't die from drowning or by hypothermia. These outlaws didn't want a day school, but they all learned a very good life lesson that night. They all wanted the liquor from the bar, but they all got cold water instead. Just gave them the best possible advice for the circumstances and this was to run for their life and to keep warm enough not to die. This is what they did.

This reminded me a very good message from the Messiah that we can read in Matthew 10, 42. 'And if anyone gives even a cup of cold water to one of these little ones because he is my disciple, I tell you the truth, he will certainly not lose his reward.'" Laughs.....

The next day the youngsters of the village were laughing and saying their neighbours came to the night school.

Just went back to his wife and he asked her: "I hope you're a not cool off yet, because I just started to warm up." "Don't worry about that my love; I'm still vibrating. There is no other like you." "What do you know about that and how can you say that?" "Because, a different woman than me would be bragging about this on the Internet." "You might just be right."

As soon as Jeannine was deeply sleeping, Just went quickly back to his village to save Raymond's ass; knowing very well that the others won't forgive him for bringing them in such a fiasco. Superhuman was still there and he was trying to figure out the extent of the damages.

"The school only has outside damages and the children will be able to continue their schooling as usual. But I'll have to bring you materials to repair all of this anyway. They didn't have the time to break through the bar and only the door is damaged and it will need to be replaced." "All of this can wait till daylight, but there is urgency to pull out of his mess the instigator of this fiasco and this before the others kill him for misleading them the way he did. Do you mind coming with me to the next village?" "Let's go right away, if you think there is rush."

Just was right; the others were getting ready to burn him alive. They had already judged him and sentenced him to death. This is often the way things happen where there is no law and order. But then, Just moved directly behind Raymond and he undone the knot behind his back and Superhuman took him away from the woodshed and he brought him to his family. Another fire was already lighted up over there. And this is how the legend of the burnt man gone directly to hell was born.

Just ordered enough materials for all of the repairs that have to be done and also to make four big signs to indicate from the four sides of the village that it is protected by good spirits of justice. He wants this to be written and French, in English and in the native language of his inhabitants. Then another legend was born and this is: The legend of the protective spirits.

There was also a third one that was about to be born. A big missionary priest together with a young fifteen years old black boy arrived at the village on a canoe. Dressed with a long black robe with a huge rosary around his belly and he had a big silver cross hanging from his neck that was coming down on his chest.

When the children first saw him, they wondered if this wasn't a witch. The missionary and the boy were each carrying a box. One box was full of nickels and pennies and the other one was full of medals and rosaries.

"Children, my father will talk to you now about the good God and about his mother." "Hey you there, it is written not to call anyone father on this earth, especially not if he is not your real father and how could you say God's mother if God had no beginning?" "We also brought you a lot of money to help you to survive."

All the children were laughing their heads off.

"We all have thousands of dollars in the bank; we certainly don't need your pennies. We were even told that pennies are not worth anything anymore." "You need medals of the holy virgin to protect you." "'You shall not make for yourself an idol in the form of anything in heaven above or on the earth beneath or in the waters below.'

We do have the Holy Spirit to protect us and He is very efficient. Where do you guys come from, to be so ignorant? We are not in 1515 anymore; we are now in 2015." "We represent God on this earth." "Who made you believe such a thing?" Laughs.....

"You should be confessing yourselves; you are blasphemers." "It is written: 'This is what the Lord says: 'Cursed is the one who trusts in man, who depends on flesh for his strength and whose heart turns away from the Lord.'

I think I read this somewhere in the Holy Bible. Jesus was telling the truth and they said he too was a blasphemer, but this was a lie and you are lying too. You should be on your way with all of your junk before the Holy Spirit chases you away from our territory." "Are you sure not to want any rosaries?" "What would be the use?" "To pray the Holy Virgin, of course." "Hear then what Jesus told us to say when we pray: 'Our Father in heaven.'

He also said that when we pray, not to keep on babbling like pagans, for they think they will be heard because of their many words. He said not to be like them, because our Father in heaven already knows what we need before we ask Him.'

Our God knows what we need and right now; we certainly do not need anything and certainly not peddlers of lies or news mongers."

"Come my boy: I heard enough of this for today." "Yes father!"

The two of them went back to their canoe and the young boy was questioning himself about what happened and he wanted to know more about it.

"These youngsters seem to know what they are talking about, isn't it father?" "You keep your mouth shut, before I throw you down into this lake." "But why are you so mad, father?" "Shut up, I said." "Yes father!"

Without saying another word, this young boy threw himself in the glacial water to go join the other children on the shore. He has just discovered on which side was the truth and on which side he wanted to be. All the kids covered him with their coats and they quickly brought him near the fire, so he can warm up. The mission direction of this young boy just changed at the same time. This was another one who will learn with the purpose of spreading the truth throughout the nations and this way continuing the Messiah's mission. The children of this village of Westimouche gave him a different name in their own language that means; 'Moses saved from the cold water.'

"What happened for you to leave your father and to risk your life this way?" "Iiiii didn'tttt haveeee theeee rightttt to speak anymore and he is no longer my faaaather." "I rather learn everything that you all know. Him, he is terribly mad right now and he was just yelling at me." "'There will be weeping and gnashing of teeth.'

This is what Jesus said. Us, we learn the messages that come from the Messiah and to wonder why he is mad; is somehow answering the question, don't you think?" "I think you are right. Do you have room for me in your community? This is only for a little while, because I have a mission at heart and this is to make the truth known everywhere I go." "If you are ready to work and to learn; then you are at home over here."

Printed in the United States
By Bookmasters